Claire Taschdjian

THE PEKING
MAN IS MISSING

BALLANTINE BOOKS • NEW YORK

For Chiang Ta-shih

and for the children of the House of Chiang:

Sung-ya, Je-han and Ma-ting

Copyright © 1977 by Claire Taschdjian

Library of Congress Catalog Card Number: 77-3806

ISBN 0-345-28434-8

This edition published by arrangement with Harper & Row,
Publishers

Manufactured in the United States of America

First Ballantine Books Edition: October 1979

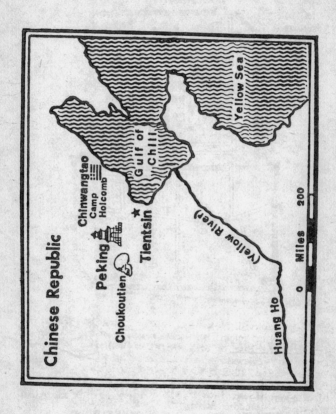

Peking

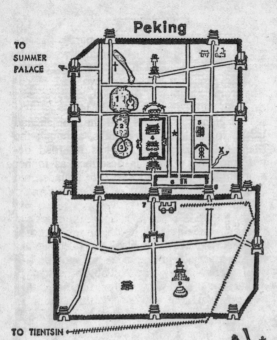

TO
SUMMER
PALACE

TO TIENTSIN ←

SUMMER PALACE AND
JADE FOUNTAIN PAGODA

TO
PEKING

READER'S GUIDE

1,2,3 NORTHERN, MIDDLE & SOUTHERN LAKE

4 FORBIDDEN CITY

5 EASTERN MARKET

6 LEGATION QUARTER

7 CHIEN MEN GATE

8 HATAMEN GATE

9 TEMPLE OF HEAVEN

✝ "ST. JOSEPH'S UNIVERSITY"

"PEKING MEDICAL SCHOOL" (PMS)

▌▌ FRENCH EMBASSY

U.S. EMBASSY & MARINE BARRACKS

CHIEN MEN STATION

★ EVVIE'S HOUSE

✗ KATHY'S HOUSE

After: Lin Yu Tang, Imperial Peking, LONDON: Elek Books, Ltd. 1961

Prologue

NEW YORK, January 27—The partly decomposed body of a middle-aged woman was discovered early this morning in the swamps of the Jamaica Bay Wildlife Refuge by two bird watchers. The woman had been strangled, and her fully clothed body stuffed into a plastic leaf bag. The Medical Examiner estimates that the woman had been dead for at least two months, although the persistent subfreezing weather has retarded decomposition. The woman is described as in her early or middle forties, 5'8", 115 pounds, red hair, hazel eyes, fair complexion. She was dressed in a blue suit, white nylon blouse and tan nylon stockings. The blouse was torn down the front but there was no evidence of a sexual attack. A badly rotted black seal coat and black fur-lined leather boots were found near the body in another leaf bag, but there was no purse. The body was removed to the City Morgue for further examination. Anyone able to identify the woman is asked to confidentially call Police at ME9-5627. (See photo.)

The photo showed the too obviously reconstituted face of a once handsome woman with short, curly hair and a thin, triangular face. The caption read: "Do you know this woman?" and repeated the invitation to impart information to the police.

Thus the *Daily News*. The *Times* apparently had not considered this news Fit to Print.

There were several people in New York City who could have identified the dead woman.

Señora Ramirez of West 126th Street had known her quite well. But the señora did not read the *Daily News*, which transcended her very limited knowledge of English. Señora Ramirez kept abreast of world affairs through *El Diario,* which, like the *Times,* had not considered the item newsworthy ("Middle-aged *gringa,*

1

not even raped, so who the hell gives a damn?").

Even if Señora Ramirez had possessed the necessary linguistic ability, she would certainly not have shared her knowledge with the police. Partly out of principle, but mainly because it might have meant explaining a certain twenty-one-inch TV console in her living room, the clothes with Bergdorf Goodman, Saks Fifth Avenue and Lord & Taylor labels, which looked so good on her daughter Margarita, and possibly also a Rolleiflex camera and a portable typewriter that had brought fifty-eight dollars at Goldman's hockshop on West 125th Street. . . .

The doorman of an apartment house on East End Avenue looked at the photo and mused, "Yeah, could be the poor lady. . . ." He decided against calling police "confidentially." Better not get involved. His duty to his family came first. What the duty to his family had to do with the dead woman was not immediately apparent to him, but hell, the cops would make him go down to the morgue to identify a "partly decomposed" corpse that had been lying around Jamaica Bay for two months. Who needed that? Let someone else do it. Like that tall, skinny character who'd been so anxious to get hold of her forwarding address. . . .

Unaware of the New York *Daily News*'s existence, Frau Katrin Peters, in Innsbruck, Austria, was trying to sort out her mementos into true keepsakes, to be taken to Vorarlberg, and trivia, for the trash can at her side. As is usual with such undertakings, she had got sidetracked by a box filled with old photographs. At the moment she was contemplating an eight-by-ten glossy. A square red stamp on its back said in Chinese and English: "Photography Department, Peking Medical School," with an inked notation underneath: "March 2, 1941."

The photograph showed a group of people posed stiffly against a carved balustrade. Frau Peters gazed fondly at the short, roly-poly figure of the Professor, front row center. This had been the last picture of him taken in Peking; a week or so later he and his wife had left for the United States. She herself stood between the Professor and tall, stooped Father Lorrain, who was smiling that sweet yet somewhat mischievous smile

2

of his. The rest of the group were Chinese members of the staff, whose names and functions she had long since forgotten. Except Ch'en, of course, who flanked the Professor on the other side. Frau Peters wondered briefly how Ch'en had managed to survive in the People's Republic. She decided to take the picture with her.

Frau Peters picked up a faded color print showing two tall uniformed young men—one dark, one blond—and two girls. One girl was tall, with short chestnut curls and long-lashed, slanted green eyes; the other was blue-eyed and chubby, her round face framed by a lank brown pageboy bob. The notation on the back said: "Tom, Bill, Evvie and Kathy. Peking, September 1941."

Frau Peters grimaced a little. Chubby then, she was now downright plump. It was a good likeness of Evvie, though. The color of her face had faded to a pale ivory, more true to the living original than the crude orangy-pink of the fresh print. Color prints were still primitive in 1941 and faded easily. . . . Joe had taken the picture. Both Joe and Tom were dead; poor Tom! She hadn't heard from Bill Snyder or Evvie in a long time. Martin had never met any of them. . . .

Frau Peters dropped the print into the trash can.

PART I

The Hijack

Peking, China: March to December 7, 1941

1

"Evvie?"

"Hmmm . . ."

"Come on, Evvie, time to get up."

"Hmm . . ."

"Come on, Evvie—it's nearly noon."

"So? *You* come *here*, Joe."

Two white arms emerged from under the covers and twined themselves around Joe's neck, pulling him down. Reluctantly Joe stiffened his neck and back and began to disengage the grip of the arms.

"Not now, Evvie. I've got to go out. Rickshaw's waiting."

"Let him wait." The arms increased their hold.

"Evvie, let go! We had all last night; we're going to have all tonight. Give a man a chance to recharge the battery. Come on now; it's a nice day."

Heavily lashed lids opened halfway over slanted green eyes. "Uh . . . okay, Joe." A yawn. The arms disappeared under the covers, the red-curled head snuggled deeper into the pillow. Evvie gave every indication of going back to sleep.

Joe grinned and jerked the covers off. Jabbing his finger into the bare rib cage, he said again, "Get up, you lazy slut! Don't steal God's beautiful day."

"Since when have you got religion? Anyway, He's got lots more. Oh, all right—I'll get up, blast you."

"Blast you," Joe mimicked. "Don't be so goddamn British."

"I'm not; I'm German—remember? Where do you have to go in such a bloody hurry?"

Joe had walked over to the dresser, carefully skirting a table which occupied most of the wall space and bore a tall structure covered with a sheet. He straightened his tie and smoothed down his hair in front of the mirror. "I'm meeting Hans; have to bring him some stuff and get some more reagents. Bunch of guys going home. . . ."

The perfectly plucked eyebrows contracted in a

frown; the eyes were suddenly hard and shrewd. "Make him give you more money, Joe. With the risk you are taking . . . I do wish you could quit."

Joe walked over to the bed, kissed his wife and said, "Soon, babe, but not yet. We need that dough bad."

Evvie sighed and scowled at the shrouded contraption by the wall. "I know, Joe. . . . Give the call of the Orient, will you?"

Joe yelled, "Amah?"

Amah bustled in, a short, dumpy figure, lacquered black hair drawn straight back into a neat bun, the hairline impeccably plucked into the perfect oval required of married women. She wore a short, starched white jacket, with a stand-up collar and frog-button fasteners, over baggy black cotton trousers. These were caught and tied at the ankle and tucked into snow-white hose, which in turn were encased in black satin slippers. In rapid, melodious Mandarin, Evvie instructed Amah to run a bath, tell Kim to prepare breakfast, and lay out the linen suit. Amah began to pick up the various items of clothing and underwear that were strewn all over the floor. Joe watched and shook his head.

"Why can't you pick up after yourself?"

"What are amahs for?"

"Still beats me how you jabber that lingo."

"Well, look—after all, I was born here; Chinese was my first language. Nothing so wonderful about that."

"Yeah; still . . . Tell Amah to be careful with the stuff in the bathroom and to clean up after you've had your bath; Kim has to set up for tonight. You got any plans for today?"

"I think I'll walk around the Morrison Street Market, maybe have a tea at the Wagons-Lits later."

Joe said, "Okay; have fun. Don't be home late, though. Bill is coming over tonight; he'll probably bring Tom. Tell Kim there'll be company for dinner."

"Joe, I don't really like Bill. He reminds me of a shark!"

"I know, baby, you've said so before. You don't have to like him; just feed him—okay?" Joe kissed Evvie again and walked out.

Bathed, dressed and fed, Evvie left the house an

hour later. Joe had been right—it was a beautiful day.

The pale-blue sky gave no hint that only yesterday it had been darkened by dirty yellow clouds composed in equal parts of dust blown in from the Gobi desert by a northwesterly gale and the local product swirled up from the unpaved hutungs—one of the periodic dust storms that dimmed the sun to a faint reddish lumines-cence and visibility to that of a pea-souper fog, creating darkness at noon and filling air, pores and nostrils with fine desert sand that irritated eyes and throat and gritted annoyingly between one's teeth.

On her way home from the Grand Hôtel des Wag-ons-Lits, Evvie caught sight of a small, sturdy figure walking smartly along Legation Street, brown pageboy bob swinging. Evvie accelerated. "Kathy?"

The other girl swirled around, startled. "Evvie!"

They hugged, then held each other at arm's length in the manner of friends who have not seen each other for a long time, exclaiming simultaneously and inevitably:

"You haven't changed a bit!"

"I didn't know you were in Peking."

"I'm married. I live here now."

"Why, Evvie, that's really *news!* Uh . . . not Hans von Albers, is it?"

"Hans! Don't be bloody silly. That would be like incest, for God's sake! No, I am Mrs. Joseph Cramer now."

Kathy let out her breath. "And who is *Mister* Joseph Cramer? Where did you meet him?"

"Well, he is an American, he came over last year, we met at Hans's. We've been married two months; we live at Nan Ho Yen."

Kathy was impressed. Nan Ho Yen—the Southern River Bank—was Peking's Park Avenue.

"Your Joe must be doing well. Those houses aren't cheap."

"Oh, we haven't a dime. The house and furniture belong to Hans. He's letting us have it." Evvie deliber-ately changed the subject. "What about you, Kathy? I thought you were in medical school in Switzerland?"

"I was, but I quit school and tried to come home last year when Mother got so ill and Father and Mother moved to Peking so that she could get treat-

9

ment at PMS. But it took so long, Evvie, with the war in Europe, and waiting endlessly for the Russian and Japanese transit visas. By the time I finally made it back, it was too late. . . . And Father died suddenly last December; a heart attack."

Evvie took Kathy's hand. "I'm so sorry, Kathy. . . . But you are staying on here?"

Kathy brightened. "Well, I've got a job. I was very lucky. After Mother's death Father worked at PMS—he said his medicine had got rusty in all those years in Shantung, he needed a refresher course—and he met the Professor there, my boss, and the Professor needed a bilingual secretary, German and English, and there I was. I work at the Paleoanatomy Laboratory, Evvie—it's marvelously interesting."

"The *what* laboratory?"

"Paleoanatomy—where they are working on the Peking Man."

"The Peking Man . . . Oh, you mean those ancient fossils. How old are they—a million years?"

"Maybe only six hundred thousand," said Kathy with a grin.

"Well, that's old enough; anyway, it must be *fascinating*," said Evvie politely.

Kathy got carried away. "Yes, it *is* fascinating. Imagine, I am actually *handling* those fossils. Although I don't know what's going to happen now. I just saw my boss off at Chien Men Station—he and his wife are being repatriated. The embassy insisted that his wife go back to the States and he said they were too old for a separation that could be indefinite, so he went along. I don't know how the work is going to go on without him."

Evvie nodded. She was aware of the exodus of "nonessential" Americans—wives, children, the elderly—whose repatriation was urged by the U.S. Embassy in view of the ever-increasing danger of war with Japan. Joe kept talking about going home—after they'd built up a stake. . . . What was Kathy saying?

". . . But at least Father Lorrain is still in charge, and maybe there won't be a war after all and the Professor will come back and we'll start digging again and maybe I'll even discover some fossils myself—"

Evvie cut her short. "Why not. You always were smarter than me, Kathy. I don't know how I'd ever have made it through school without you doing my chemistry and physics for me—and of course Hans to do my math assignments," she added loyally, giving credit where credit was due. "But you must tell Joe about your job. He'll be *so* interested. Joe knows about these things; he's a scientist."

"Is he! What kind of a scientist, Evvie?"

"Joe . . . he's . . . uh . . . Joe's a chemist. I say, are you doing anything special right now?"

Kathy said she had no particular plans for the rest of the day.

"Then why don't you come home with me, meet Joe, have a drink and stay for dinner?"

Walking through the eastern gate of the Legation Quarter, they reached Hatamen Street, hailed rickshaws and were swiftly borne toward Tung Chang Ang Chieh, the southernmost of the four broad thoroughfares that enclosed the square Imperial City.

The late afternoon was still pleasantly warm and the rickshaw coolies had shed their long padded gowns, which lay neatly folded at their passengers' feet. The coolies' bare brown backs glistened with sweat as they trotted along Tung Chang Ang Chieh. The air was filled with the sounds and smells of Peking: the cries, chants and clappers of the street vendors; the spicy aroma of their wares mingling with the undefinable smell of dust, open sewers, camel dung and incense which characterized the city in the spring. Small donkeys clop-clopped along, carrying one or more riders of either or both sexes, or pulling two-wheeled, blue canopied carts that conveyed apparently limitless numbers of passengers. Rickshaw coolies shouted cheerfully to one another. The radios in the open street stalls were blaring a commercial for cod liver oil, delivered in a fruity belly voice that seemed to slither with the product it recommended. The street sounds merged with the flutelike piping of reed whistles tied to the tail feathers of pigeons that rose and dipped in silvery flocks in the blue hazy sky over the dark evergreens and distant golden roofs of the Forbidden City.

The gently rocking motion of the rickshaw in the

11

balmy, multi-scented spring breeze was conducive to meditation and free flow of thought. In view of their unexpected reunion, Kathy and Evvie naturally thought about each other and about the beginning of their somewhat incongruous friendship.

They were as disparate in looks and personality as a race horse and a Clydesdale, Evvie having the pale fragility of an ivory figurine, Kathy with the sturdy body and apple cheeks of a Swiss peasant girl. Evvie could and did eat like a horse, never losing her look of elegant emaciation; Kathy had to watch her diet. Evvie draped in a towel managed to look like a *Vogue* cover girl; Kathy appeared rugged and wholesome no matter what she wore. Evvie's hair, naturally curly and the color of richly polished mahogany, was cut in an artless short crop; Kathy's limp brown hair would not hold a wave even in the dry climate of North China.

Evvie relished night life and detested outdoor activity in any form; Kathy swam, played tennis and ice-skated, and despised late nights and the smoke-filled air of nightclubs.

However, these differences tended to facilitate their friendship, since neither girl threatened competition for the other.

Their initially forced association was brought about by similar, heavily middle-class European backgrounds.

Katrin Ewers' parents had been medical missionaries who had joined a small British mission hospital some two hundred miles inland of the Chinese Treaty Port of Tientsin when Kathy was just learning to talk. Growing up at the mission, Kathy quickly became trilingual, effortlessly speaking Chinese with the servants and her playmates, guttural Swiss German with her parents, and British-accented "China Coast English" at the mission's elementary and grammar schools.

After completing grammar school, Kathy was sent to the German school in Tientsin for the four-year course that would qualify her for study at a Swiss or German university.

The Zimmermanns were happy to welcome their Evvie's "nice little classmate" as a boarder in the Victorian mansion to which young Mr. Zimmermann had brought his bride after the Boxer Rebellion, and where Evvie had been born when her parents were already middle-aged. For once they resisted Evvie's violent objections to the arrangement ("She's going to pray out loud and try to save my soul"); Kathy was installed, and Dr. and Mrs. Ewers returned to Shantung, happy in the thought that their young daughter was well looked after in a solidly respectable Christian household.

Neither set of parents ever learned of Evvie's after-school and nocturnal activities. Contrary to Evvie's unvoiced fears, the "goody-goody mission brat" not only failed to "snitch," but even seemed fascinated when she first surprised Evvie in the process of weighing out small quantities of a white powder on a postage scale.

Thereafter Kathy would sit cross-legged on Evvie's bed and watch as Evvie deftly weighed the powder and then wrapped the little portions in paper and cellophane, chatting gaily about her good friend Hans von Albers, whom she "owed" for doing her math homework. Kathy never found out whether Evvie received money in addition to solved math problems for her services, although she never seemed short of cash and apparently did not mind losing, sometimes heavily, at the races, the only outdoor activity she enjoyed.

Kathy usually was half asleep when Evvie crept out the window to distribute her packages and, that duty discharged, kept assignations with various commissioned members of whatever armies and navies happened to be stationed in Tientsin at the time, to come creeping back the same way shortly before dawn.

Kathy knew, of course, that what Evvie was doing was wicked and sinful, but it was part of Evvie's glamour and sophistication, which she admired deeply, humbly and without envy. Besides, a little heroin-pushing did not seem too reprehensible in a country where the heavy, sweetish odor of opium hung heavily in the air on a summer's night, and where many Westerners were as accustomed to their daily opium pipe as they were to cocktails before dinner; some were even known to have cut short their year's furlough when they ran out of supplies in their homeland.

Dr. and Mrs. Ewers did not require such supplies

13

when, after Kathy's graduation, they went home on their sabbatical leave to enroll their daughter at the medical school in Basel.

The recent Anschluss with Austria, and the subsequent invasion of Czechoslovakia and Poland, followed by the outbreak of World War II, did not seriously interfere with Kathy's studies in neutral Switzerland, despite the sporadic fighting at the nearby French-German border. But mail from China arrived with increasing irregularity and often with great delay, and the news about Mrs. Ewers' health became ever more alarming. When in the spring of 1940 Kathy finally returned to China, it was only to keep house for her father and take typing lessons, since Peking Medical School did not accept foreign students. Soon after she had started in her job at the Paleoanatomy Laboratory her father died, and she was left alone in a small Chinese house off Hatamen Street with her amah left by way of a family. Amah had been part of Kathy's life since she could remember, as nursemaid, teacher, servant and chaperone. But neither Amah's devotion nor the Professor's kindness could relieve Kathy's loneliness after her father's death. There were few datable young men left in Peking, although there was no lack of middle-aged grass widowers eager to show a pretty young woman a good time—for a price that Kathy considered far too high for an afternoon game of tennis at the Peking Club and drinks and dinner afterward.

Kathy had become a loner, less from choice than from necessity, and she was happy to have found Evvie again.

As the rickshaws turned north into Nan Ho Yen, Kathy began to wonder about Evvie's husband, a chemist—which meant he was probably stodgy and respectable. Perhaps Evvie had reformed? And they had met at von Albers'; Hans must have reformed too. Perhaps he had gone into real estate—after all, he owned the house Evvie and Joe lived in. . . .

While Kathy was spectulating about Joe and Evvie's well-born German landlord, Evvie's thoughts, also, had returned from the Tientsin past to the Peking present. She had just decided that Kathy, though proven trust-

14

worthy, had better not know too much about Joe's chemistry, when the rickshaws stopped in front of a red-lacquered gate which was flanked by two elaborately carved stone lions. Evvie paid the coolies and operated the heavy brass knocker.

2

The red gate was opened immediately by a smiling houseboy in immaculate white. A painted spirit wall blocked direct access to the courtyard and the house beyond. Evil spirits, able to proceed only in a straight line, would bounce off this obstacle, but Kathy and Evvie walked around it, crossed the courtyard and entered the living room. This was a low-slung pavilion with an overhanging blue-tiled roof. The overhang was supported by tall red-lacquered pillars and roofed over a paved veranda, which connected by walkways with the bedroom and kitchen pavilions right-angled on either side of the living room. The three pavilions flanked the square, paved courtyard in which tubbed oleanders and pomegranate bushes were budding fatly. Gold and black fish with telescope eyes and delicate, veil-like fins undulated in a circular goldfish pond at the center of the courtyard, in the shade of two gnarled jujube trees.

The houseboy announced, "Missie come home," whereupon a baritone emating from behind the back of an overstuffed chair said, "Hiya, babe. You don't mind if I don't get up, do you? . . . Bring drink for Missie, Kim."

Kim? thought Kathy. A Korean houseboy?

"Joe," said Evvie, "look whom I found on Legation Street. Kathy, meet Joe. Joe, I've told you about Kathy—she's living right here in Peking and working at PMS."

Joe rose and shook hands. "PMS, eh? Nice to meet you, Kathy. Meet Bill and Tom. Kim, bring drink for Missie Kathy."

After which he sank back into his chair. Two tall young men, one fair, the other brunet, had risen politely when the ladies entered the room. It was not immediately apparent to Kathy which was Bill and which was Tom, but for the moment she concentrated on Evvie's husband. He reminded her of Clark Gable; perhaps it was the hairline mustache and the slightly protruding ears. But Joe's features were coarser and more irregular than the movie star's, and his nose seemed too porous and engorged with small veins for a man in his late twenties, as Kathy estimated his age. His grin was friendly, his handshake warm and firm.

Tom Aiken was the dark-haired, Bill Snyder the blond young man, and both were U.S. Marines, members of the Legation Guard, Tom a Pfc., Bill a corporal.

Evvie and Kathy settled down with the cocktail and sherry served them by the Korean houseboy, Kim. The conversation resumed, easily, drawlingly and about nothing in particular. Evvie's mention of Kathy's job at PMS—"What was the name of that laboratory?"—aroused momentary interest. Joe showed himself unexpectedly knowledgeable. "Human fossils six hundred thousand years old, eh? Pithecanthropus, Sinanthropus, Eoanthropus—all that sort of thing. Boy, I've got to see all those anthropussies. You giving a guided tour, Kathy?"

He grinned innocently at Kathy over the rim of his glass. Evvie said, "Really, Joe." Bill Snyder converted a titter into a cough. Tom Aiken blushed.

Kathy, not quite sure what the byplay was all about, said, "The fossils are on display, Joe, and I do give a guided tour for visitors; it's part of my job. I'll be happy to show you around the laboratory. Uh . . . Evvie says you are a chemist?"

Joe shot a quick glance at Evvie, who was slouching in a second armchair, her back against one armrest, her knees over the other, balancing her drink on her stomach. "Yeah, yeah, a chemist, that's right," said Joe, then to Evvie, "Hey, baby, since you're up, why don't you get me a fresh pack of cigarettes from the dining room?"

Evvie obediently disentangled herself and went to fetch the cigarettes. As if to change the subject, Bill

Snyder, the blond Marine, asked if he, too, might visit the laboratory. Tom said, "Me too?"

Kathy smiled. "Sure; come anytime."

Kim came in to announce that dinner was served, and the group went into the dining division of the pavilion, which was partitioned from the living room by elaborately carved room dividers. The dinner conversation turned to the Japanese, who were cordially detested by everyone present, on general principles, and in particular because they were directly responsible for the ten-o'clock curfew that was rigorously enforced by the U.S. provost marshal's office, in hopes of preventing clashes between drunken Japanese soldiers and drunken U.S. Marines. The curfew was ruining the latter's enjoyment of Peking night life.

More drinks were consumed after dinner, until the Haig & Haig Pinch bottle at Joe's elbow was almost empty. Evvie watched the decreasing Scotch level with a worried expression, but said nothing.

An elderly coolie shuffled in with an armload of logs and a bucket of coal, bowed and grinned, built a fire in the grate and departed with another bow and grin, both of which went as unnoticed as the coolie himself.

At nine-thirty Evvie began to yawn delicately. The two Marines rose, cursing the curfew. Kathy said she had to get up early to go to work. They took their leave and stood for a moment talking in the courtyard. The lights in the bedroom pavilion on their left came on almost immediately, although the living room remained lit.

It was a fine, clear night. Kathy decided to walk part of the way, making use of her two unexpected escorts. Walking south toward the Legation Quarter, Kathy found out more about the two Marines. Both had been stationed in Peking for more than a year and were due to return "Stateside" in December. Bill Snyder came from Texas. He had dropped out of college to enlist in the Marine Corps and "see the world." He was planning to quit the Corps after his tour of duty and finish his work for a degree in biology and "maybe go on to med school if there's no war." This explained Snyder's apparent interest in visiting the Paleoanatomy Laboratory.

Tom Aiken was from Vermont. His father owned a dairy farm near Woodbury. "You wouldn't never have heard of the place, Kathy, but it sure is purty country—all woods and hills, not brown and flat like here. But farming don't pay; it's a hard life, 'specially in the winter." Tom was thinking of becoming a "thirty-year man" in the Marine Corps. "Could do a lot worse, you know. Pay is good, and I'll make top sergeant one of these days; I'll get a pension, and I'll be only about fifty-five when I get out and kin start something else. The life ain't so bad, lessen there's a war, of course."

Kathy asked if they had known Joe Cramer in the States. No, they had met him and Evvie here, at the Enlisted Men's Club. "He's a real nice guy, and Evvie, she's got class. She ain't stuckup like the other American dames around here. These bitches—sorry, Kathy —these *ladies* wouldn't even invite an enlisted man into their kitchens." Kathy reflected somewhat guiltily that this was true enough. The rigid class standards prevailing in Western communities east of Suez decreed that a man in uniform had to be at least a second lieutenant to be socially acceptable. Dating a private soldier or a noncom was unthinkable in the world in which Kathy had grown up.

They reached Legation Street, where their ways parted. They said goodbye, nice meeting you, see you again at your lab for sure, then the two Marines turned west toward the barracks. Kathy hailed a rickshaw, which carried her east, across Hatamen Street, past the massive, looming silhouette of Hatamen Gate into narrow, dusty, winding Kan Mien Hutung—"Dry Noodle Lane."

Dry Noodle Lane was deserted except for an occasional mongrel which slunk by silently, and here and there a street hawker with his portable stand, selling hard-boiled eggs, sesamum buns or deep-fried, cruller-like cakes. But the night air was filled with sounds— the chants and clapping of the hawkers, the distant howling of dogs, and the screech of Chinese opera blaring forth from radios behind the gray walls that lined the hutung.

Kathy's thoughts were vaguely troubled. Joe and Evvie had seemed unnecessarily evasive about Joe's profession. If he was a chemist, why hadn't he talked about his work, considering that both she and Bill Snyder knew enough chemistry to understand what he was talking about?

Then there was the matter of the houseboy, Kim. Why a Korean, in a city that boasted the best-trained and most sought-after Chinese servants in the country, an overabundance of them now that so many foreign families had left. And Evvie, China born and bred, the lady of the house, who presumably hired the servants—Evvie certainly shared the local dislike for the Koreans and their Japanese overlords, the word "Korean" being synonymous in North China with vice and organized crime, from drug traffic to prostitution. Of course, Evvie had always been pretty broad-minded about drug traffic. . . .

The coolie stopped in front of a red gate, less grand and guarded by a much smaller pair of lions, more the size of Pekingese dogs, than their counterparts at 58 Nan Ho Yen. Amah had been waiting up and greeted her young mistress with, "Have you eaten?" the Chinese equivalent of "Good morning," "Good afternoon" and "Good evening." Kathy replied affirmatively in Mandarin and asked for a bath. She sat in the yellow earthenware Soochow tub with her knees to her chest, soaking up to her neck in the warm water while Amah scrubbed her back, then toweled her dry and helped her slip into her nightgown.

Kathy was almost asleep when it occurred to her that Evvie had not offered to show her around the house, surely an unusual omission for a bride of only two months. Another small mystery . . . Kathy slept.

Feng, the unnoticed coolie, could have enlightened Kathy on all counts. Feng knew exactly what kind of chemistry Joe performed, why the house, especially the bedroom, was out of bounds to all visitors except Corporal William Snyder, USMC, and why a Korean, not a Chinese, number one boy ran the household. Who had better qualified for such observations than the coolie, the lowest of the low in the strict caste system of upperclass Chinese servants, the first to get up in the morning, the last to retire at night, the poorest paid but hardest working of the staff, bullied by the number one boy, and a nonperson to his employers, who barely knew his name and would not recognize his face if they met him in the street.

Feng smiled thoughtfully to himself as he prepared for bed. Kim and his masters were going to get what was coming to them; the knife was being sharpened every night, to be ready when the right moment came. . . .

Feng stretched out on the scrubbed kitchen table, rested his clean-shaven head on a rolling pin and fell asleep.

3

At eight-thirty on Monday morning Kathy parked her bicycle against the carved marble balustrade that flanked the shallow flight of steps leading to the west wing of Peking Medical School and entered her small office. Kathy's desk and typewriter table were crammed into a corner near the single window, which faced east. All available wall space was crowded with bookcases, shelves and filing cabinets, which were overflowing with books, journals, correspondence, manuscripts and specimen trays that had been accumulating ever since the laboratory had come into existence some thirteen years before.

Kathy sat down at her desk and began to sort the mail, separating what she herself would answer from what was to be forwarded to the Professor in New York. From her window she had a view across the courtyard of the east wing, which was an exact replica of the west wing. Looking far to the left, she could, if she wished, catch a glimpse of the Administration Building, which faced south and was built in the same pseudo-Chinese style as east wing and west wing, with a green-tiled, sloping roof. Behind Administration lay another square courtyard, surrounded by the main hospital buildings. Other courtyards and buildings extended behind the east wing, including Jackson Hall, where Father Lorrain's laboratories were situated. The whole complex of courtyards and white, green-roofed buildings that constituted Peking Medical School occupied two city blocks between Hatamen Street and Morrison Street and was only a short distance from Nan Ho Yen.

Kathy went across the hall to the Professor's laboratory, to open the safe where the fossils were kept. The room was spotless, but it already had the chilly, deserted air of an apartment long left unoccupied. There was not a speck of dust on the Professor's workbench, facing the window. The bare surface of his redwood desk was polished to a rich glow and the glassed-in bookcases and wall cabinets were gleaming. A collection of neolithic skulls from Mongolia stared vacantly at the room through empty black sockets, as though awaiting the Professor's calipers.

Ch'en, the technician, came in and together he and Kathy removed one of the Peking skulls from the safe and deposited it reverently on a felt mat in the large, dust-free laboratory next door, where Ch'en was preparing to make hollow casts of the specimens.

In his ankle-length blue cotton gown, Ch'en seemed even taller and lankier than he was. He looked eighteen, but Kathy thought he was probably nearer twenty-five. Ch'en had never been known to speak or react to English, and it was taken for granted that he didn't know the language.

In fact, Ch'en was twenty-nine years old and his English was as perfect as his Japanese and his Korean, but he had good reasons for keeping these accomplishments to himself. Nobody else in Peking knew about them, not even the owner of a stall selling sesamum cakes in the Eastern Market on Morrison Street, with whom Ch'en chatted once in a while when he bought one or two of the crisp, hot *shaoping* for his supper.

Ch'en knew as much about Kathy and the Professor, indeed about every member of the laboratory staff, from Father Lorrain down to the coolies who scrubbed the floors, as they knew themselves. Ch'en respected the Professor's and Father Lorrain's scientific competence and tolerated Kathy, whom he considered frivolous, socially useless and rather stupid. He might have liked the Professor and Father Lorrain as persons, had he permitted himself to like anyone, let alone a "foreign devil" and a priest to boot. But Ch'en was trained to control his emotions, at least as far as affection was concerned, although he had been encouraged to hate foreign devils, dispensers of "opium for the people," the Japanese and the Kuomintang, which he did, impartially and with intensity.

Kathy, of course, was completely unaware of this. She loved to listen to Ch'en's accounts of the excavations, delivered in melodious Mandarin, of how he himself had sifted the little pea-sized wrist bone of Peking Man out of a pile of excavated rubble and had witnessed the discovery of the last of the five skulls.

The excavations had been suspended in 1937 after the Japanese invasion of North China, but the wealth of specimens recovered during the years of field work was still being worked up at PMS. The Professor had been measuring, x-raying, describing and interpreting the human remains in the west wing laboratory; at Jackson Hall Father Lorrain and his technicians were doing similar studies on the plants, the animals and the geological specimens that had been part of Peking Man's environment.

Ch'en was a skillful artist and technician. He had performed the delicate tasks of cleaning, shellacking and labeling each specimen, then piercing fragments of broken skulls together like jigsaw puzzles, shaping replicas of missing pieces from plaster of Paris to fill the gaps. He had made the solid plaster casts of the restored skulls, painting them realistically to resemble the originals. Duplicates of the casts had been sent to every major museum and paleontological laboratory in the world. Under the Professor's guidance, via an interpreter, Ch'en had reconstructed the composite life-size head of a Peking Woman, had sculpted the skull and fleshed the bones. The finished product was promptly and somewhat prissily christened "Nellie" by the laboratory staff. Nellie sat on her pedestal in a corner of the laboratory, watching inscrutably from beneath the heavy overhang of her eyebrows as Ch'en assembled the materials needed for the intricate long-term project that would result in exact replicas of both inner and outer surfaces of each of the five skulls, as fragile as the originals.

Kathy looked on for a while, then went back to her office. She picked up the manuscript that the Professor had left for her to edit and prepare for publication. The Professor had learned to master the English language since his emigration from Nazi Germany to the United States six years previously, but he continued to think in his native German. Sometimes it was difficult to convert the Professor's labyrinthine phrases into more idiomatic English, but today Kathy found it impossible. Three attempts to earn her salary ended crumpled up in the wastebasket.

Kathy stared out the window, but the east wing was uninspiring. She walked into the hall and gazed at the oversized bronze busts of Neanderthal and Cro-Magnon Man in their glass cabinets—the founders of Peking Medical School, she had told visitors on her first day on the job, failing to notice the explanatory plaques. It was not a happy memory. Blushing in retrospect, Kathy abandoned the "founders" and ambled aimlessly into the laboratory to watch Ch'en construct a grid of small rectangular Plasticine compartments across the crown of the Locus E skull, to be filled with plaster of Paris in preparation for the mold from which the outer surface of the skull would be cast. Normally the procedure was fascinating to watch; today it palled quickly. Kathy returned to her office, had another unsuccessful go at the Professor's Teutonic phraseology and dropped it with relief when Father Lorrain shambled in to pick up his mail and stay for a chat.

Lunchtime finally came. Kathy rode her bicycle home, ate the lunch that Amah had ready for her, rested awhile, then rode back to the lab and tried to kill the rest of the afternoon.

Shortly before five o'clock, Tom Aiken walked in. So he *had* meant last night's "See you again soon."

"Just happened to be in the neighborhood," he mumbled. "You said drop in anytime."

Kathy tried to conceal her pleasure. "Sure, Tom. Nice to see you. Did you come for the guided tour?"

"Well . . . uh . . . maybe another time." Tom seemed a little awed by the scientific atmosphere. "Say, that's quite a setup you have here. You look like a doctor in that white coat. Did you read all them books

23

and magazines on the shelves?" The thought appeared to scare him.

Kathy reassured him. "No, I didn't. Not *all* of them, anyway. And I have to wear the lab coat; it's regulations." She took the forbidding garment off. Tom seemed to feel that this restored her to femininity and approachability. "I was wondering was you doing anything special tonight? It's nice out; I thought maybe you'd like to go for a walk and have dinner with me? And there's a movie at the barracks. Maybe you'd like to see it?"

"I'd love to, Tom. I'll be ready in a few minutes."

Ch'en came in to say he was ready to return the skull to the safe. He ignored Tom except for a brief glance, but Ch'en's many hidden accomplishments included a photographic memory. Tom was quickly appraised and evaluated as an American serviceman, the usual illiterate clod, but possibly needing watching, especially if the little *kuniang* (unmarried lady of rank) took up with him, which seemed likely.

The evening of the day that had begun so drearily turned out to be very enjoyable. Kathy rode her bicycle alongside Tom's rickshaw. "I have to go home and change first. Come and see where I live."

Tom admired the one-pavilion house with its small paved courtyard. "Doll's house for a living doll," he said gallantly.

He went on to say that Chinese houses were unlike any he had ever seen. Certainly there was no resemblance to the frame houses of New England. "Yeah, I kinda like them houses. They're cute, like something out of a play." He agreed that it made sense to have a bike and that he was going to "get him one" if Kathy would ride around with him and show him the city. "Not much fun, going alone or with the guys. . . ."

He refused a drink and sipped with rather marked reluctance at the cup of jasmine tea that Amah served him.

They took rickshaws to Central Park, which was part of the Imperial City, and walked among the evergreens, to which the cranes and herons were now returning to roost after their day's fishing in the three artificial lakes of the Winter Palace.

Although Tom was "only" an enlisted man, it turned out that he and Kathy had a lot in common. Like Kathy, he liked the outdoors, especially hiking, fishing and skiing. Besides, he had nice eyes—not brown, as she had thought last night, but a deep blue that seemed even darker because of the long black lashes. He became quite eloquent as he talked, with a slightly nasal twang that was sometimes hard to understand, about green, wooded hills and clear lakes and the ski slopes of Mount Mansfield. Kathy visualized Vermont as somewhat like her native Switzerland and said so.

Oh, I didn't know you was German."

"I am not," said Kathy indignantly. "I am Swiss. It's like saying an American is the same as a Canadian."

"Uh . . . sorry, Kathy. But I wouldn't hold it against you even if you *was* a Kraut."

Kathy gave up. Tom became more personal. "I ain't much of a one for drinking and parties, Kathy, and I don't dance too good. I hope you don't mind."

"That's all right, Tom. I am not too good at that kind of stuff myself."

"Well, not much of a chance for nightclubbing now anyways, what with curfew at ten P.M. and restricted liberty. They're always afraid if one of us beats up a Jap it's going to trigger the war."

Tom took Kathy to dinner at the Enlisted Men's Club, where they ran into Joe and Evvie in the company of Snyder and Snyder's girlfriend, the Grand Duchess Tanya Petrovna. Tanya was luscious like an overripe pear and earned her living as an "entertainer," as did tens of thousands of grand duchesses all over China—all, like Tanya, first cousins of the Romanoffs and compelled to leave their vast estates behind when they fled from the Bolshevik Revolution.

After the movie at the barracks, Joe and Snyder made a date to visit the Peking Man as soon as Snyder had "liberty," then Tom walked Kathy home. He kissed her quickly and shyly, said, "You're cute. See you day after tomorrow for sure," and got into a rickshaw, telling the coolie to go chop-chop so that he would reach the barracks before the 10 P.M. deadline.

Kathy did see Tom two days later, but he didn't come alone. Joe and Snyder were with him, proclaiming loudly that they couldn't wait to see the famous fossils, while Tom's scowl said clearly that he wouldn't mind waiting a lifetime.

But Joe and Snyder listened with unexpected interest and attention to the routine lecture Kathy gave to all visitors. The fossils told their own story; Kathy only translated. Peking Man, six hundred thousand years ago, had walked upright just as humans did now; he had known fire and cooked his meat, cutting it up with crudely hewn stone implements. He had been a cannibal, breaking the skull and sucking the brains of his fellows, though apparently for ritual rather than nutritional purposes. He had been a man, notwithstanding his beetle-browed, sloping skull and chinless, apelike snout. He was one of the oldest representatives of mankind known at the time, and a contemporary of Java Man. In fact, the discovery of the first Peking skull had finally resolved the thirty-year-old controversy over the more fragmentary Java skull. *Pithecanthropus erectus,* the "upright apeman" of Java, had been a man and not a large ape; he had been a contemporary and close relative of Peking Man, as had been further confirmed by the recent finds of additional Java skulls.

With the aid of the actual fossils and plaster casts, Kathy demonstrated how Peking Man and Java Man stood intermediate between the great apes and modern man. The expansion of the human brain and reduction of the snoutlike face, the acquisition of a forehead and a chin, could be traced step by step from the Asian fossils via Neanderthal Man, to Cro-Magnon Man, who some twenty thousand years ago had completed the transition from low-browed, massive-boned "apeman" to fragile modern "highbrow."

This evidence of the gradual transformation and "humanization" of man in the course of five hundred millennia had led Kathy's boss, the Professor, to see evolution as a directed trend, inherent within a species and largely independent of the environment, a view which contradicted the random, haphazard environmental weeding process of natural selection. In the rarefied scientific circles in which the Professor moved as a recognized authority, this was rank heresy, which had called forth a great deal of mutual name-calling in learned monographs, with the Professor giving as good as he got.

Snyder, the ex-biology student, seemed slightly scandalized by the audacity with which the Professor demolished a sacred cow like natural selection. Then he said, "Hey, you've left out Piltdown Man. I was taught that he was the granddaddy of us all."

Kathy grinned. "The Professor says he's an anatomical impossibility—the jaw belongs to an ape, and the skull is modern—so we've bounced him off the family tree."

"Tsk, tsk." Snyder shook his head and sighed. "Here I thought he was my great-grandpa, and now your Professor calls him a phony. I'll never get over it."

Fingering the fossils reverently, Joe now asked, with a quick side glance at Snyder, what they were worth in dollars and cents. Kathy smiled. "They are unique. They're priceless. You can't express their value in terms of money."

Joe persisted. "You say this setup here and the excavations were financed by the Morgan Foundation. That's American money. Why aren't those fossils in the States? They are ours by rights, aren't they?"

Kathy explained that the Chinese government had permitted the excavations and construction of the laboratories only under the condition, solemnized by contract with the Morgan Foundation, that these relics of the remote ancestors of the Chinese people were never to leave the soil of China.

"That explains it," said Joe. Then he said, thoughtfully, "I'll bet there isn't a museum in the West or in Japan that wouldn't give its eyeteeth to have these prize specimens in its collection." Again he and Snyder exchanged a look.

Kathy showed the two men around the laboratories. They stopped for a while in the large workroom, admiring Nellie on her pedestal and watching Ch'en at work on the hollow casts. Ch'en took no apparent notice of the visitors, but their faces were immediately registered and filed in the permanent portrait gallery of his infallible memory.

Leaving an obviously relieved Tom behind, Joe and Snyder thanked Kathy for the educational afternoon and took their leave. They walked in silence for a while. Then Joe asked, "Are you thinking what I'm thinking?"

"I dunno . . . maybe. What *are* you thinking, Joe?"

"Well, those bones, you know—they got to be worth a lot of dough to *somebody*. A million, at least."

Snyder nodded. "That's exactly what I've been thinking too. What's on your mind?"

"Well, of course you couldn't *sell* anything like that to a private collector or to a museum in the States or in Japan, but . . . I bet the Morgan Foundation would have a real red face if those bones were to disappear. I bet they'd pay any amount to get them back without publicity before the Chink government in Chungking gets wind of it. Know what I mean?"

Snyder grinned. "Sure. You mean like the Lindbergh baby. Beautiful. Except the guy got caught and burned—remember? You got any ideas?"

"Well, I'm thinking. . . . Theoretically it shouldn't be too tough to get into that lab, and the safe looks flimsy enough. And I noticed that security at PMS is pretty lax; they got guards at the gates, but it seems like anybody can walk in and out without being challenged or searched."

Snyder frowned. "Yeah, but—"

"Hold it—I said *theoretically*. In practice it's a different kind of ball game altogether. First of all, we stick out like sore thumbs among the Chinks. *Somebody* would notice us for sure. Second, they'd question Kathy and that Chink lab technician right away and would be onto us in no time. Third, where would we *keep* the things? The cops would come searching the house the next day."

"Yeah, and the MP's would be searching the barracks at the same time."

"What about Tanya's?"

Snyder shook his head. "That'd be too risky, Joe. She'd be sure to blab—or else to try to shake me down. Let's leave Tanya out of it."

Joe nodded. "We've just got to wait, Bill, see how things develop. Anyway, there's no rush. Something's sure to come up."

"You're right. But we can't wait forever; remember, I'm due back Stateside in December."

"Well, listen—this may be just the thing. I've been planning to take Evvie home soon's I've got enough dough out of Hans. I'll book passage for around the time you are due to leave. We'll get the fossils to the States and make the contact from there. You can take anything in your luggage; you don't have to go through customs like a civilian—or at least they aren't that particular about servicemen."

Snyder said this would be a minor worry; he'd take care of that problem if and when it came up. The major headache would be getting the fossils out of PMS.

Joe said, "Look, we've got till December. The less time we have the stuff in our possession before we leave, the better our chances of getting away with it. We'll just have to play it by ear. In the meantime, couldn't you jolly up to little Miss Darwin a bit, get her to play along—know what I mean?"

Snyder protested with a vehemence that seemed somewhat disproportionate.

"What—*me* make out with that overgrown Heidi? You got to be kidding, Joe, for Chrissakes! She's a *missionary* kid; but she's a *virgin*, yet. *And* I'd louse up my setup with Tanya. Nothing doing, Joe! Let Aiken handle that end; he seems to like the idea."

"Okay, okay. Don't get your bowels in an uproar. It was just a thought. Makes no never mind to me who gets to deflower the little broad. Let Aiken have the pleasure, by all means. Main thing is, we may need them *both*. I'll get Evvie to have them to the house a lot; old friends and all that, you know? And maybe implicate them both a little in our work, just in case we have to put the screws on. Anyway, if it doesn't work out and we can't get our hands on the fossils, what have we lost?"

"Only a million bucks, that's all," said Snyder glumly.

Joe grinned and nudged Snyder. "Aw, come on, Bill. Don't act as if you were destitute. We're doing all right out of von Albers. You aren't even running any risk for your money. All you have to do is hand the stuff over to the guys going home, and *they* have the headache of getting it into the country, not you. Me, I'm going to blow myself up one of these days. . . . Well, hell, so who wants to live forever? I'm on borrowed time. . . . Look, we're making out okay, even without the fossils."

"Yeah, sure, Joe. But boy, a *million!*"

"Cheer up, Bill. We may collect it yet—you never know. Anyway, it's only going to be half a million apiece, or a third if we have to split with Aiken. But I guess you'll be able to live on your share! Okay?"

"Aiken . . . yeah,". said Snyder thoughtfully. "Sure, Joe. Okay."

4

The season of weekly dust storms which in Peking passed for spring came to an end. Suddenly, abruptly and without transition, it was summer.

Western-style houses disappeared underneath a shell of "pongs," straw mats mounted on a bamboo scaffolding which were closed at dawn and rolled up after sundown, shading the house during the day's heat and exposing it to a cooling breeze at night. Itinerant sellers of ice cream and improbably pink, lime-green and orange soft drinks loudly advertised their wares, whose comsumption contributed significantly to the rising incidence of *tutzupuhao*, the seasonal diarrhea. The Asian cuckoo clamored incessantly for "one more bottle"; hoopoes tripped on the lawns, their feathered crests raised like Indian war bonnets, their shrill cries blending into the symphony of Peking sounds. The smell of open sewers was intensified and mingled with the pungent aroma of green incense coils used to repel the flies and mosquitoes, which had suddenly appeared out of nowhere. The acrid odor of opium hung heavily in the air.

The populace squatted in front of their doorways, sunning and painstakingly delousing their padded winter gowns after six months' uninterrupted wear. The women were shaping mixtures of coal dust and mud into potato-sized balls, which were dried in the sun to be used as fuel come winter. The white acacias along Tung Chang Ang Chieh had bloomed, transiently covering up the permanent smells with their heavy scent; the more delicate perfume of the powderpuff-like pink mimosas would last through the summer. The lotus growing in the moat surrounding the Forbidden City and in the three artificial lakes of the Winter Palace had opened their pink succulent blooms, each as large as a child's head. The oleanders and pomegranate trees in the courtyard at 58 Nan Ho Yen were covered with red and orange blossoms. Children played hopscotch and diavolo in the hutungs and on windy days flew their splendid butterfly- or goldfish-shaped kites on the Parade Grounds surrounding the Legation Quarter.

The attrition of the American community continued. More dependents of military and diplomatic personnel, and whole families from the business and missionary communities, left with every train for Shanghai and Tsingtao to catch a President liner home. Marines returning Stateside after their two-year tour were not replaced.

Other foreigners stayed. The Dutch, the Belgians, the Norwegians and Danes had no homeland to go back to; the French had no desire to return to Vichy France. The Germans and Italians stayed because they had nothing to worry about. After Germany's invasion of Russia everybody stayed, because there was no choice. The last link with Europe, the Trans-Siberian railroad, was severed and the door to the West slammed shut.

The exodus from Peking did not involve only Westerners. Whole classes of medical students and their instructors, taking portable equipment with them, disappeared overnight from PMS, making their way west to Szechuan Province to continue their studies free from Japanese domination. Members of the medical staff also headed for Free China, and the hospital, though still functional, became restricted in the services it was able to offer.

Work at the Paleoanatomy Laboratory had settled into a somewhat tedious routine. Kathy finished the Professor's manuscript and mailed it to New York, then started Anglicizing one of Father Lorrain's arti-

31

cles, which was a literal translation from the French. The first of the hollow skull casts had been shipped off to New York, and Ch'en was working on the second.

Visitors kept coming—scholarly residents of Peking and Tientsin, professors and their students from the four local universities. The visits were a welcome interruption of the general somnolence created in equal parts of heat and boredom. One day Professor Peters of St. Joseph's University in the north city came with ten students, left them in Kathy's charge and departed for a chat with Father Lorrain in Jackson Hall. Kathy delivered her lecture, relieved that Dr. Peters had not chosen to stay. She had met him before when he had visited the Professor and was awed by his erudition, but irritated by his tendency to ask questions that she could not answer. Otherwise she dismissed him as an ungainly, balding old man of at least fifty; actually, Dr. Peters was in his early thirties.

As Westerners left, more Japanese seemed to arrive. A good number of the newcomers appeared to be anthropologists. Not a week passed but that a pair of them—they always traveled in pairs, like nuns—visited the laboratory, claiming personal acquaintance with the Professor, expressing admiration for his work and regret at his absence, and requesting to see the fossils.

They all looked alike to Kathy. Their hair stood up in bristle cuts; horn-rimmed glasses perched uneasily on the tip of snub noses; polite smiles revealed inordinate amounts of oversized front teeth. Their ill-fitting Western suits all seemed to have been cut by the same incompetent tailor. However, their comments, uttered in sibilant German or English interspersed with many "Ah ssso's" and audible intakes of breath, were relevant and knowledgeable.

Kathy thought they were funny little men and entertained the company at 58 Nan Ho Yen with imitations. Father Lorrain did not think the little men were at all funny; neither did Ch'en.

Father Lorrain insisted on being present at these visits, ostensibly to honor the distinguished visitors in the Professor's absence. After the third such visit in as many weeks, Father Lorrain had a conference with Mr. Mitchell, administrator of PMS. He then instructed

Kathy not to display the fossils to visitors anymore and to use casts exclusively to illustrate her lecture.

Ch'en carefully but unobstrusively memorized the names and faces of the visiting scientists. After each visit he went to buy a *shaoping* or two at the stall in the Morrison Street Market. He also took to working late at the laboratory, pleading the pressing need to get the casts finished. Unaware that this "overtime" covered the entire night, Father Lorrain had no objection to Ch'en's zeal, just so long as the fossils were locked in the safe when Kathy left at 5:00 P.M.

"Smart move," Joe said approvingly when Kathy explained why she had to deny his request to see the fossils again. "Guess that one look will have to last me; I don't think we'll be coming back to China for a long time."

"What do you mean, Joe?"

"Didn't Evvie tell you? We're going home in December. It's about time Evvie met my folks. Also, we've got to get her citizenship under way. She has to live in the States three years before she is naturalized; she won't get anything as long as we live abroad."

"Why are you waiting till December? Why not leave earlier?"

"First sailing I was able to get," said Joe curtly, considering it unnecessary to explain that he himself had chosen the date to coincide as closely as possible with that of Snyder's departure.

Kathy thought herself lucky to be Swiss. Unlike German women, she would not lose her citizenship if she married a foreign national—an American, for instance.

Kathy's relationship with Tom had deepened into something they both called love. They saw each other whenever Tom had liberty. True to his promise, he had "got him" a bicycle, and she had become his guide through the city.

They wandered through the courtyards and halls of the Forbidden City, stood in the anteroom to the Emperor's throne hall, where hapless mandarins, aroused at 3 A.M. and compelled to wait for hours for the audience to which they had been summoned, had carried small *shetzu* dogs in their wide sleeves to serve as spittoons, since this vital commodity was not provided by

33

the imperial household. Use of the marble floor could cost the offender his queued head. Tom received this bit of historical information with a mixture of amusement and disgust.

At the Lama Temple in the north city, they shuddered in mock horror at the sculptures depicting in explicit, gory detail the tortures that monsters would inflict on evildoers once they reached the Nether World.

"Look at that guy's guts spilling out."

"Yes; isn't it like something out of Hieronymus Bosch?"

"Huh?"

"Weirdo Flemish painter," mumbled Kathy, and hastily changed the subject.

They rode their bicycles through the tangled park that surrounded the Temple of Heaven and along the mile-long marble avenue that led from the temple, with its soaring, three-tiered blue roof, to the snow-white altar, whose roof was the open sky and whose center was the Center of the World. Here the yellow-robed Emperor, the Son of Heaven, had worshipped twice a year, invoking the blessings of his Parent on his people.

"He was probably kowtowing right here where we are standing," Kathy demonstrated, kneeling down and hitting her forehead against the marble floor. Tom slapped her behind and asked, only half jokingly, "Hey, quit that. How would you like to be raped right here in the Center of the World?" and when she rose hastily, "Come on. What's in that basket? I'm getting kind of hungry."

Tom would pick Kathy up after work whenever he had liberty. "What's on the program today?"

"Let's go rowing on Nan Hai." Or "Let's walk around Pei Hai."

And they'd end the day eating *chiaotzu*—"like ravioli," said Tom, "but where's the tomato sauce?"—in the restaurant high up on the bottle-shaped Great White Dagoba, watching dusk descend in a gentle blue mist over the Northern Lake.

On weekends they rode out to the Summer Palace, walking in the footsteps of the wicked Empress Dowager and giggling at the "Chinese Navy," the atrocious marble boat that the Empress had constructed with funds intended for the real thing.

Kathy never tired of just walking through the streets of the city. Tom tagged along willingly, though unable to overcome his shock at her tendency to buy and unconcernedly consume the sweetmeats hawked by the street vendors. "Look at the flies! How can you eat this filth? Look at the guy's hands! He probably hasn't washed in years."

Kathy munched with relish. "Don't worry! I grew up in this country! I'm immune to all the bugs; I've never even had a worm."

Tom never learned to appreciate the fact that the out-come of the biannual examination for "ova and parasites" was a routine topic at Peking dinner parties.

Kathy, on the other hand, had to counteract Tom's inclination to buy grossly overpriced brass Buddhas or garish scarves and kimonos lavishly embroidered with writhing dragons. Regretfully he let himself be pulled away: "Mom and my sister would have liked that."

"Come on, Tom. This is just tourist stuff; it's not even real silk. And that Buddha was probably made in Czechoslovakia!"

But the street life was an unending delight. Tom had started to take pictures of the more picturesque shop signs: "Nobody is going to believe this when I tell them. I've got to show them *proof.*"

And he clicked away at the PEKING FROZEN SUCKER COMPANY, which manufactured ice cream, the window of a tailor shop that proclaimed: LADIES HAVE FITS UP-STAIRS; he stood speechless with awe in front of INSER-TION OF FALSE TEETH AND EYES, LATEST METHODISTS.

Tom enjoyed the sightseeing, but Kathy sensed that he remained unaffected by the enchantment that Kublai Khan's "Xanadu" held for her. Peking would remain forever alien to him. He would interrupt her expressions of rapture about this, that or the other crimson-pillared, golden-roofed palace with descriptions of the green mountains and trout brooks of Vermont, the fishing in summer, the skiing in winter; he couldn't wait to show them to Kathy! He liked Chinese food and became reasonably adept in the use of chopsticks, but remained essentially, as he termed it, "a steak and potatoes man." This taste was indulged in frequently at the Enlisted Men's Club, usually in the company of the Cramers, Snyder, and the Grand Duchess Tanya Petrovna.

Steaks, ice cream sodas, Coca-Colas at the Enlisted Men's Club, dances and movies at the barracks. This was Tom's home ground, a small piece of the United States. Here, not at the Temple of Heaven or in the Forbidden City, he felt at ease.

Both Tom and Kathy were aware of the differences in their backgrounds and educational levels. There was, for instance, Tom's grammar. Kathy tried, persistently and quite unsuccessfully, to discourage his use of double negatives and of constructions like "I woulda went." Tom took these language lessons in good humor, calling her his "little schoolmarm." He also called her "little limey," while admitting privately that Kathy's British-accented China Coast English occasionally got on his nerves.

When Kathy talked about going back to college and getting her degree, he balked—"You don't need no college degree to be a Marine sergeant's wife"—and categorically rejected suggestions that he might attend officers training school: "Ain't got the brains for it, honey. I barely made it through eighth grade."

Both suppressed vague misgivings about their basic incompatibility and concentrated on what they did have in common—a fondness for the outdoors and, chiefly, the healthy passion of two young people in love. One possible obstacle to mutual bliss had been removed by a negative answer to a delicately worded question: Tom was not one of the clean-cut young Americans who regularly contributed "specimens" to Dr. Detwyler's special research laboratory in the Department of Dermatology and Syphilology of PMS.

When Tom was too occupied at Kan Mien Hutung to make the 10 P.M. curfew, he could always leave at 5:30 A.M. and be in time for Reveille. Amah, mission-bred and a strait-laced Methodist., disapproved visibly and audibly of the goings on, hinting darkly that the Old Master and the Old Mistress would have been greatly distressed by the *kuniang*'s sinfulness.

Since Kathy was a "nice" girl, and both she and

Tom had strict Puritan backgrounds, the subject of marriage came up with increasing frequency.

By the end of June they were engaged. Kathy wore the gold ring with the Marine Corps emblem that Tom had had made for her by one of the skilled goldsmiths outside Hatamen Gate.

Tom would return to the States in December as scheduled, would send for her as soon as possible, and they would be married from his parents' home in Woodbury, Vermont.

What free time Kathy did not spend with Tom she spent with Evvie. Evvie was always at home and always glad to see Kathy; she seemed to have few if any other friends. Being congenitally opposed to physical exercise in any form, Evvie pointed out, reasonably, that in this heat no place could be more comfortable than the courtyard at 58 Nan Ho Yen. Coolness rose from the courtyard's wetted-down flagstones, and spread from the spray of the fountain in the center of the little goldfish pond. Lounge chairs were set out by the pond in the shade of the two jujube trees. Evvie and Kathy, dressed in sunsuits, reclined there sipping iced tea, as companionably as in the old days at the Tientsin Country Club.

Evvie became a little more forthcoming, but her girlish confidences about Joe left a great deal to be desired.

"Where did Joe study chemistry?"

"Uh . . . Iowa State, I think."

Since neither Kathy nor Evvie was familiar with American universities, this meant precisely nothing.

"Does he have a doctorate in chemistry?"

"Uh . . . not really."

"Well, did he get a master's or a bachelor's?"

"Uh . . . no, not really."

"Oh?"

"Well, he took two years of chemistry . . . but, well, Joe's got this *problem* . . . and then something came up. He had some trouble; he had to quit school."

Evvie did not elaborate on the "trouble" that had curtailed Joe's academic career. The "problem" did not need explaining—it was only too obviously responsible for the dilated veins on Joe's nose and for the amount of Haig & Haig Pinch that was consumed at 58 Nan Ho Yen.

"Joe is doing all right," said Evvie defensively. "He does some free-lance writing and photography, and chemistry. He's got a darkroom and a laboratory."

"It's a small house. Where do you have room for a darkroom and a laboratory?"

It turned out that Joe was using the bedroom.

"The bedroom?"

"Well, the bathroom is next door, and he needs running water and a sink."

That was plausible. It also explained why Kathy had never been shown the bedroom; it was probably in such a mess that Evvie was ashamed to have visitors see it. Kathy felt relieved at this simple solution to the "mystery."

"What kind of chemistry is Joe doing? Organic? Inorganic?"

But Evvie was very vague about this—or was "evasive" a better word?

"I don't really know, Kathy. . . . Let's go in; dinner will be ready in a little while."

At any rate, Joe didn't seem to be much of a chemist, or he was an exceptionally clumsy one, since he frequently appeared with his eyebrows and mustache singed and his hands bandaged because of burns.

Bill Snyder was a frequent visitor, and Evvie did not seem to mind if he saw the presumable mess in the bedroom; he seemed to have free access to these off-limits premises.

Sequestered there, Joe and Snyder continued to discuss the "operation." They had agreed that it was impossible to remove the fossils from PMS without risking immediate exposure. However, it seemed increasingly likely, in view of the steadily deteriorating political situation, that sooner or later the fossils would be shipped to the United States for safekeeping. Who was more likely to affect this transport than the U.S. Embassy or the U.S. Marines? This would inevitably entail transfer of the goods from PMS to the embassy or to the barracks next door. A hijack between these two points was the obvious solution to their problem.

Joe and Snyder proceeded to refine their plan on the basis of this contingency. After kicking the matter back and forth, they decided to leave Kathy out of it.

"She can't really help, and we'd be traced through her right away."

"But we'll need Aiken," said Joe.

Snyder agreed but expressed his doubts.

"Trouble is, Aiken is such a *straight* guy. He'd never go along with something like this operation. Let's face it, Joe—what it amounts to is kidnapping or at least grand theft and extortion."

"No," said Joe thoughtfully. "I guess he wouldn't play along—not unless he had no choice."

"Meaning we've got to get something on him?"

"Exactly."

"Like what?"

"How about a drug rap?" suggested Joe. "You could plant a little package among his belongings, discover it and threaten him with exposure unless he plays ball with us."

Snyder considered. "Nope, Joe, better not. It might backfire. Besides, Hans wouldn't like it; it could blow the business. See what I mean?"

Joe saw. "You got a better idea?"

Snyder rose. "Give me a little time, Joe. I'll come up with something."

"Okay; just don't take too long. You never know when the break is going to come; might be tomorrow for all we know."

"That would be a little premature. . . . Right, I'll sleep on it."

5

The summer got hotter and reached the period when heat and humidity remained near one hundred around the clock. Evvie invited Kathy to spend her two-week vacation at the Zimmermanns' beach home in Peitaiho, a seaside resort some 180 miles east of Peking. Joe remained in Peking, explaining that he was behind in his work and had to catch up.

Bill Snyder, an expert wangler, wangled a temporary transfer for himself and Pfc. Aiken to the U.S. naval base at Chinwangtao, near Peitaiho. This permitted Snyder to explore the layout and storage facilities of the base, where he and, it was to be hoped, the Peking Man would embark for Stateside come December.

While performing perfunctory duty, investigating the base and loafing on the beach in Peitaiho with Evvie, Kathy and Tom, Snyder kept thinking of ways to "get something" on Aiken. The inspiration came one morning shortly before they were all due to go back to Peking.

Upon their return, Snyder lost no time telling Joe about it. Joe smirked, called it "perfect" and suggested one or two minor refinements.

"When do you want to do it, Bill?"

"Well, it's got to be a weekend. Maybe weekend after next? I've got to line up a little help. Also, we have to get Kathy out of the way. And I'll need a Mickey ... you know?"

"Leave Kathy and the Mickey to me. Weekend after next it is."

The Friday preceding the weekend in question was very hot and humid. At Joe's suggestion, Evvie gave an engagement party for Kathy and Tom. Kathy enjoyed Kim's excellent cooking but became quite ill during the night. She put it down to an attack of *tutzupuhao,* nothing unusual at that time of year, and thought no more about it. However, on Saturday she felt too weak to keep her evening date with Tom.

Tom sat disconsolately on his bunk. Snyder appeared.

"What's the matter, Tom? No date?"

"Naw. Kathy's sick."

"Tell you what. I haven't got a date either; Tanya's busy. Let's you and I go out and paint the town red. It's been a long time since you and I've been out on the town together."

The two set off visiting one joint after another along Hatamen Street. When Tom began to show the desired signs of extreme drunkenness, Snyder hired two rickshaws and gave a certain address in the red-light district outside Chien Men Gate. This place, whose occupants and clientele were exclusively male, was not "off limits" to U.S. servicemen for the sole reason that its existence was unknown to the provost marshal's office.

Snyder introduced the half-conscious Tom to a willowy young Chinese in a green brocade gown, who declared himself charmed to make Tom's acquaintance. Snyder ordered one last vodka for Tom and slipped into it the chloral hydrate provided by Joe. Tom, well primed, passed out almost immediately.

"Come on, Chang."

Snyder and the young Chinese carried the unconscious Tom into a small back room with mirrored walls and ceiling and deposited him face up on the bed that occupied most of the available space.

Snyder immediately got busy. He unzipped Tom's trousers and unbuttoned the undershorts. Chang, watching, said with some regret, "Nice-looking guy. You know, I wouldn't mind . . ."

"Never mind what you wouldn't mind. Gimme the egg white."

Chang, tittering, handed Snyder a small dish.

"Go get a couple of rickshaws."

While Chang was gone, Snyder proceeded to distribute the egg white on Tom's person and clothing in the appropriate places. He allowed a moment for the viscous material to dry, then restored Tom's clothing to a semblance of order.

Chang returned. Together they maneuvered Tom's limp form through the doors and dumped him in one of the waiting rickshaws. Money changed hands.

"Thanks, Chang. You'll hear from me in a couple of days. You know what to do. There'll be another twenty when the job is finished."

The willowy Chang grinned. "You're welcome, Bill. Always glad to help out a business friend."

"Yeah, I know you don't mind a little moonlighting. Just so von A. doesn't get to hear about it."

"Sure thing. Take it easy. Don't take any wooden nickels. See you later, alligator," said Chang, who prided himself on his idiomatic American. He looked hopefully at Snyder for the obligatory response "On the Nile, crocodile," but Snyder merely closed his eyes

41

with an expression of long suffering and entered his rickshaw.

Returned to the barracks, Snyder called for help. "This guy has really had it," he explained to the young private who helped carry Tom in and get him settled on his bunk.

"Sure looks like one hell of a night," agreed the private admiringly, and withdrew.

Tom awoke on Sunday morning with a blinding, throbbing headache and a foul taste in his mouth. A heavy weight seemed to crush his ankles. Tom dimly associated the pressure with a blurred silhouette at the foot of his bunk. The silhouette was speaking with Snyder's voice, the decibels hitting like body blows.

"Well, Tom, you really had yourself a night, boy! How do you feel?"

"Lousy. What happened? I don't remember a thing—just that joint on Hatamen Street. But I didn't drink that much, did I?"

"You mean to say you don't remember Chien Men? The joint? The young fellow?"

"What young fellow? What joint? What are you talking about? Jeez, my head is splitting. I'm sick, man."

"Here, have some coffee. You'd *better* remember, Tom; you could be in big trouble."

"What the hell do you mean, Snyder, for crying out loud?"

"Take a look at yourself . . . your clothes."

Tom raised himself slowly and painfully. Blearily he tried to focus on his disheveled clothing, fingered the stiffened cloth of his trousers.

"I don't understand," he said desperately. "How, Snyder . . . where . . . who with? For God's sake, Snyder!"

"Why, Tom, there was this young Chink. I tried to pull you back, boy, but there was no holding you. You took off with him to the backroom—don't you remember?"

"I swear to God, I don't. I've never done nothing like that in my life, not even as a boy. . . . I'm no fag! You've *got* to believe me, Bill."

"Why, sure, I believe you, if you say so. . . . But,

man, I *saw* you, and so did a dozen people in that joint, and the Chink—what if he puts the bite on you?"

Tom had sobered under the influence of the coffee and the shock.

"You mean *blackmail?* Oh, my God! If this comes out . . . that means stockade and court-martial and dishonorable discharge. Bill, what *am* I going to do?"

"Well, look, take it easy; there's nothing you can do right now. The next move is up to the Chink. *If* he makes one. Anyway, I'll certainly keep this under my hat; you can rely on that. And if that Chink does make trouble, maybe I can take care of it for you."

"My God, Bill, thanks. Thanks for being a buddy."

"That's what buddies are for. Anyway, I haven't done anything yet."

The distraught Tom at least didn't have to wait long. Snyder considered a softening-up period of two days sufficient, not because he was sorry for Tom, but because he felt pressed for time, mindful of Joe's warning that the break could come any day. The sooner he was ready for it, the better. Accordingly, word went out to the "Chink," who made his move.

A note was delivered to Tom by messenger. In the neat Spencerian handwriting taught at American mission schools, it addressed Tom as "My dear Mr. Aiken," and demanded in succinct, impeccable English that Mr. Aiken meet the undersigned at 9 P.M. tomorrow at a certain address outside Chien Men Gate and hand over two thousand dollars in cash. Otherwise the undersigned would be compelled to present Mr. Aiken's commanding officer with a detailed account, names of witnesses and "pictorial evidence" of Mr. Aiken's rape of the undersigned last Saturday night; signed, "Yours very sincerely."

Tom, frantic, showed the note to Snyder. Snyder decided approvingly that Chang rated a five-dollar bonus for a superb job. The imaginary pictorial evidence was a touch of genius!

Snyder pocketed the note and said, "Okay, we've got a date, a place and a time, and the Chink is going to meet you in person. You are going to stay home, and I'll go instead. Just leave it to me. I promise you this is the last *anybody* will ever hear of this business."

43

Tom managed to live through the following day, pleading duty as an excuse for not meeting Kathy. He sat on his bunk, chain smoking and awaiting Snyder's return.

Snyder was back by nine forty-five, grinning and rubbing his hands.

"Relax, buddy. Your worries are over. I beat the shit out of that little fairy and promised him more of the same if we ever had another peep out of him. I got the pictures and negatives off him too, and destroyed them. You can stop worrying, really. I guarantee it."

"Judas Priest! I don't know how to thank you."

"Forget it. One of these days I'm going to collect."

6

September came. Heat and humidity abated. The cicadas had stopped their incessant maddening shrilling and had gone to wherever they went in the fall. A steady rain of brown, datelike jujubes plopped on the flagstones, and the pomegranate trees were heavy with fruit in the courtyard at 58 Nan Ho Yen. The days were warm and still, the nights were cool.

Tom Aiken didn't appreciate the fact that Peking had entered upon its best season. He refused to eat the jujubes, which, though sweet, were also richly endowed with pectin and puckered the mouth, and turned down the pomegranates, which were just seeds surrounded by a little pink juice and certainly did not justify their literary reputation. Tom was nervous and irritable these days; he slept badly and was losing weight. Kathy was worried, but his answers to her concerned questions and suggestions that he see a doctor were evasive, or he blamed his condition on "an intestinal bug— nothing to worry about, honey." When Kathy persisted, he blew up and yelled at her to "stop her goddamn nagging!" only to apologize profusely afterward for his outburst.

But as the weeks went by without a further sign from the "Chink," Tom cautiously began to relax and to dare hope that his trouble had really blown over, and he gradually became his old self again.

The days got shorter and cooler, and the briskness of autumn was in the crystal-clear air. Camel caravans became an increasingly frequent sight, bringing coal from the Mentoukou mines northwest of the city. The beasts plodded along the main streets, looking disdainfully down their somewhat Semitic noses, or squatted in the hutungs, chewing their cud with large yellow teeth and blocking traffic.

The Chinese resurrected and donned their padded gowns; the Westerners took furs and woolens out of mothballs. The coal balls made during spring and summer were put to use in small stoves, yielding little heat, an abundance of carbon monoxide and large residues of ash.

On a chilly night in October, Ch'en's "overtime" finally paid off.

He had been spending uncomfortable nights—first uncomfortably hot and sticky, now uncomfortably cold—sleeping fitfully on the hard stone floor between two workbenches, getting up cramped and stiff to leave PMS when the night shift went off duty, just before the cleaning crews reached the laboratories, and returning an hour and a half later for his normal day's work.

In the middle of that October night he suddenly jerked out of a restless doze. Scrabbling sounds came from the Professor's laboratory next door, which showed a faint glow of illumination. Hunched over, Ch'en crept soundlessly on stocking feet around the shielding workbenches to the open door. A flashlight was resting on a wall shelf in a corner of the Professor's laboratory, casting its beam on the safe. The beam focused on a hand steadying a stethoscope against the safe door while the other hand was fiddling delicately with the dial.

Ch'en turned the light switch by the door. The prowler gave a startled outcry and twitched involuntarily, dropping the stethoscope with a clatter.

For a brief moment Ch'en and the prowler confronted each other in silence. The prowler's short blue jacket and black trousers tied at the ankles proclaimed "coolie." The bandy legs inside the trousers said

45

"Japanese." This visual evidence was reinforced acoustically when the prowler burst into fluent but all too sibilant Mandarin, explaining volubly that he had been sent by the Housekeeping Department to clean the paleoanatomy laboratories, pointing to a mop and a pail in support of his legitimacy.

Ch'en gravely accepted the explanation, ignoring the incriminating evidence of the stethoscope and the flashlight. Leaving more drastic measures of punishment to the "coolie's" superiors, he directed and supervised the most thorough cleaning job the two laboratories, the hall and Kathy's office had enjoyed in years. At day break he dismissed the "coolie," who scuttled off exhaustedly into oblivion, his "face" lost irretrievably and his career finished for good.

After which Ch'en called a rickshaw and was conveyed at a rapid pace to the Morrison Street Market, where he had an urgent talk with the *shaoping* baker, who had just opened shop for the breakfast business.

Minutes later a message went from Peking to a mud hut in a village twenty miles west of the city, in countryside that was shunned, for excllent reasons, by Japanese patrols. From there the message was relayed to the temporary allies of the mud hut's occupants— the Nationalist government in Chungking.

The message caused a great deal of soul-searching at the highest levels, culminating in a conference between the head of the government, his English-speaking wife and the American ambassador.

The response was relayed back to Peking by the same underground postal route, except that it bypassed the mud hut in the countryside and went directly to Mr. Mitchell, administrator of PMS.

By that time, the middle of November, the last hollow cast of the Peking skulls, so delicately shaped and realistically colored by Ch'en's artist's hands that it could easily be mistaken for the original, had been shipped off to the Professor in New York.

Having received his orders from Chungking, Mr. Mitchell instructed Kathy via Father Lorrain to pack up the fossils, using materials and containers that were promptly provided by the medical school's carpentry shop.

Neither the American ambassador nor Mr. Mitchell, not Father Lorrain and certainly not Kathy, ever learned what had prompted the sudden reversal of Chiang Kai-shek's government regarding the everlasting repose of the Ancestral Remains on the soil of China.

Kathy mentioned the new development that evening at 58 Nan Ho Yen. Joe and Snyder exchanged a rapid glance.

"All of a sudden?" asked Joe. "I thought the fossils were supposed to remain in China forever."

Kathy explained that the Chinese government at Chungking had finally sent word for the fossils to be shipped to the United States for safekeeping.

Joe expressed concern. "Hope you packed them real careful. Wouldn't it be awful if these irreplaceable things got damaged in transit!"

Kathy reassured him. Each skull was wrapped very carefully in absorbent cotton, embedded in wood shavings, and fitting tightly into an individual carton.

"Well, I damn well hope they won't fall out of those cartons. Seems a pretty flimsy way of packing something this precious."

"Oh, no, the cartons are stiff cardboard, the lids are taped down. The fossils can't possibly fall out. And the fit is so tight, they can't rattle around and break."

"Even so, these things shouldn't be shipped in *cartons*. Don't tell me the Morgan Foundation can't afford a wooden crate!"

"Come on, Joe, don't be silly! Of course the cartons aren't going to be shipped as is. They all went into a wooden box."

"Well, that's more like it. What kind of a box?"

"You're really worried about them, aren't you, Joe? A redwood chest with a lid, if you must know."

"Redwood? You mean like lawn furniture—that kind of wood and that color?"

Kathy assented.

"Must be a pretty big box. How many cartons does it have to hold?"

"Well, it's about the size of a footlocker, and the cartons . . . let's see, there is one for each skull—that's five—and one for the smaller pieces like teeth and jaws and so on. They fit just nicely into the chest.

I think the PMS carpenter made it to measure."

Joe voiced the hope that the chest wasn't so conspicuous that everybody could guess at a glance what was in it.

"Oh, no; the box isn't even marked."

"Just a little old redwood box, eh? Maybe not even locked?"

Kathy explained patiently that the box was fitted with a circular Chinese-type brass hasp and lock, another look with Snyder, who responded with an imwhich seemed to relieve Joe's worries. He exchanged perceptible wink.

"When do you think they'll be shipped?" Joe asked presently. "From where? Do you know?"

Kathy didn't know. She assumed they'd be shipped from Chinwangtao, probably by the next sailing.

"That's the *Harrison.* On the tenth of December. That's the boat we're sailing on!" exclaimed Tom, Snyder, Joe and Evvie almost in unison.

That evening Snyder stayed on after Tom and Kathy had left. He and Joe went into conference in the bedroom, having barely been able to control their mirth. They hugged each other, shaking with laughter.

"Can you beat that stupidity? She might as well have given us a photograph."

"Yeah, in color yet."

Joe sobered up. "Can't be more than a matter of days now. Get your footlocker over here first thing tomorrow, as soon as you have a chance."

"Sure; in the evening, after dark."

"Think you can manage to get to drive the truck? There's sure to be a truck to pick up the stuff from PMS."

"No sweat. That's usually volunteer work, and I'll make sure to be the first to volunteer. I'll order Aiken to go with me."

"Great. Looks like we're all set. Let's keep our eyes and ears open and our fingers crossed."

The day after the redwood chest had been packed and locked, Father Lorrain and Mr. Mitchell came to the laboratory in the company of a coolie equipped with a dolly.

Kathy handed over the key to Mr. Mitchell. The

chest was placed on the dolly, and a small procession consisting of Father Lorrain, Mr. Mitchell, Kathy and Ch'en escorted the Peking Man in his redwood coffin through hallways, into the elevator, and along several catacomb-like passages traversed by water and steam pipes, to the walk-in safe in the basement.

Mr. Mitchell twiddled the dial and the heavy steel door opened. The dolly was pushed in. The redwood chest was deposited gently among the numerous other crates and packing cases with which the vault was filled.

The heavy vault door closed behind them.

Kathy and Ch'en went back to the laboratory with a sense of bereavement, as if they were returning from the funeral of a close friend.

After that Ch'en made it his business to patrol the basement several times a day to keep abreast of possible developments.

7

At ten o'clock on the morning of Thursday, December 4, 1941 (Peking time), a truck backed out of the U.S. Marine compound under a lowering gray sky from which an occasional snowflake drifted vertically in the still air to melt immediately upon the pavement.

The truck turned east on Legation Street, then north toward Morrison.

The driver, a corporal, spoke to his companion, a Pfc. "Okay, Tom. You owe me. Time's come to pay up."

"Sure thing, Bill. Anything you say."

"All you have to do is drive the truck on the way back and stop at Joe's for about fifteen minutes."

"Stop at Joe's? I don't understand. The sarge said come back directly without stopping on the way."

"I heard what the sarge said. *I* say we are going back via Nan Ho Yen and stop at Joe's. You stay in the cab. That's an order, Aiken! And you keep your lips buttoned, y'hear?"

"Sure; okay, Snyder, if you say so. Fifteen minutes can't make that much of a difference."

"That's the spirit, kid."

Snyder backed the truck against the loading platform at the delivery entrance of PMS. He and Tom got out, lowered the tailgate and, with the help of PMS coolies, began to load the crates and packing cases that were stacked on the platform. Snyder assigned the places on the truck, leaving an inconspicuous redwood chest with a circular brass lock to the last. The chest was finally placed directly behind the tailgate.

Ch'en, having observed the emptying of the vault during his morning's inspection walk, was on hand to watch the proceedings and mentally noted the interesting coincidence that the two Marines loading the truck had been frequent visitors to the laboratory.

The sporadic snowfall had ceased. Tom started the truck. He had become increasingly uneasy about Snyder's loading maneuver, having recognized the redwood chest from Kathy's description. And now that unauthorized stop at Joe's . . . Tom began to put two and two together.

"Snyder . . . That last box—isn't that the one with the fossils?"

"Your guess is as good as mine, boy."

"What are you going to do with it?"

"Never you mind. You just drive and stop at Joe's like I told you."

"Snyder! You can't think . . . you wouldn't dare!"

"You just shut up, Aiken, and do as you're told." Snyder paused, then said thoughtfully and deliberately, "You know, Tom, those photos are really *something*. Those Chinks sure knew how to use a camera and flashlight. Wonder what the colonel would say if he saw them."

Tom's stomach contracted. "The p-pictures," he stammered. "I thought . . . you said . . ."

"You thought I'd destroyed them? Wrong, Tom. But nobody but me will ever see them. *If* you're a good boy, that is. If you're a real good boy and do as you're told, I'll even give them back to you someday and you can destroy them yourself. How's that?"

"Why, you dirty, lousy, rotten . . ."

"Easy, boy! Now stop here and stay in the cab, and no peeking, hear?"

Tom, still stunned, pulled up in front of 58 Nan Ho Yen. Snyder reached over and gave a short honk on the horn, then got out and went to the back of the truck, where Joe joined him almost immediately and helped him lower the tailgate.

"Sure nobody's home?" asked Snyder.

"Sure, Bill. Kim's out marketing. Amah's in the back doing the laundry, and Evvie's still asleep; she won't wake up till afternoon. We had a late night last night." Joe smirked. "I made sure she'd be good and tired today."

They quickly unloaded the redwood chest and carried it into the house. Tom, remaining in the cab as ordered and watching through the rear-view mirror, guessed rather than really saw what was going on.

Joe had been mistaken. Feng, the coolie, the "invisible man," was observing the transaction from the kitchen. Although it seemed to have no direct bearing on his own assignment, the carrying in of the redwood box was sufficiently unusual to be committed to his memory, which was almost as faultless as Ch'en's.

Joe and Snyder transported the chest into the basement, where Snyder's footlocker stood open and ready, the bottom padded with regulation and civilian type underwear. More of Snyder's wardrobe, and an assortment of screwdrivers, lay at hand.

Snyder rapidly and skillfully unscrewed the back hinges and raised the box lid from behind. He pulled out the cartons from between two layers of excelsior and passed them to Joe one by one. Joe stowed the cartons in the footlocker, then handed Snyder several cartons filled with beakers, Erlenmeyer flasks and other small chemical glassware, which Snyder inserted between the two layers of excelsior. The fit was perfect. He closed the lid, and while he refastened the hinges on the chest, Joe covered the cartons in the footlocker with Snyder's clothing, closed and locked it, and put the keys in his pocket. Then he and Snyder carried the redwood chest back and reloaded it on the truck. The whole operation had taken less than fifteen minutes, a fact duly noted by Feng.

Snyder took over the driver's seat and drove back to the Marine compound. The sergeant was waiting for them.

"Took your time, didn't you?" he said.

"Hell, Sarge, there was an awful lot of boxes," said Snyder aggrievedly.

"Sure, Snyder," said the sergeant sarcastically. "I know you wore yourself out as usual. Start unloading. The colonel and the major are going to have their names stenciled on this lot. Stand by to reload."

The unloading and stenciling took about two hours. The colonel's name went on the redwood chest. Snyder grinned. The colonel hadn't even bothered to look at his "luggage." *Somebody* was going to be surprised. Snyder'd give part of his million—*half* million—to see the face of the recipient when he opened the chest and found a chemistry set instead of the Peking Man.

The cases were reloaded on the truck and covered with a tarpaulin. The sergeant returned and said, "Snyder and Aiken. Your liberty for tonight is canceled. You'll report at 0700 hours tomorrow. You'll ride guard on the freight train that will take this consignment to Chinwangtao. You've brought it here; you may as well stay with it all the way. You'll be able to make the afternoon train back, easy."

That night, stretched out on his bunk, his hands folded under his head, Snyder gave himself up to pleasurable thoughts. The operation had gone unexpectedly smoothly, without a hitch anywhere. Apparently the PMS boxes weren't going to be opened—certainly not here in Peking, and probably not in Chinwangtao either. Even if they were, it had been smart of Joe to substitute the chemical equipment, which might well have come from PMS. Also, it was a break, his being able to keep the redwood chest under observation on the train and in Chinwangtao. Plus, he'd be able to keep an eye on Aiken and see that he didn't do something stupid, like maybe confessing to the colonel. Aiken, of course, would try to search Snyder's belongings for the pictures. Well, let him search his little heart out; he couldn't find something that didn't exist. Catching Aiken in the act might even be a good thing, enable Snyder to tighten the screws a little. But Aiken was the only witness. Sooner of later he'd have to do something about Aiken . . . an accident . . . preferably sooner; maybe on the boat.

Snyder, of course, was not aware of the existence of a second, far more reliable witness—Feng, who by now had found an opportunity to slip into the basement and copy down Snyder's name and serial number from the stenciled lettering on the footlocker.

Aiken was one of Snyder's problems. Another was that Snyder had planned to retrieve his footlocker that very evening, but the canceling of liberty and the trip to Chinwangtao had fouled him up; he'd be back too late from the four-hour journey to pick it up tomorrow. That left Saturday at the earliest. . . . That footlocker *had* to get on board the *Harrison;* the whole operation depended on it. Well, Saturday or even Sunday would be time enough to get it back in time for his own departure on Monday.

Once the footlocker was safely in the hold of the *Harrison,* Snyder's problems would be over. There would be no inspection at San Diego, and he'd just take off for his sister's home in Harlingen, Texas, start his discharge proceedings from there and wait for Joe to get in touch. Then they'd meet someplace and Joe would take over. Joe was a smart cookie; he'd know just how to put on the bite for the ransom. The whole thing shouldn't take more than maybe two weeks after their arrival Stateside; say the end of January. Then they'd both be half a million richer . . . provided the problem of Aiken had been taken care of.

Snyder fell asleep with a smile on his face.

Tom Aiken also was kept awake by problems. That sonofabitch Snyder! Keeping those pictures instead of destroying them as he'd sworn he had done! Using them now to blackmail Tom into compounding a felony or at least being an accessory to something illegal. As Snyder had surmised, Tom considered searching for the pictures, but he discarded the idea. Snyder was too smart to keep this kind of stuff in his locker, what with inspections and all. He probably had the pictures stashed someplace else, maybe at Joe's or Tanya's. Tom then thought—again as Snyder had guessed—of throwing himself on the colonel's mercy and confessing. But . . . what exactly did he have to confess? That he'd blacked out and didn't remember a thing about that night? His lame story against Snyder's hard evidence; an eyewitness account, *and* the pictures, *and* the extortion note—the bastard had kept that too, Tom now remembered. No, the best he could hope for was avoidance of a court-martial; he would still face a dishonorable discharge and a complete ruin of his whole future.

And today's monkey business . . . Tom was convinced there *was* monkey business, but what had he actually witnessed? An unauthorized stop at Nan Ho Yen. He had been ordered to make that stop by Snyder, who outranked him and therefore bore the responsibility. And Snyder would probably come up with a good excuse, like having to go to the bathroom, something like that.

Tom had seen a box being carried into the house and out again fifteen minutes later. The point was, he had seen a box, but was it *the* box? Had something been taken out, or had something been put in? He had no way of knowing. What were Snyder and Joe up to? Surely they wouldn't be dumb enough to steal those ancient bones—who could they sell them to? More likely Joe or Snyder was smuggling something into the U.S. But one way or the other, Tom had no proof of anything and wouldn't even be able to identify the box that had been unloaded and reloaded at 58 Nan Ho Yen, having seen the transaction only in the rear-view mirror. No, he had nothing to gain by going to the colonel. Snyder had screwed him properly. Anyway, it was too late now; tomorrow the whole truckload was going to Chinwangtao, and he with it. Good thing liberty had been canceled for tonight and he hadn't had to face Kathy; not tomorrow either, and maybe by Saturday he'd feel better. Maybe Snyder had what he wanted now and would get off his back. . . . Tom drifted into a troubled sleep.

8

━━━━━━━━━━━━━━━━

Snow had begun to fall in earnest during the night and was swirling in a rising wind the next morning. Two inches had to be swept off the tarpaulins covering the two trucks that stood in the Marine compound ready for departure. What had been swept off was speedily replaced as the trucks rumbled slowly toward Chien Men Station, less than half a mile away. The falling snow veiled the massive outline of Chien Men Gate like a billowing gauze curtain.

The trucks pulled up at the station. The tarpaulins were swept again, and the drivers and guards began loading the consignments into two boxcars. The drivers said ironically, "Bye. Have a *pleasant* trip," and left. Snyder, Tom and two other guards, clutching their carbines and heavily weighted with side arms, climbed into their respective boxcars. Tom and Snyder took their seats on PMS crates.

The train was an hour late pulling out of Chien Men Station. It chugged along at not more than forty miles an hour, then stopped suddenly in the countryside between Peking and Tientsin, sitting there for some two hours and becoming rapidly blanketed by snow while the tracks were being repaired. The Chinese Communist Eighth Army, the famed Palou, had been busy during the night. The Palou were conducting a systematic and highly successful guerrilla campaign against Japanese convoys and installations in the open farmlands around Peking and Tientsin and with great regularity blew up sizable stretches of railroad track between the two cities.

Snyder sat on his packing case, fuming. He fumed at the delay—they'd sure as hell miss the afternoon train back to Peking. He fumed at the Chinese engineer, who had wasted an hour that morning. Snyder was assailed by a fleeting but intense feeling of patriotism; such delays were unthinkable in the good old U.S.A., where trains left and arrived on time. He had a vision of mile-long Southern Pacific and Santa Fe goods trains, powered by diesel engines instead of that filthy coal, moving at speed over gleaming tracks across the plains of Texas. . . . Goddamn the Chinks and their inefficiency!

Snyder also fumed at the sarge for assigning him to this duty so soon before he himself was to leave for Chinwangtao anyway, and at himself for not having tried to get out of this trip. Snyder's anger concentrated like light rays refracted through a magnifying glass and focused on Tom Aiken, who was sitting on another packing case, staring morosely at his feet. Snyder gripped his carbine more tightly. The urge to let Aiken have it was overpowering, but Snyder fought it down. No use working himself up over a situation he couldn't change. They'd get back by the early train tomorrow and he'd still have plenty of time to pick up his footlocker in the evening, or even on Sunday.

The time margin had shrunk somewhat, but not yet critically so.

Snyder soothed himself by thinking about the operation. Joe would call him in Harlingen. They'd decide where to meet. Snyder would have liked to make Laredo their joint base of operations; all he'd have to do then was walk across the bridge into Mexico with his share of the money. But of course that was *out*. The recipients of the fossils, whoever they were, and the potential dispensers of the ransom money were in New York. New York would therefore have to be the headquarters. By the time he and Joe arrived in New York the loss of the fossils would already have been discovered, for Snyder was sure that the intended recipient would lose no time getting his treasures into a safe place immediately.

Snyder didn't see how the operation could possibly fail—unless he got stuck on this goddamn trip! Even so, Joe was smart enough to take the footlocker back to the barracks in time if he, Snyder, didn't show up— although this was a lot riskier than if Snyder took it back himself. Well, perhaps he was worrying unnecessarily. Chances were still good that he'd get his footlocker back where it belonged by tomorrow evening.

The train began to move. The Palou apparently had

confined last night's activities to just that one stretch of track.

It was cold and penetratingly damp in the unheated boxcar. The two Marines shivered in their greatcoats; their fingers became numb despite fur-lined gloves and they had difficulty holding on to their carbines, but Tom, in a deep depression, was barely aware of his physical discomfort. He felt hopelessly trapped. Snyder held all the aces. Tom would remain under the threat of blackmail indefinitely. No knowing what Snyder's next demand would be and when it would be delivered. Tom couldn't even quit the service unless he was willing to face a dishonorable discharge. He felt he'd rather die. Of course, he couldn't possibly marry Kathy with this cloud over his head. Well, no need to make a big production out of breaking the engagement; he'd just fade quietly. That would be easy once he was back in the States. Might be for the best, for both of them. They weren't really suited. Kathy could be fun and was a nice lay, but Tom was getting fed up with her constant nagging about his grammar. She always made him feel that he wasn't quite good enough for her. . . . No, the break would be better for both of them. Kathy would find someone else, maybe a college professor who spoke the proper King's English.

The train finally pulled into Chinwangtao in the late afternoon, after numerous further stops during which the tracks were cleared of snowdrifts. The afternoon train for Peking had of course long since departed. Snyder and Tom had to spend the night at the base, but were glad of the chance to thaw out and of the hot meal that was awaiting them.

They assisted in the unloading of the boxcars and supervised the storage of the consignments in the godowns, warehouses, where they were added to huge stacks of packing cases from Tientsin and Fengtai which were already awaiting the arrival of the S.S. *President Harrison.* Snyder heaved a sigh of relief. Nobody was going to bother opening anything now; the contents of the redwood chest would be left untouched until they reached their final destination.

The Peking Marines would return on the morning train. Even with delays, they should be home in the early afternoon. Snyder would have plenty of time to go to Nan Ho Yen and collect his footlocker. And at least they'd be traveling comfortably in a heated carriage.

As that Friday afternoon wore on, Joe looked at his watch with increasing frequency. By 7 P.M. he was sure Snyder would not show up. He suggested to Evvie that they drop in at the club for a while, just for a change of scenery. Evvie agreed. It had stopped snowing, and the air was unbelievably pure and clean. At the club, Joe learned what he had come to learn—that Snyder and Aiken had escorted "stuff" to Chinwangtao, had been expected back tonight, but apparently had been delayed. "Maybe the Palou, or the snow'n all." They'd be back tomorrow for sure.

Joe was relieved. He inferred from this intelligence that the PMS shipment had not been inspected at the Peking barracks, and was by now safely in Chinwangtao, where inspection was even more unlikely. One major hurdle had been overcome. By Wednesday next week Snyder and his footlocker would be safely on board the *Harrison;* he and Evvie would join him at Tsingtao two days later, and the success of the operation would be pretty well assured. If Snyder still didn't show up tomorrow, Joe himself would return the footlocker to the barracks.

Joe turned his mind to other matters. "Let's get home, honey." Back at 58 Nan Ho Yen, he announced, "Guess I'll go do a little work."

"Oh, Joe, must you? You promised no more. You've already packed most of the apparatus."

"Just this one more time, honey. I swear it's the last time. We need the stake for when we get home to the U.S. Hans promised a bonus if I'd do this last job. We can't afford to pass up a thousand bucks."

Joe kissed Evvie on the tip of her nose, slapped her behind, picked up a half-full fifth of Haig & Haig, and closed the bedroom door behind him.

There was absolutely no reason why Saturday's return trip from Chinwangtao to Peking should have been any faster than Friday's trip from Peking to Chinwangtao. To be sure, the snowfall had stopped and the tracks were clear of drifts, but the Palou had really outdone themselves that night, blowing up a Japanese troop train as well as miles of track between Tientsin and Peking. When the train finally crawled into Tientsin station with two hours' delay, word was received that train service to Peking was suspended and would not resume until the next day, at the earliest.

The English-speaking radio and English-language newspaper, both Japanese-controlled, blamed "bandits" and promised dire reprisals. Everyone else knew it had been the Palou and cheered silently. Everybody, that was, except Snyder, who suddenly felt nauseated, as though he had been struck a body blow, and Tom Aiken, who didn't care whether or not he ever got back to Peking.

The small group of Peking Marines were conducted to the Tientsin barracks. Snyder's hopes revived when he was told that they'd be taken back to Peking by truck if the trains weren't running tomorrow. Being a sensible man, he resigned himself to the inevitable and made use of the opportunity to catch up on his sleep.

9

At 6 A.M. that Saturday morning, three hours before Snyder and Tom were to embark at Chinwangtao for their frustrated return trip to Peking, Kathy was awakened by a violent rattling at her front door. Presently Amah came in with a cup of tea and a note. The rickshaw coolie who had delivered the note was waiting outside, Amah said.

Kathy, still dazed with sleep, sipped tea and stared stupidly at the note, which said: "Kathy, *please* come to the German Hospital *right away*. *Emergency!!!* Evvie." The words "please," "right away" and "emergency" were heavily underscored.

When the message began to sink in, Kathy's first thought was that Evvie had had a miscarriage, but as far as she knew, Evvie wasn't pregnant; she would have told her friend. Kathy gulped her tea while she dressed hurriedly, and ten minutes later she was on her way to the German Hospital, in the Legation Quarter.

The German deaconess sister behind the information desk informed Kathy that Herr Cramer was in room 203; he was on the critical list and no visitors were allowed. Frau Cramer had sent for her, Kathy explained, and Sister thought it would be all right for Fräulein Ewers to go up. *Herr* Cramer, thought Kathy on her way to the second floor. So it was Joe. . . .

Kathy found Evvie in the corridor, huddled in her fur coat, her hair disheveled, her face without makeup, tear-streaked and pale. Evvie's amah perched on the edge of a chair at a respectful distance, rocking to and fro and keening softly, "Aiyah, aiyah."

"Kathy, thank God you are here!" Evvie threw herself into Kathy's arms.

"Evvie, for God's sake, what happened?"

"Oh, Kathy, it's Joe. He's burned. The still blew up. He threw himself on the flames. He had no clothes on. . . . He's *burned!*"

Kathy held Evvie tightly. "Evvie, dear, tell me . . . what exactly happened?"

Evvie babbled a tearful, incoherent account. Kathy gathered that Joe had been distilling ether in the bedroom for Hans von Albers; it was used for the extraction of heroin (so *that* was Joe's "chemistry"; no wonder he hadn't cared to talk about it). The still had exploded. Joe, wearing only his undershorts, had thrown himself on the flames with his almost naked body. Hearing Joe's screams, Evvie and Kim had rushed into the bedroom. Kim had poured water on the remaining flames and put out the fire. They had wrapped the screaming Joe in blankets and got him to the German Hospital. "It was to be the last time, Kathy. Joe said we needed the money—Hans promised him a bonus—and now he's *burned,* all over his body and *inside* . . . his lungs. Oh, Kathy, what's going to happen—what am I going to do? He isn't going to *die,* is he, Kathy? Say Joe isn't going to die!"

Kathy shook the hysterically weeping Evvie. "Evvie! Listen to me! I am going to call your father and ask him to come up here as soon as possible. Then I'll get you some coffee. And I'm sending your amah home.

Pull yourself together, Evvie! Joe needs you now; you can't afford to go to pieces. Do you hear me, Evvie?"

Evvie sniffed, blew her nose and straightened her shoulders. "You're right, Kathy. Thanks. Yes, call Vati, ask him to come quickly. And coffee would be fine. I'm going back to Joe."

Evvie disappeared behind the door of room 203, which bore a large sign: NO VISITORS.

Kathy dismissed the moaning amah—who stopped in midmoan and scuttled off quickly—then tackled the complex matter of a long-distance call to Tientsin.

Evvie sat down beside her husband's bed. A deaconess sister sat on the other side. A package lay on that bed, swathed in bandages from head to foot. Tubes running from fluid-filled bottles suspended from racks terminated somewhere under the bandages that covered Joe's arms. Only his eyes, mouth and nostrils were visible. The eyes were bloodshot, red-rimmed and lashless; the lips and nostrils were cracked and crusted. His breathing was labored and stertorous, but he was conscious. His lips formed a soundless "Evvie." She bent over him. "Yes, Joe, darling. I'm here. Don't try to talk, darling."

Joe moved his eyes toward the sister, then back to Evvie, his look imploring, his lips moving soundlessly. Evvie understood. "Please, Schwester Ulla, can I be alone with him for a few minutes?" Joe closed his eyes, relieved. The sister hesitated. "I am not supposed to leave the patient, Frau Cramer."

"Please, Schwester!"

"All right then, but only for a few minutes. I'll be right outside the door." The sister left.

An expression of urgency appeared in Joe's eyes. "Evvie," he croaked. Evvie bent over him.

"Evvie, listen. Important! Snyder's footlocker . . . in basement. Keys my pants pocket. . . . Hang on to footlocker . . . very valuable . . . a crime. Tell nobody about footlocker!" He repeated painfully, "Tell nobody, Evvie. Swear, Evvie!"

Evvie raised her right hand. "I swear, Joe, I'll tell nobody, *ever*. Do you want me to return the footlocker to Snyder?"

But Joe was seized with a fit of coughing, spitting up

blood clots and bits of blackened tissue into the basin that Evvie quickly held to his lips. The sound brought Sister Ulla back. Joe sank back exhausted and closed his eyes. Sister Ulla said gently, "He is asleep, Frau Cramer. Let him rest." She made a note in the chart, then resumed her seat by the patient's bedside.

Evvie sat numbly, waiting for Kathy to return and thinking over what Joe had said. She'd take care of the footlocker and talk to nobody about it except to Bill Snyder when he came back from Chinwangtao.

Kathy returned with coffee, knocked and beckoned to Evvie from the doorway. Sister Ulla said, "He is asleep, Frau Cramer. Go have your coffee. I'll call you the moment he wakes up."

They sat down in the small vistors' lounge at the end of the corridor and sipped their coffee.

"I spoke to your father, Evvie. He said he'd leave within the hour. He is driving; there are no trains. It's now eight o'clock. He should be here by noon at the latest. He asked me to reserve two rooms at the Wagons-Lits; I've done that too."

"Thanks, Kathy," said Evvie abstractedly. "I'm glad Vati is coming. . . . Listen, Kathy, don't tell Vati about the ether. He must never know about that. I'll tell him Joe fell asleep with a burning cigarette." She finished her coffee.

"Let's go back to the room, Kathy. I'm sure Sister will let you stay; we'll be very quiet."

The morning dragged on. There was a brief interlude when the doctors came on rounds. Kathy and Evvie waited in the corridor, then resumed their vigil by the bedside, not talking, Evvie keeping her eyes fixed on Joe.

Joe's hoarse breathing was the only sound in the room. Evvie thought: *Nobody,* Joe said, tell *nobody.* He made me swear. . . . I'll have to get the keys out of his pocket as soon as I get home, first thing.

There seemed to be a sudden change. Kathy had barely realized that the rasping, racking sounds from the bed had ceased when Evvie screamed, "He's not breathing—my God, he's stopped breathing. Call the doctor!"

Sister Ulla put a stethoscope to Joe's bandaged

chest, then rushed out and came back with the doctor. The doctor made a brief examination, then softly gave an order. The flow of the intravenous fluids was stopped, the tubes removed from Joe's arms. The sister gently closed Joe's eyes and drew the sheet over his face. Evvie stood dumbly for a moment, then wailed, "He's dead—oh, God, he's dead. Joe, Joe!"

Evvie refused a sedative. Kathy said quietly. "Herr Doktor, give me the tablets. I'll see that Frau Cramer takes them later." The doctor gave Kathy a quick, searching look, handed over four tablets and said, "Two now, two more after six hours if she needs it." Kathy nodded and pocketed the small box.

Kathy put her arm around Evvie. "Let's go down and wait for your father, Evvie. There's nothing we can do here. Your father should arrive any minute; he said he'd come directly to the hospital."

Evvie allowed herself to be led out of the room. They sat in the hospital lounge, waiting for Mr. Zimmermann.

Evvie was deathly pale. Suddenly she said, "He's paid it back."

"What do you mean, Evvie?"

"Joe always said he was living on borrowed time. He did time in the States—drunken driving. He killed a child. He always said he'd have to pay it back someday; but he never did stop drinking. There was nothing I could do about it. He was drunk last night. . . . Don't tell Vati; he doesn't know."

Evvie fell quiet.

Kathy said nothing. There was nothing to say. So this had been Joe's "trouble," the reason he had had to leave college. What a waste! Although now it no longer made a difference. . . .

Mr. Zimmermann finally walked in. Evvie clung to her father and began to weep uncontrolledly. "He's dead, Vati. Joe is dead!"

Mr. Zimmermann murmured, "Evchen, *armes* Evchen," helplessly stroking his daughter's hair and waiting till the wild sobbing subsided. Then he said, "Evchen, I want you to take the car. Perhaps Katrin will go with you. Wang will drive you home; pick up your things and meet me at the Wagons-Lits. I'll make

63

the necessary arrangements here. We'll stay at the hotel until we can go back to Tientsin."

The footlocker . . . the keys . . .

Evvie straightened up. "Yes, Vati."

When Kathy made to get out of the car at 58 Nan Ho Yen, Evvie restrained her. "No, Kathy, you stay in the car. I can manage by myself. I'll call if I need help."

"But, Evvie—"

Evvie suddenly screamed, "I said wait in the car. I want to go by myself, do you hear? I want to go by myself!"

Kathy, taken aback by this outburst, quickly soothed her friend. "Of course, Evvie. Just call if you need me."

When Evvie knocked on the red lacquer gate, it unexpectedly swung open. She did not consciously register surprise at the unlocked gate, and walked in, calling, "Kim! Amah!" There was no response.

Evvie did not detour to the servants' quarters in the back courtyard. Had she done so, she would have discovered the sight that earlier had caused her amah to scream, then rapidly bundle up her belongings and escape from this accursed house to seek refuge with her relatives in the north city. Kim had not answered Evvie's call because he was lying behind the kitchen pavilion in a pool of congealed blood, his eyes staring sightless into the blue sky, his throat a gaping slash from ear to ear. Feng, the coolie, was nowhere in sight.

But Evvie walked directly into the house, which was chilly and dank. It smelled acridly of smoke and scorched matter; dirty glasses and overflowing ashtrays still stood on the living room table. Evvie took no notice. She went straight into the bedroom. Broken glass crunched underfoot; the bedding was charred; undefinable black debris floated in puddles on the floor. Ignoring this also, Evvie kicked aside a nearly empty Haig & Haig bottle, went to the closet and picked up Joe's pants, which were lying on the floor. Evvie swallowed hard. She searched the pockets and withdrew a ring with two small brass keys. Then, as in a trance, she went down to the basement and found Snyder's footlocker.

Evvie forced herself to think. The locker bore Snyder's name and serial number. She couldn't take it with her without Vati asking a lot of questions. She couldn't leave it in the empty house either—where *were* those servants? "Very valuable," Joe had said. . . . Evvie made her decision.

A steamer trunk initialled "O.Z." stood in readiness, already packed for her and Joe's departure. Evvie dumped out the contents, then unlocked the footlocker. She stared uncomprehendingly at what it revealed. "Very valuable"—surely Joe couldn't have meant Snyder's fatigues. It must be the cartons that she found underneath the pieces of military apparel. Sealed cartons . . . where had she heard of sealed cartons? But Evvie did not try to remember now. She transferred the cartons to the steamer trunk and locked it. She threw what clothing the steamer trunk had contained on top of Snyder's belongings in the footlocker, locked that also and went back upstairs.

In the sodden bedroom she dragged a suitcase from the closet and piled in whatever lingerie and toilet articles came to hand. She slung Joe's Rolleiflex camera and accessory case around her neck, took his portable typewriter, picked up the suitcase and carried the articles out to the car. She instructed Wang, the chauffeur, to bring the footlocker and the trunk from the basement, apologizing for the absence of her servants.

While they were waiting for Wang, Evvie turned to Kathy. "Kathy, there was a footlocker in the basement that belongs to Bill Snyder. I can't leave it in the house—the servants are gone—and I can't take it to Tientsin. Will you keep it for Bill until he can pick it up?"

Kathy said she'd be glad to.

Wang returned with the footlocker, then went back for the steamer trunk.

On the way to Kan Mien Hutung, Evvie said suddenly, "Kathy, come back to Tientsin with me! I need you, Kathy."

Kathy said this was impossible. PMS would check on her if she didn't report for work on Monday, but she would come down the following weekend. "I promise, Evvie, and I'll stay with you tonight at the Wagons-Lits; the room has two beds."

At Kan Mien Hutung, Wang carried in the footlocker while Kathy quickly packed an overnight case.

They went on to the Grand Hôtel des Wagons-Lits. Kathy remembered with a pang that Joe had always called it the "Waggons Litz" to tease Evvie. She gathered from the fleeting expression of pain on Evvie's face that Evvie remembered also.

They went up to the room. "Come, Evvie. Undress and get into bed and take your pills now."

Evvie was undressing when a thought occurred to Kathy. "Evvie, shouldn't I notify von Albers? It was his house after all; shouldn't he know?"

Evvie became violently agitated. "No," she screamed. "I don't give a damn about Hans. Hans murdered Joe—he made Joe work for him and distill that ether. Joe was going to quit. Hans made him do it. Hans is a murderer; he killed Joe—he killed my Joe! I am going to kill *him*," and she began to weep bitterly.

Kathy tried to calm her down. "Of course, Evvie. Now take these pills and rest. Joe would want you to."

Obediently, Evvie swallowed the tablets. The sedative worked quickly on her empty stomach and five minutes later she was in a deep sleep.

Kathy, feeling exhausted herself, went down to the lobby to await Mr. Zimmermann. He came in presently, looking gray and ten years older. He sat down beside Kathy on a sofa, leaned his head against the backrest and closed his eyes. "I am getting old, Katrin," he said in German. "*Armes* Evchen! That man, that Joe—what did we know about him? *Ein hergelaufner Mensch,* a nobody; no background, no breeding. We were opposed to the marriage. We always hoped Evchen would marry Hans von Albers— fine old family—but Evchen, she had her heart set on Joe. How could we stop her? She was of age."

Gently squeezing his wrinkled, age-spotted hand, Kathy thought: True, there was a lot you didn't know, Father Zimmermann, about your Evchen and about nobly born Hans—not to mention Joe, that "nobody."

Mr. Zimmermann patted Kathy's hand and pulled himself together. "He'll be cremated tomorrow morning at ten o'clock outside the East Gate. The hearse will leave from the hospital. You'll come, Katrin?"

Kathy assured him she would and told him that she was staying with Evvie that night. Mr. Zimmermann was pleased. "I am glad. I didn't quite like to ask you. Why don't we go upstairs? You could use a rest and I certainly could. It's been a strenuous trip. The Japs stopped the car every five minutes; they always get obnoxious when they have trouble with the Palou. God bless the Führer and the Axis," he added ironically. "A German passport certainly helps these days."

Mr. Zimmermann had no use for the Nazis, although like most China Germans, he had been impressed with the cleanliness of the streets and the punctuality of the trains when he had last visited Berlin in 1938. He had been away from his Fatherland too long to remember that the streets had been clean and the trains had also run on time in the Weimar Republic and before that under the Kaiser.

He now rose and they went up to their rooms. Evvie was sound asleep. Kathy flopped down on the other bed and followed suit.

Kathy awoke with a jolt in the middle of the night, suddenly realizing what it was that had been nagging at her since the visit to Nan Ho Yen; the unlocked gate and the missing servants. It was inexplicable. Kim, whatever his national origins, was a good, responsible number one boy; it was entirely unlike him to desert the house of which he was in charge and leave the front door open to boot. It was very disturbing.

She decided to talk the problem over with Tom and Snyder tomorrow.

Evvie's deep and regular breathing and the sounds of snoring from Mr. Zimmermann's connecting room next door lulled Kathy back to sleep.

Feng, the Cramers' coolie, who possessed the answers to all Kathy's questions, was by then close to his destination, a walled village some twenty miles west of Peking. Walking steadily, he presently reached a thatched mud hut, where he reported to his superior officer.

Feng received praise for a job well done.

"The German comes next. The American turtle's egg seems to have saved us the trouble by liquidating himself. That should be the end of the drug snydicate that has been poisoning our people."

Feng mentioned the redwood chest that had been carried in and out of the house, and the presence of the footlocker in the basement. He handed the slip with Snyder's name and serial number to the commissar.

"I do not know what this means, Comrade Feng," said the commissar. "But the information may be significant. Rest now; you will receive your next assignment within a few days."

The information became very significant less than a week later.

10

By the time, late on Sunday afternoon, Snyder and Aiken finally reached the U.S. Marine compound on Legation Street, Evvie had returned to the Victorian mansion in Tientsin, had silently endured her mother's tearful embraces, and had stored the steamer trunk in the basement. There it blended with other large pieces of luggage, covered with faded North German Lloyd labels, that had accompanied young Mr. Zimmermann on his first journey to China shortly after the Boxer Rebellion.

Snyder was welcomed with three pieces of disturbing information.

The first was a note from Kathy, which had been delivered in the early afternoon. It informed Snyder of Joe's sudden death and cremation, and of Evvie's return to Tientsin that morning. "Evvie left your footlocker with me," the note continued. "She did not want to take it with her and could not leave it at the house because the servants were gone. You can pick it up at my house any evening. I am enclosing the keys."

Snyder was stunned. Joe dead—"burned to death." It was impossible to believe. The poor guy! So he had paid back his "borrowed time," but at what exorbitant interest! Well, at least the footlocker was safe; he'd go and get it from Kathy right away.

This occasioned the second blow. All liberty was canceled, the sergeant said. Colonel's orders.

"But, Sarge, I've got to pick up some of my stuff from Tanya's." The sergeant grinned appreciatively; he had met the luscious grand duchess at club dances. "It's got to go on the truck with me tomorrow."

"Sorry, Snyder," said the sergeant, looking longingly at a ten-dollar bill that was dangling carelessly from Snyder's hand. "Colonel's orders. There's nothing I can do about it tonight. But I'll tell you what—I'll assign you some duty in town early tomorrow morning; that'll give you time to say goodbye to Tanya"—he leered and closed one eye—"and you can get your stuff back here in time before we take off. How's that?"

Snyder said that would be okay and repocketed the ten-spot.

The third item of news was a piece of scuttlebutt. The S.S. *President Harrison* would depart from Chinwangtao on Wednesday, December 10, as scheduled, but would sail for the Philippines instead of San Diego. Nobody seemed able to substantiate this information, not even the sergeant. Only the colonel knew for sure, and he wasn't saying. But something was definitely up; there had been a lot of burning of papers in the colonel's office and in the embassy next door during the past couple of days.

Snyder concentrated on what affected him personally. How long would they be stuck in the Philippines? he asked. He was due for discharge, his tour was finished, he had made plans and was expected at home. The sergeant thought that guys up for discharge would probably be shipped home from the Philippines; no problem there. Snyder resigned himself. The layover would probably not be for more than a week. He'd still get himself and his footlocker back Stateside.

Snyder began to consider the implications of Joe's death for the operation. It was now up to himself entirely. Well, it shouldn't be too hard to compose a letter, piecing it together in the traditional manner from newspaper cutouts. Or maybe a phone call? Snyder was sure he'd be able to manage. And there would be no splitting of the ransom money now—the whole million would be his! Maybe he'd ask for *two* million; even that was peanuts to the Morgan Foundation.

Snyder felt no obligation whatsoever toward Evvie. Tough on her! He proceeded to rationalize his proposed plan of action. After all, what had been Joe's contribution? The idea of the snatch had come simultaneously to both of them. Joe had just furnished a temporary hiding place. All the risk of the hijack and subsequent transport and smuggling of the fossils into the States was his, Snyder's, alone. Also, Joe, though an accomplice, was also a witness and therefore a potential danger, which was now eliminated. That left only Aiken. . . . The need to get rid of Aiken was becoming imperative.

Snyder began devising and discarding possible ways and means of disposing of Aiken, but fell asleep without coming to a decision.

Snyder needn't have worried. As it happened, he was relieved of all decision-making, and his personal problems dissolved into nothingness, before daybreak. Although he would find time for a silent prayer of thanks that his footlocker was at the home of a neutral national, and not at the U.S. Marine barracks.

Before daybreak, then, on Monday, December 8, 1941 (China time), a heavily armed Japanese detachment led by a captain entered the U.S. Marine barracks in Peking after a brief scuffle with the sentries at the gate.

When the colonel, his staff, and the forty members of the Peking Legation Guard were assembled, the Japanese captain informed them in precise English that a state of war existed between the Japanese Empire and the United States. The colonel and his men were to surrender and lay down their arms forthwith.

The colonel complied, relying on the Boxer Protocol of 1901, which guaranteed diplomatic status and immediate repatriation to U.S. Marines.

The colonel's assumption that the Japanese would honor this agreement was mistaken, as were also any subsequent assumptions he may have made regarding the Japanese attitude toward the Geneva Convention concerning the humane treatment of prisoners of war.

PART II

The Search

Peking, China: December 8, 1941, to Spring 1946

11

On Monday morning, December 8, Kathy awoke earlier than usual. She woke with a start, her mind suddenly flooded with images of the preceding two days, which she had not had time to assimilate and evaluate consciously during that period of stress. Now she was unable to suppress the memory of the last chapter of the sudden tragedy that had played itself out in less than forty-eight hours.

The Zimmermanns' Mercedes had been the only car to follow the "hearse," little better than a truck, bearing the "casket," a crude pine box. Evvie, Mr. Zimmermann and herself had been the only mourners. Evvie had been in a state resembling catatonia, not speaking, not crying, obeying mechanically when told to dress, eat, sit in the car. She sat motionless, staring emptily ahead, her clenched fist cold and unresponsive in Kathy's hand, as the small procession made its way through the East Gate into the countryside. Even the snow, sparkling in the sun under a deep-blue sky, could not hide the desolation and stench of the "badlands," the city's vast garbage dumps, populated only by rats and by packs of lean, mangy mongrels, which snarled at one another as they scraped in the snow to get at the refuse underneath.

Whether by chance or design, the small crematorium was located in this area of corruption and decay.

Evvie, without uttering a sound, stubbornly resisted efforts to make her leave the car. Kathy stayed with her. Mr. Zimmermann, after a whispered converation with a Japanese official in a black kimono, went to witness the cremation through a small window. A Buddhist priest in yellow robes, with shaven head, stood by chanting softly and fingering carved wooden beads. Kathy silently mouthed the words of the Twenty-third Psalm.

The whole process took less than fifteen minutes. The priest then presented Evvie with a small square bamboo box.

Then they had returned to the hotel, Evvie, remaining rigid and stony-faced, clutching the box in her lap. While Mr. Zimmermann collected and loaded the two suitcases, Kathy quickly scribbled a note to Snyder. The car had dropped her at the western gate of the Legation Quarter. Kathy had looked up at the forty-year-old inscription over the bullet-scarred gate. LEST WE FORGET, it said there, in memory of the Boxer Rebellion and the siege of the Legation Quarter. How appropriate the words seemed today. . . . Kathy had left the note for Snyder at the gate of the Marine barracks, learning from the sentry that Tom and Snyder had not yet returned, and that liberty for tonight had been canceled.

Kathy felt that these memories would haunt her for the rest of her life, and she experienced an unreasonable and unfair resentment toward Tom for not having been with her during this emotional crisis.

It was still early when Kathy had bathed, dressed and breakfasted, too early for the *Peking Gazette* to be delivered. She decided to walk to the laboratory.

It was colder than yesterday, but clear and beautiful. The air was like champagne, and Kathy's spirits revived during her brisk walk along Kan Mien Hutung, the snow crunching under her boots. Hatamen Street seemed unusually busy. There seemed to be a lot of Japanese troops about, marching in squadrons, or mounted on their splendid horses, so much more impressive than the shaggy Mongolian ponies that were indigenous to North China. The Japanese wore black face masks, a protection against cold or infection, or both, since they wore white surgical masks during the rest of the year.

The gate at PMS was guarded by a Japanese sentry. He barked raucously at Kathy, barring her way with his bayonet, and then prodding it at her with unmistakable shooing movements. Kathy stood uncomprehendingly.

Ch'en appeared. "There is war," he said in Mandarin. "PMS is occupied by the Eastern Dwarfs." Kathy shot an apprehensive look at the sentry, who fortunately did not seem to understand Chinese. "The *kuniang* had better go home." Ch'en hesitated and

74

cleared his throat. Never forgo an opportunity to obtain information. He said diffidently, "If the *kuniang* permits, I will escort her part of the way. The streets may not be safe."

Kathy was glad of the company. "Thank you, Ch'en; that is very kind of you." They walked toward Hatamen Street. Ch'en began to probe. "I wonder where the fossils are now." Kathy replied that to her direct knowledge they were still in the PMS vault, although that seemed improbable. "I suppose they must have been taken to Chinwangtao to be shipped on the *Harrison*. I guess they must still be there now."

Ch'en agreed. So the *kuniang* had not witnessed the removal of the redwood chest four days ago. "I trust the *kuniang*'s American friends are in good health," he observed courteously. "It is to be feared that the *kuniang* will not see her military friends for a while. It is hoped that *kuniang* was at least able to spend the last few days with them."

Kathy's Mandarin was not adequate to an expression of her anguish about Tom. "I have not seen Tom for almost a week," she said. "I heard that he went to Chinwangtao and had not returned yesterday afternoon, although he was expected."

So Tom had gone to Chinwangtao, possibly guarding a shipment? What about Snyder?

"Your friend's friend, Szu Nai-du"—Ch'en was not going to give himself away by pronouncing the name correctly. "No doubt he was able to reassure the *kuniang* about her friend's well-being?"

"No; he went to Chinwangtao too. I don't know where Tom is; I don't know when I'll see him again!" Kathy's voice became choked.

Ch'en recognized the symptoms of an imminent hysterical outburst. Having gathered what information the *kuniang* had to impart—precious little—he hastened to take his leave before she erupted into tears.

"Perhaps the *kuniang* will excuse me. I have some business to attend to. If the *kuniang* will permit me to summon a rickshaw to take her home?"

The rickshaw was summoned. Kathy again thanked Ch'en for his kindness. Ch'en bowed courteously, his hands clasped in front of his chest. He then hurried off in the direction of Morrison Street.

Kan Mien Hutung was the last place Kathy wished to go. She was in a state of bewilderment. That Japanese sentry with his threatening bayonet . . . Ch'en had said "war." Very gradually the implications began to sink in. Father Lorrain would be able to explain. Kathy directed the coolie to the French Embassy in the Legation Quarter.

Father Lorrain lived and worked with two other priest-scientists in the Geological Institute, next door to the French Embassy. The institute had well-equipped laboratories, as well as spartan, cell-like living quarters, a refectory and a chapel for its three occupants.

The French Embassy was located in a side street of the Legation Quarter. Nothing there seemed out of the ordinary. The gate was guarded as always by two doll-like Annamite soliders, and more of them were drilling on the small parade ground in front of the embassy.

Kathy entered the adjoining institute. A conference was in progress in the refectory. The air was blue and thick with the smoke of Gauloises, three of them stuck to priestly lower lips, the butts of others smoldering in a large, overflowing ashtray.

Father Lorrain, his two confreres and Dr. Detwyler were seated at the table, listening to a French broadcast.

Dr. Detwyler was professor of dermatology and syphilology at PMS. He, Kathy, one or two missionary families and the manager of the Grand Hôtel des Wagons-Lits represented the Swiss colony of Peking. Dr. Detwyler was a tall, portly man with an egg-shaped head. The smooth fullness of his face was accented by a center part in his short, thinning hair. His gaze was mild and benevolent behind gold-rimmed spectacles. His general air of bland saintliness camouflaged a mordant wit and Dr. Detwyler's major passions: the coffee-bean-shaped *Neisseria gonorrheae* and the tiny corkscrew *Treponema pallidum,* which were the subject of his special research, and *Phthirus pubis,* the crab louse, which was his hobby. Dr. Detwyler never tired of extolling the habits, habitats and special adaptations to the single-minded mode of transmission of

76

these wonders of creation, especially at dinner parties, and preferably if his audience included ambassadors' wives, female missionaries and Catholic clerics.

He rose when Kathy entered and gave her a courtly little bow. Father Lorrain shut off the radio with a muttered *"Rien de nouveau"* and turned to Kathy. "Ah, Katee, how nice of you to come."

"Father, I came to hear . . . I went to PMS; it's occupied by the Japanese. Ch'en said there is *war*. What has happened?"

Father Lorrain imparted what news he had, sketchy but all of it disastrous. The Japanese had launched a massive air attack on the U.S. fleet at Pearl Harbor early that morning, taking the Americans by surprise. The American fleet seemed to have been largely or totally destroyed. The S.S. *President Harrison* had been sunk off Shanghai. American and British diplomatic personnel were under house arrest in their embassies; the American Legation Guard were prisoners of war at the barracks.

Father Lorrain continued. Mr. Mitchell and other high-ranking PMS administrators and department heads had been arrested before dawn and taken to a place somewhere in the east city. This last piece of intelligence had been passed along the grapevine originating with Mr. Mitchell's houseboy and ending with the houseboy at the institute.

Kathy's reaction of stunned incredulity was representative of that prevailing in the entire foreign community of Peking that morning, with the exception of the Germans and the Italians, who were already getting out the champagne.

Kathy's lower lip began to quiver. Father Lorrain was as unwilling as Ch'en to cope with female hysterics. "I am happy you came, Katee. I have some work for you that I was going to bring to PMS this morning. I would be grateful if you could do it here." He took Kathy by the elbow, and before she knew it, she was settled in Father Lorrain's office behind his portable typewriter. After a while the ruse succeeded. Kathy began to concentrate on the manuscript written in small, beautifully neat longhand, and to transcribe Father Lorrain's Gallicisms into more idiomatic English.

Father Lorrain gave Kathy lunch. "It would be good for you, Katee, if you came to work here for the time being, until we know what happens at PMS. I have enough work for you, and so have Father Lautrec and Father Marin. We are in need of a secretary, and we have sufficient funds to offer you a salary if PMS remains closed."

This was a happy suggestion. Kathy had not had time to think about a livelihood if she were to lose her job.

She gave some thought to this problem that evening. She certainly would need a job. She was forced to stay in Peking for the duration of the war. She had to forget about going to the United States or returning to Switzerland. There was some money in a bank in Tientsin, but she did not know if it was accessible. The Japanese might freeze all foreign accounts, for all she knew. It boiled down to "wait and see."

Her thoughts returned to Tom. Kathy had no concept of what it was like to be a prisoner of war. But there was something called the Geneva Convention ensuring humane treatment for prisoners. Perhaps Tom was better off in prison camp than as an active combatant; at least he would not be in physical danger. The Leathernecks always got the toughest and most dangerous jobs, Tom had told her rather proudly. He was probably well out of it! They would be able to write to each other, she could send him packages. . . .

There was certainly no reason why Katrin Ewers should have been less naïve in these assumptions than, say, the commanding officer of the U.S. Marines in China.

12

The job at the Geological Institute was a godsend in more than its financial aspects. Father Lorrain's visions of man's past and future encompassed stretches of time that reduced the present to a mere watch in the night, and however abstruse and only dimly understood they were, they helped Kathy to retain her sanity during the following weeks. Disasters came cascading with the rapidity and impact of a rock slide, leaving people numbed and reeling. H.M.S. *Repulse* and H.M.S. *Prince of Wales*, Britain's newest and mightiest battleships, were bombed and sunk before the war was a week old; Hong Kong and Singapore fell; the Philippines were attacked; British and American troops were in retreat everywhere.

The Japanese-controlled English-language radio crowed, and the Japanese-controlled *Peking Gazette* was jubilant with the victories of the armies of Greater Japan. The puppet Chinese newspapers had immediately added a mute "dog" radical to the ideograms denoting "England" and "America," an affront that remained lost on most foreigners, except for a few scholars, who chuckled at the Oriental subtlety of the insult.

There were rumors, later confirmed, that the U.S. Marines of the Peking Legation Guard had been transferred to Kiangwan prison camp near Shanghai.

The Japanese had invented the concept of the "civilian prisoner of war," meaning that civilians could be confined and kept incommunicado wherever it pleased their captors. Mr. Mitchell and his colleagues fell into this category. Their whereabouts was pinpointed thanks to the Chinese grapevine, but their fate inside the heavily guarded villa in the east city was unknown. Even Dr. Detwyler, who was in due course appointed acting Swiss consul, with an office in the "Waggons Litz" Hotel, was consistently refused access to the prisoners.

Armbands made their appearance, issued by the Japanese military, their wearing made compulsory under threat of imprisonment. Only "friendly enemies," the German and Italian Axis allies of Japan, were exempt from displaying these marks of distinction. "Neutral enemies," like the Vichy French, the Swiss or the Swedes, wore green; "enemy enemies"—American, British, Norwegian, Dutch—wore red. (The classification, reflecting the Japanese attitude toward Westerners, had been proposed by the German chargé d'affaires, who was also reported as having referred to his country's newly Aryanized allies as "only recently climbed down from trees.")

Radios had to be handed in to the Japanese military, who sealed the shortwave circuits. Many people removed the seal immediately after their set was returned to them; others, including the Chinese puppet premier, refrained from handing in their sets in the first place, concealing them instead in closets and cabinets and keeping a long-wave set on display. Thanks to these illicit sources of Allied broadcasts, the foreign community of Peking remained well informed and up to date on developments all through the war years. Those who lacked shortwave sets could always tune in at midnight on New Delhi, the only Allied long-wave station within range, and listen to the depressing news prefaced by the station's signal—the thin, reedy piping of a snake charmer's flute.

Early in January 1942, the Japanese permitted neutral and Chinese PMS personnel to return, even restoring their salaries for one last month, and permitting them to remove personal belongings, which were checked, and the removers frisked, by the armed sentries at the gates.

Ch'en did not return, and Kathy worried about him. He had never concealed his hatred for the "Eastern Dwarfs." She feared that he might be imprisoned and being tortured by the Japanese gendarmerie, the dreaded Kempetai, who were equivalent in reputation and brutal efficiency to the German Gestapo.

But Kathy needn't have worried. After meeting her at PMS that Monday, December 8, Ch'en had taken a leisurely walk to the Eastern Market on Morrison Street. There he had purchased and consumed his customary *shaoping* and held a brief chat with the vendor. As a result of this conversation, Ch'en had gone "over the wall" that night and made his way north through the countryside to a mud-walled village and thatched mud hut which were identical twins to those farther south that Feng, the coolie, had reached less than a week before. The occupants of the premises were the same, deeming it prudent to change their headquarters frequently.

Ch'en made his report concerning the loading of the fossils on an American truck on December 4. He described and named the two Marines who had supervised the loading, mentioning that the redwood box with the fossils had been loaded last, ready to be the first unloaded. He added the information extracted from Kathy that morning—that the same two Marines had apparently accompanied the shipment to Chinwangtao on December 5.

Ch'en's report was received by the Commissar for Cultural Affairs, whose rank corresponded to that of a lieutenant colonel. Commissar Liu came from Hunan Province. His five-toned southern Mandarin and native inability to distinguish between the sounds of *h* and *f*, *l* and *n*, made his speech difficult to understand for his northern Chinese comrades. Commissar Liu was also the possessor of a doctorate in anthropology from the University of Chicago, where he had been a student of the Professor's before the latter had assumed the directorship of the Paleoanatomy Laboratory at PMS. Commissar Dr. Liu also had received extensive training in Moscow, which had covered a wide range of subjects unrelated to anthropology except in the broadest possible sense.

The commissar now evaluated Ch'en's report in silence. Then he said, "Did you say that one of the American turtles' eggs was named Snyder and that he had frequently visited the laboratory?"

Ch'en assented. The commissar sent for his opposite number in charge of drug traffic, who in turn sent for Feng. Feng repeated his report of the unloading and reloading of a redwood chest at 58 Nan Ho Yen on Thursday, December 4, and the presence in the basement of a footlocker bearing Snyder's name and serial number. Feng had not checked it again before departing from the premises early Saturday morning after taking care of Kim.

Commissar Liu's reasoning paralleled Tom's on the trip to Chinwangtao:

"There are several possibilities. Snyder and his accomplice may have put something *into* the redwood box to be smuggled to America. Perhaps narcotics. However, this would be discovered immediately by the intended recipient of the box, unless this person was also an accomplice of Snyder's and Cramer's."

Both Ch'en and the commissar smiled involuntarily

at the thought of the Professor as a receiver and pusher of heroin. Ch'en said so. The commissar agreed:

"No, it is more likely that Snyder and Cramer hijacked the fossils. They probably transferred them to Snyder's footlocker and left them at Cramer's house. It is unfortunate that the house was not watched while Cramer was in the hospital."

Feng's superior bridled at this implied criticism and said stiffly that Feng's orders, like his own, had been restricted specifically to surveillance of the drug syndicate and liquidation of its members. "Comrade Feng faithfully obeyed his orders, which did *not* include watching the contents of Cramer's basement. He was explicitly instructed to return here immediately after liquidating that Korean turtle's egg, so as not to imperil himself."

Commissar Liu said soothingly, "I am aware of this, Comrade. Comrade Feng is to be commended, not only for faithfully carrying out his orders but also for being observant. The problem now is to establish the whereabouts of the footlocker. There are several possibilities: One, the footlocker may still be in the house. Two, Snyder recovered the footlocker. The only time he could have done so was on Wednesday evening, prior to his departure for Chinwangtao, or after his return on Sunday afternoon. Or Cramer may have returned the footlocker to the barracks during Snyder's absence. Or either Cramer or Snyder himself took the footlocker to the home of Snyder's Russian girlfriend. These possibilities must be checked out."

Messengers were summoned and given certain instructions.

Commissar Liu continued to consider possibilities. "Could the *tai-tai* [married woman—i.e., Evvie] have been implicated in the theft and removed the footlocker?"

Feng considered this theoretically possible but highly improbable. "The *tai-tai* is an empty-headed, frivolous young woman. She never got up before noon. She rarely left the house, and I did not observe her leaving with or without a footlocker on Thursday or Friday; besides, there was a heavy snowfall. By Friday night the *tai-tai* was hysterical due to her husband's accident. She would not have left his bedside to dispose of the footlocker."

"Comrade Ch'en, do you consider it possible that Miss Ewers was implicated in the theft?"

Ch'en denied the possibility, having an opinion of Kathy's intellect similar to Feng's of Evvie's. Both young women were ruled out on these grounds and on the basis of the general consensus that women were too inferior to be trusted as accomplices in a conspiracy of this magnitude.

Commissar Liu terminated the conference. "We must assume that the footlocker is either still at the house, or that Snyder or his girlfriend have it in their possession. If Snyder has it, it is either at the barracks or in Chinwangtao. In either case, the Japanese will find the fossils and we shall hear about it shortly. Our further plans will depend on the information we receive. You, Comrade Ch'en, will then be instructed accordingly."

The lawlessness in Peking was deplorable. That night, both the derelict house on Nan Ho Yen and Tanya Petrovna's apartment were broken into. Tanya discovered the burglary in the early morning hours when she returned from "work." The apartment was in shambles, but nothing had been stolen except for a few pieces of not very valuable jewelry. Tanya notified the police, but the burglars were never apprehended and she subsequently bought back her jewelry from an itinerant vendor who claimed he had found it in the street.

Information was duly passed on to Commissar Liu. Nothing but the bare walls were left at the Nan Ho Yen house; no footlocker answering the description had been found at Tanya Petrovna's apartment, nor anywhere in the Thieves' Market outside Chien Men Gate.

After taking over the American naval base and disarming the occupants, the Japanese troops had lost no time in thoroughly and efficiently looting the crates and packing cases awaiting the S.S. *President Harrison*. There had been several redwood chests, one of them containing chemical glassware, now crushed to powder under heavy Japanese boots, the other holding only personal effects. No bones of any description had emerged from any of the looted receptacles. A certain amount of unopened officers' luggage had been transferred to Tientsin, where it was now stored in the Swiss Warehouse. It could not now be ascertained whether the footlocker in question was among these pieces. Investigation would continue.

About the time this intelligence from Chinwangtao and Tientsin reached Commissar Liu in his mud hut, the Peking Marines were transferred to Kiangwan prison camp near Shanghai, the first lap of the *via dolorosa* that led to Hokkaido, famous for its cheese and notorious for its hostile, forbidding climate. The event was duly reported by the *Peking Gazette*, illustrated by photographs showing the Legation Guard embarking at Chien Men Station under Japanese guard.

Ch'en identified Snyder in the picture, but the likeness was too fuzzy for enlargement. Accordingly, a roll of Leica film disappeared mysteriously several days later from the files of the White Russian photographer who had taken the picture in the *Gazette*. One of the thirty-six negatives on this roll yielded an excellent portrait of Snyder, which was added to Commissar Liu's Peking Man file.

Commissar Liu concluded that the fossils had certainly not been in the redwood chest where they were supposed to be. This left Snyder's footlocker, now presumably in Shanghai or in the Tientsin warehouse, as the logical container of the relics. It seemed more than likely that the Japanese would conduct a search once the fossils were missed.

Plans were made accordingly. A Korean named Moon, disembarking at Shanghai, was brutally beaten to death and the corpse stripped into anonymity within ten minutes after the victim had set foot on Chinese soil. Ch'en then received his instructions.

Early in 1942 Colonel Yoshi Kimura was summoned to the Imperial Palace in Kyoto and received certain orders from Emperor Hirohito himself, along with an appointment as head of the Kempetai within the North China Expeditionary Forces, with headquarters in Peking.

Colonel Kimura arrived in Peking and set up house-keeping in an elegant Chinese villa in the north city. This necessitated a staff of servants. There was no lack of well-trained, English-speaking houseboys and cooks who had lost their jobs when the American and British embassies and private homes had closed. However, these Chinese could not be trusted with regard to their fondness for Japan. Also, Colonel Kimura, though fluent in English, preferred a Japanese-speaking staff.

One particular applicant excelled in his qualifications—a tall, lanky Korean named Moon, who spoke fluent Japanese and Chinese and also admitted to a knowledge of English. Moon had served as number one houseboy to the Mitsubishi representative in Johannesburg, South Africa, until his master's recent repatriation. He had disembarked at Shanghai and come north to find a suitable position. Moon presented impeccable credentials, which were confirmed by Mr. and Mrs. Yoshiwara, recently of Johannesburg, now residing in Osaka. Moon was hired and proved highly satisfactory, fully justifying the Yoshiwaras' letters of recommendation.

As befitted the dignity of an upper servant, Moon was reserved and aloof with his subordinates, although he did not object to sharing an occasional glass of beer with Corporal Hata, the colonel's orderly and personal servant. The consumption of Asahi beer was a major sacrifice for the cause; just how great, Commissar Liu for one would never learn. Fortunately, one glass of the brew was usually sufficient to render Corporal Hata relaxed and exceedingly garrulous.

Moon was permitted an occasional afternoon or evening off. He took delight in exploring Peking during that time, developing a particular fondness for the Eastern Market on Morrison Street and a taste for Chinese baked goods. The *shaoping* at a particular stall near the west entrance of the market were of exceptional quality. Moon rarely missed a chance to munch on one of these crisp delicacies, while chatting amiably with the vendor.

13

The foreign residents of Peking, whatever the color of their armbands, or even in their absence, were beginning to experience at first hand what life was like in an enemy-occupied country. The fact that their Chinese hosts had lived and suffered under Japanese occupation for almost five years had affected them only peripherally thus far, interfering slightly with social activities and convenience. Of course, there had been occasional "slapping incidents" when Westerners had failed to show respect to the Emperor by not bowing to Japanese sentries, each of whom was the Son of the Sun incarnate while on duty. Now the bowing was compulsory, and omission punishable by imprisonment.

Ditches were dug along all major streets. At the sound of the siren announcing an air raid drill, anyone hapless enough to be caught in the streets had to crouch in the ditch until the all-clear signal sounded, which often was not for several hours. All travel required a permit, which could be obtained, if at all, only after endless waiting. Identity cards, bearing the owner's photo and printed in Japanese, Chinese and quaint English, were issued and had to be carried and produced upon request at all times. An excursion to the Summer Palace, some twenty miles outside Peking, assumed the complexity of a major expedition and seemed hardly worth the trouble.

But human beings are adaptable, and the foreign community began, albeit resentfully, to come to terms with the restrictions of personal freedom, the insecurity and the feeling of being totally at the mercy of the hated invaders.

PMS was converted to a military hospital. The fossils and geological specimens remaining in the paleoanatomy laboratories were taken to museums in Japan or simply thrown out. The discards gradually found their way to the Thieves' Market outside Chien Men or into the hands of itinerant street hawkers, who offered them back for sale at the Geological Institute.

In time the whole collection was stored almost intact at the institute.

About this time the *Peking Gazette* and the Chinese puppet press began a passionate crusade against the (Dog) American Thieves who had systematically robbed China of some of her most sacred national relics. These included Sun Yat-sen's cancerous liver, which, embalmed in a formalin-filled specimen jar, had been part of PMS's pathology collection since the death in 1925 of its late owner, the Father of the Chinese Republic.

Also about this time, Kathy Ewers received the first of several visits. A thoroughly disapproving Amah handed her two visiting cards, imprinted respectively: "Captain Ken Omura" and "Lieutenant Yiro Matsuhashi," and with much grumbling obeyed Kathy's instructions to admit the visitors and prepare tea.

The two Japanese officers entered Kathy's living room. Both wore Western suits. The shorter man's was ill cut, hanging on him in awkward folds and creases and emphasizing his bandy legs. The other man was unusually tall and straight-legged for a Japanese. His tweed suit was obviously custom tailored of imported Scottish material. There was a greenish glint to the eyes under their Mongolian lid fold; the bristle-cut hair had a reddish tinge, and, improbably, the man's nose was freckled.

The tall, freckled man introduced himself and his companion in faultless, Oxford-accented English. "This is Lieutenant Matsuhashi." The lieutenant smiled toothily, hissed and bowed. "I am Captain Omura—no apostrophe." He bowed stiffly but forbore to hiss.

Two leather folders were flipped open, flashed at Kathy and repocketed immediately. The humor of the captain's allusion to his part-Irish ancentry was entirely lost on Kathy. Not so the significance of the leather folders. This was her first personal acquaintance with the Kempetai. Hiding her apprehension, Kathy, too, bowed courteously, and pointing to the sofa, invited her callers to be seated. They sat, each in a corner, the captain having taken care to hitch up his immaculately creased trousers. Kathy offered cigarettes, which were accepted, and pointed to the ashtray at the captain's elbow. The ashtray, in the company of a potted poinsettia, rested on an embroidered shawl which in turn shrouded Snyder's footlocker, now promoted into an end table. Amah served tea, her expression saying clearly that she wished it were poison.

"We came to ask you a few questions, Miss Ewers," said the captain politely. Lieutenant Matsuhashi remained silent at this and all subsequent interviews, and Kathy assumed that he neither spoke nor understood English.

Captain Omura was dedicated to his work. His field of specialization might be termed "foreign relations." He was expert at extracting information from Westerners of all nationalities, suiting his methods to his subject's passport. He particularly relished interrogating Britishers. He reveled in the power he now had over these arrogant snobs, who, because of his Eurasian ancestry, had denied him access to their daughters, their drawing rooms and to the managerial positions to which he was entitlted by way of his superior intelligence and university education. The snubs Ken Omura had endured as a "half-caste" had bred in him a sadistic hatred of all Westerners. This included Japan's German allies, to whom until recently he had been a "non-Aryan," on a par with Jews and similar scum.

His hatred made Captain Omura a valuable officer in the Kempetai. His intelligence really was superior, and his self-control such that he knew exactly how far he could let himself go, and what methods in his almost unlimited arsenal to use with each of his suspects. Mr. Mitchell, for instance . . . highly satisfactory with regard to the mechanics, though unfortunately not as to outcome of the "interview."

Captain Omura had received his present assignment directly from Colonel Kimura and was aware of its importance to the Emperor himself. With this young woman he would have to be gentlemanly and display the charm inherited from his mother, the late Maggie O'Brien Omura. Since the captain prided himself on being a gentleman and could turn the charm on and off at will, this presented no problem.

"What exactly was your function at PMS, Miss Ewers?" he inquired suavely. Kathy explained that she was just a secretary.

"What kind of work did you do? What were your duties?"

Kathy replied that she was expected mainly to deal with the correspondence and to edit and type up the Professor's manuscripts. She was still doing this type of work for Father Lorrain.

"When the Professor left, were you left in charge of the Peking Man fossils?"

"Oh, no, sir. I was just the secretary. I just obeyed orders; I was not in charge of anything."

"Who then was in charge? Who gave you your orders?"

"Well, the Professor left instructions. . . ."

"Where are the fossils now, Miss Ewers?"

"Why, as far as I know, they are still in the vault of PMS." (No need to volunteer information which was after all based only on hearsay.)

"When were the fossils placed in the vault?"

Kathy's reply confirmed information that had been elicited the day before from Mr. Mitchell in a far less gentlemanly manner.

"Why at such a late date? The Professor left Peking early last March."

Kathy explained that work on the hollow casts had required access to the skulls until November.

"Why were the fossils removed to the vault at all? Why were they not left in the laboratory safe?"

Kathy thought that the Professor had left the orders with Mr. Mitchell. After all, she was young and inexperienced, and also in too inferior a position to be entrusted with the responsibility for these precious relics, said Kathy, hunching her shoulders, spreading her palms, raising her eyebrows and opening blue eyes wide to impress upon Captain Omura her youth, inexperience and inferior social status.

The captain gave no indication that this maneuver half amused and half irritated him. How stupid did she think he was? But he revised his opinion of the suspect. Miss Ewers was perhaps not quite so naïve and simple as he had thought. He decided to do a little impressing himself and suddenly switched to fluent German.

"Wie waren die Fossilien verpackt, gnädiges Fräulein?"

Kathy was visibly taken aback.

"Ja, Sie wundern sich, dass ich mit Ihrer Muttersprache vertraut bin?"

Kathy hastened to compliment him on the excellence of his pronunciation and vocabulary.

"Bitte, beantworten Sie meine Frage—wie waren die Fossilien verpackt?"

Feeling that he had made his point, he repeated the question in English. "How were the fossils packed?"

Kathy described the redwood chest—"Dimensions? . . . Height? . . . Width? . . . Depth?"—the brass lock—"Diameter?"—the absence of markings; the six sealed cartons containing the fossils.

Captain Omura took notes. He then made her repeat the description, point by point. When there were no inconsistencies, he and the mute Lieutenant Matsuhashi rose. The lieutenant bowed and hissed. The captain said, "Thank you, Miss Ewers. You have been most helpful. *Auf Wiedersehen.*" He bowed slightly. They left.

Captain Omura's *"Auf Weidersehen"* had sounded ominous. Kathy felt that she had not seen the last of her sinister visitors. She was disturbed and uneasy, exactly as Captain Omura had intended her to feel after his departure.

Kathy was tempted to go to the institute immediately to discuss the situation with Father Lorrain. Then she thought better of it. She might be watched. It would be wiser to wait till tomorrow, when she had to go there as a matter of ordinary daily routine.

Father Lorrain listened to Kathy's report with interest and some apprehension. Kathy implied that she could have done with some forewarning about this visit.

"Katee, I did not know that you would be questioned. In fact, it was better that you had not been coached, and that your answers were spontaneous and unrehearsed. You have done very well." He frowned. "What disturbs me most is that the fossils seem to be missing. They should have been discovered at Chin-wangtao. I cannot think what might have gone wrong."

Kathy agreed that it was most disturbing. They speculated for a while but were unable to find even an implausible explanation for the disappearance. Father Lorrain said, "It seems clear that the Japanese are conducting a search. No doubt they will come here and question me. They will also question you again. I suggest that we cooperate fully. At the present time the recovery of the fossils is more important than the question of ownership. I would prefer to see them safe in the hands of Japanese scientists to having them lost or destroyed through someone's ignorance."

Kathy agreed.

Father Lorrain had predicted correctly. Within hours, two Japanese visitors were announced. Captain Omura and his silent partner were ushered in. The scene was an exact replica of yesterday's visit to Kan Mien Hutung; folders were flourished and there were bows and hisses. Except that Captain Omura addressed Father Lorrain in flawless French and conducted the interrogation in the same language. His questions were similar to those he had put to Kathy, but went somewhat further. The captain elicited the information of the fossils' removal to Chinwangtao and the intended shipment to the United States. However, Father Lorrain was unable to furnish details as to the methods of transport and storage once the redwood chest was in the hands of the U.S. Marines.

After repeated attempts to trap Father Lorrain into contradictions—which were noted with some amusement by the Jesuit—Captain Omura was satisfied that the priest was telling the truth. He politely requested a tour through the institute, which was granted with pleasure. The tour was as thorough as it was fruitless and boring for the captain.

Father Lorrain insisted that his visitors examine every bone on display, open every box in the basement and inspect the contents—a surfeit of rocks, animal bones and teeth of all sizes and descriptions, but no human remains. Moreover, Father Lorrain insisted on expounding at length on the age, site of recovery and scientific significance of each specimen, including the

Latin name: *"Eh bien, voilà, c'est extrêmement intéressant, un Siphneus du Miocène supérieur de la Chine . . ."* or "Observe this tooth of *Aeluropus* from the Oligocene of Szechuan . . ." until Captain Omura's head was reeling. He begged Father Lorrain not to trouble himself, but Father Lorrain was relentless. "No trouble at all, *mon capitaine*. It is a pleasure. *J'insiste*. Now, here we have a femur fragment of *Hipparion*. Observe the intact trochanter . . . Upper Pliocene."

Captain Omura and Lieutenant Matsuhashi had great difficulty concealing their exasperation, and their relief at finally being able to take their leave from the learned Frenchman. Father Lorrain gravely thanked them for their interest in paleontology and hoped they would visit him again soon.

Father Lorrain and Kathy were as exhausted as their visitors. They sank into chairs, tea was brought, and Father Lorrain lit a Gauloise. "Well"—he grinned—"I don't think we shall see these two types again for a while; at least not here." Again Father Lorrain's prediction proved correct.

During the next several weeks Captain Omura and Lieutenant Matsuhashi did a considerable amount of traveling. Information that had come almost effortlessly to Commissar Liu was now gathered the hard way, piece by piece, by exhaustive and exhausting interrogation, and with infuriatingly negative results.

Meanwhile a search in Peking for the Chinese technician Ch'en was unsuccessful. The man seemed to have vanished into thin air, like all too many of his compatriots in whom the Kempetai were interested. The search for Ch'en did not include the home of the Kempetai's commanding officer, where the tall Korean houseboy Moon continued to serve his master with devotion and efficiency.

The Thieves' Market outside Chien Men Gate was turned upside down, resulting in much damage, loss of property and an increase in the hatred the businessmen bore the Japanese, but in nothing else.

Questioning of the Japanese officers and men at Chinwangtao and Camp Holcomb produced the information that none of the redwood chests "confiscated" from the enemy on December 8 had contained bones, human or otherwise. The private who had disposed of the chemical glassware wisely refrained from disclosing his method of "confiscating" enemy property; at any rate, he was not asked.

Interrogation of the Marines at Kiangwan prison camp near Shanghai was more exhausting and equally fruitless. The colonel acknowledged receiving a shipment from PMS, but professed himself ignorant of its contents. The men were sullen. They didn't know nothing and they didn't remember nothing. There might have been some redwood boxes, there might not; who'd remember? A corporal named Snyder admitted that he'd "picked up some stuff at PMS and ridden herd on it to Chinwangtao the next day"; he didn't remember any particular pieces. Neither did a Pfc. named Aiken, who had accompanied the corporal on both assignments. Reinforcement of the questioning by more drastic measures failed to stimulate the American memories. A suggestion from a Private Goldstein from Brooklyn that the Japanese troops knew a lot more than the Americans about the contents of the shipments for the *Harrison* was received with particular expressions of displeasure.

Captain Omura and his partner returned to Peking.

Snyder, though hurting all over, felt relieved. The Japs had not located the fossils, meaning his footlocker was still safe.

Kathy had begun to think that perhaps she had seen the last of Captain Omura and Lieutenant Matsuhashi after all. She was disabused of this happy notion when the two Kempetai officers visited her again unexpectedly after an absence of several weeks. The visit was brief, and so was Captain Omura's manner. The Irish charm was conspicuously absent.

"Miss Ewers," he said, "you will be ready tomorrow at 1300 hours to accompany us to Tientsin. Be prepared for an overnight stay."

"B-but," stammered Kathy, taken aback, "I have no permit to travel."

Captain Omura's estimate of Miss Ewers' intelligence dropped several notches. He borrowed an expression from the picturesque speech of his enemies.

"Dumb broad," he muttered under his breath, then said patiently, "You will not require a travel permit, Miss Ewers."

14

Mr. Zimmermann was still thanking his stars that his son-in-law's tragic death, as long as it had to happen, had happened when it did. Twenty-four hours later, and he and Evvie would not have been able to return to Tientsin, regardless of the German passport and the swastika pennant on the car's front fender.

Evvie herself remained oblivious of the narrow escape she and her father had had. The landslide of historical disasters beginning on December 8 also left her untouched, and so did more personal events following her return to Tientsin.

Joe's ashes were interred in the German cemetery in a simple ceremony attended only by the Zimmermanns and a few close friends of the family. There were flowers, including a spectacularly expensive wreath from Mr. and Mrs. Hans von Albers. The service was conducted in German by old Pastor Heineke, who had baptized and confirmed Evvie, and had married her and Joe Cramer less than a year before in the same language.

Evvie stood rigidly and without tears by the graveside while Pastor Heineke spoke movingly of being in death in the midst of life and of Life Everlasting. She dutifully scooped up a handful of soil and dropped it on the grave, shook hands with Pastor Heineke with a toneless *"Danke, Herr Pastor,"* and returned home with her parents.

Evvie remained withdrawn from reality for a long time, moving and performing mechanically, barely speaking. She suffered from nightmares in which she relived the horrors of Joe's death—the white bundle on the bed, the rasping breathing, the bloody matter frothing from his lips as he coughed up his scorched lungs piecemeal. Evvie had always been sheltered from the gorier aspects of life and death. It was the brutally sudden confrontation with the violent destruction of a human life rather than the loss of her husband which induced in her the state of shock from which it took her so long to recover. However, one night she broke into a paroxysmal fit of weeping which was followed by a deep, dreamless sleep. After that her youth and healthy constitution began to assert themselves. The nightmares became less frequent. Evvie began to accompany her mother to teas and mahjongg parties although both bored her to tears.

Hans von Albers called on her. He again expressed his sympathies and pressed upon her an envelope containing ten American one-hundred-dollar-bills—Joe's last payment plus the promised bonus.

"You won't be able to use it now, Evvie, but this war isn't going to last forever."

Evvie was tempted to tear up the money and throw the shreds in Hans's pink, fleshy face, but thought better of it and put the envelope in her pocket. After all, Joe had given his life for this "stake"; it was only right that she should keep it. Joe would want her to. . . . She turned away. Von Albers tactfully took his leave.

This was the last time Evvie saw Hans von Albers. He left for a "business trip" shortly after and didn't return. By the time his remains were discovered in the swamplands outside Tientsin, they had become unidentifiable. Feng and his superior had closed the book on this particular assignment.

On April 20, the German consul general in Tientsin gave a party to celebrate the Führer's birthday. Like many of their friends, the Zimmermanns attended, less out of the urge to celebrate an event they wished had never happened, than for reasons of prudence. Evvie, though technically no longer a German national and therefore free to stay away, went because it was a break in the monotony.

It was a splendid party. The consulate general was lavishly decked out with red swastika flags and greenery. Portraits of the Führer in all sizes, and occupying all available wall space, stared magnetically down on the crowd. The entire German community was present. Many of the men wore uniform, black or brown, but not field gray. There were a number of stalwart individuals whom no one had ever met before, who spoke German with an American accent. These were "Bundt" Germans, who had been expelled from the United States and had got stuck in China when their homeward journey via Siberia was blocked by Germany's invasion of Russia. Many of them had American wives, who after the war would be seen crowding American consular offices claiming restoration of their American citizenship and repatriation, and becoming most abusive when both requests were refused.

The gathering was, however, international, with numerous Italians, some French consular officers, an abundance of uniformed Japanese and a few South Americans.

Evvie stood in a corner, sipping champagne and observing with some amusement that nobody seemed inclined to entertain the Japanese except two very junior vice consuls, who had obviously been assigned this disagreeable duty.

A darkly handsome young man who had been watching her for a while walked over and introduced himself in charmingly accented English.

"If the señorita will permit me?"

Evvie suppressed the Joe-type reply "Be my guest," and graciously inclined her head.

"My name is Pablo Álvarez. I regret that I do not speak Germen. Is the señorita enjoying the party?"

Evvie smiled. The sound of English was refreshing in these heavily Teutonic surroundings.

"I prefer to speak English, Mr. Álvarez. I am Evamarie Cramer—Mrs. Cramer."

"Ah, señora, I beg pardon. The señora is perhaps American-born and is here with her husband, passing through?"

Evvie was not flattered by this allusion to the Bundt Germans and their American spouses. "No," she said. "I live in Tientsin. My husband is—was American."

Señor Álvarez seemed to understand. He tactfully did not pursue the matter further. Instead he led Evvie to a seat, brought her another glass of champagne and a plate of canapés, pulled up a chair and began to converse about his impressions of China.

He was a vice consul at the Cuban Consulate in

Shanghai, he said, posted temporarily to Tientsin. He had come to China shortly before Pearl Harbor, on transfer from Manila. "At least in Manila they speak Spanish," he sighed. "Although I must consider myself fortunate to have escaped the fighting. It must have been very terrible—much destruction, much suffering. . . . But I do not wish to distress the señora."

Evvie found young Señor Álvarez agreeable and easy to talk to despite his somewhat stilted and highly literate English and formal manner, so different from the slangy speech and easy familiarity of young Americans. The looks he gave her were far less formal than his conversation and manners. Such a look accompanied his inquiry if he might call on the señora. He bowed and kissed Evvie's hand. Permission to call was granted.

Señor Álvarez called the next day, bearing a bouquet of roses. Mrs. Zimmermann was enchanted by his breeding and manners, and by the possible prospects for her daughter, even though, most regrettably, Señor Álvarez was a Catholic.

The friendship developed and progressed rapidly. Pablo and Evvie enjoyed each other's company and sharing what social recreation Tientsin had left to offer. The promises implicit in Pablo's glances were far from empty, and their fulfillment turned out to be highly satisfactory. Evvie's nightmares ceased, dispelled by Pablo's frequent presence after the Zimmermanns had retired. Evvie began to feel young and gay again, and when she thought of Joe it was with a feeling of regret rather than the ache of irretrievable loss.

In due course Pablo called on Mr. Zimmermann and formally asked for his daughter's hand in marriage. As soon as Mr. Zimmermann had recovered from shock at this display of almost extinct old-world courtesy, he was happy to give his consent. In deference to Evvie's recent bereavement, there was no formal announcement of the engagement, and the wedding would be decently postponed, but Kathy received a cheerful note from her friend, and was happy that Evvie had begun to live again.

15

Kathy had notified Father Lorrain, and Father Lorrain had notified Dr. Detwyler, of her impending trip to Tientsin. The two Kempetai officers appeared at her house at precisely 1300 hours. For reasons that remained obscure to Kathy, both had chosen to travel in uniform. Japanese uniforms were an unbecoming gray-green color and poorly cut of cheap material, usually sagging in limp creases, as though their wearers had slept in them. However, Captain Omura was an exception. His uniform was faultlessly pressed and cut, having been constructed from imported English material by a bespoke tailor on Nanking Road in Shanghai.

The train was crowded with Japanese, military and civilian; there were also sleek-looking Chinese, who seemed to be thriving in the Greater East Asia Coprosperity Sphere inaugurated by Japan. The Chinese attendant served tea with conspicuous churlishness. Expertly utilizing a jolt of the train, he spilled tea on the lieutenant. Lieutenant Matsuhashi, quick to recognize an insult from another Oriental, rose with a snarl to retaliate. A glance from Omura made him sink back into his seat. The attendant then set down the teapot in such a way that the spout pointed toward the captain, so as to convey the message "Get the hell out of here, you turtle's egg!" Kathy suppressed a giggle. The captain seemed oblivious of the insult.

Captain Omura proceeded to brief Kathy on the purpose of the trip. "We have information that the fossils may be stored in the Swiss Warehouse in Tientsin. You, Miss Ewers, will help us to identify the redwood chest and the fossils when they are found."

Kathy assured the captain of her full cooperation. Her assurances were received with an absent nod. The captain seemed preoccupied and in a bad mood. Since he did not choose to take her into his confidence, Kathy could not know about the extremely unpleasant interview the captain had had with his superior officer,

Colonel Kimura, upon his return from his unsuccessful mission to Kiangwan prison camp. The hour had been late, and Captain Omura had had to report to the colonel at his home. Since the colonel never bothered to keep his voice down, anyone within hearing distance had become privy to Captain Omura's failure to obtain information as to the fossils' whereabouts. Moon, who had been part of the audience, had learned nothing new, but it was always useful to have information confirmed. The colonel had been most outspoken. As a result, Captain Omura was banking heavily on the present quest. He dared not think of the consequences if this search in the last possible hiding place also proved unsuccessful.

In Tientsin the traveling party was met by two uniformed, heavily armed privates. They bowed, hissed and smiled, displaying an extraordinarily large number of oversized front teeth.

Rickshaws were summoned. Kathy felt humiliated and embarrassed at having to appear in public in this kind of company. She tried to look independent, pretending that her rickshaw had got in between those of the four Japanese by a chance of traffic.

The rickshaws pulled up in front of the offices of the Swiss Moving and Storage Company in the British Concession. Kathy had no choice but to follow her companions into the office. The reception was frigid. Kathy cringed under a battery of dirty looks from the three Chinese typists and two White Russian clerks. She recognized the manager. Peter Rosanoff had been at school with her and Evvie. Peter did not get up to greet the visitors. He continued to examine the papers in front of him, finally raised his head and said languidly, "Yes?"

Captain Omura, inwardly seething at the insolence, said coldly that he and his "associates" wished to search the warehouse for contraband. The word "associates" caused Peter to shoot a particularly scathing and contemptuous glance at Kathy. Kathy felt like sinking into the ground, too mortified to feel heartened by this display of anti-Japanese sentiment.

Peter Rosanoff said icily that it was almost closing time.

"Come back at eight-thirty tomorrow morning. I will make arrangements for you to be admitted to the warehouse then. Goodbye."

His glance returned to the papers on his desk.

Back in the street, Captain Omura tried to recover his composure and his manners. He asked if Kathy would give him and the lieutenant the pleasure of her company at dinner, and if he could book a room for her at the Palace Hotel. Kathy, having had her fill of the captain and the lieutenant for the day, thanked him for both offers but begged to be excused. She said that she would like to use this opportunity to see some old friends from her school days. The captain did not object and, surprisingly, did not inquire about names and addresses.

The four Japanese hailed rickshaws, bowed to her, and left her standing in front of the office of the Swiss Moving and Storage Company.

Kathy went back in. Peter Rosanoff was tidying his desk. "Yes?" he said.

"Peter, listen to me! I was *forced* to come here with these Japs! They are after some stuff from PMS; they made me come along to identify it. I work—used to work there."

"That's *your* business, Katrin," said Peter in a slightly more conciliatory tone.

"Peter, may I use your phone?"

"Help yourself. That will be fifty cents, Chinese. We don't accept Japanese money."

Kathy gave the operator Evvie's number. Mrs. Zimmermann answered.

"Mrs. Zimmermann, this is Katrin. I am in Tientsin. May I come over? And may I spend the night?"

"Katrin, how delightful! Of *course* you must come, and you must stay as long as you can! Evvie will be *so* happy to see you! She is out just now, taking her Spanish lesson, you know—she is getting very fluent—but she will be back for dinner."

Kathy said she would be at the Zimmermanns' in about fifteen minutes. She plonked some coins down in front of Peter.

"Thank you, Peter. Here's your fifty cents—and I don't carry Jap money."

Peter grinned and pocketed the coins. "Okay, Katrin; no hard feelings. See you tomorrow. Good hunting. I hope the bastards won't find whatever it is they are after."

Mrs. Zimmermann greeted Kathy with a fond embrace, made her sit down and rang for tea. Then she launched into a recital of Evvie's recovery and accomplishments.

"She is getting to be really fluent in Spanish; so helpful for a diplomat's wife, don't you think? Wait until you meet Pablo; he is delightful and Evvie couldn't be happier. Such a gentleman, such excellent manners! He comes from an excellent family—Spanish aristocracy, you know. Of course you must come to the wedding, Katrin, sometime in the fall; after all, Evvie is still in mourning for that Joe. One must preserve appearances, mustn't one? But now you must tell me all about yourself."

Kathy was spared an exhaustive autobiography by the return of Evvie, accompanied by Pablo. Introductions and mutual appraisals were made. Kathy and Pablo both liked what they saw. Kathy was happy to see the striking improvement in Evvie's looks and demeanor; she was radiant and bubbling with gaiety. Kathy silently thanked Pablo for his part in her friend's recovery.

"Kathy, what are you doing in Tientsin? How did you manage to get a travel permit? Why didn't you let us know you were coming? How long can you stay?"

Kathy explained the unexpected suddenness and purpose of her trip. "Tomorrow the Japs are going to search the American luggage in the Swiss Warehouse. I do hope the fossils will turn up—even if it means they'll fall into the hands of the Japanese."

Evvie's heart skipped a beat. The fossils! She had never opened the cartons in the steamer trunk in the basement, but now she knew intuitively what they contained. And here was Kathy with the Kempetai, searching for them. Evvie swallowed.

"Kathy, those fossils . . . they are very valuable, aren't they?"

Kathy explained, as she had done once before, that they were priceless.

Evvie became rather silent. Pablo suggested a night on the town, with drinks, dinner and dancing to celebrate this unexpected reunion. But Kathy said she needed a good night's sleep; she would need to have her wits about her for tomorrow's search. Evvie pleaded a headache. Pablo left soon after dinner and the young women retired early. Evvie, delighted though she was to see Kathy again, found it hard to simulate the gaiety to be expected of someone newly betrothed. She was relieved when Kathy, too tired to notice Evvie's preoccupation, said she was "ready to hit the sack."

Evvie lay awake, thinking hard. There was no doubt about it; she had those fossils in the basement, bequeathed to her by Joe. Joe . . . he and Snyder must have cooked up the heist between them. What a supercolossal nerve! Evvie sat up in bed, hugging her knees, and shook with silent laughter. What a joke on the Japanese! Evvie stuffed the blanket in her mouth to choke off the laughter. Then she began to sober up. The situation wasn't really that funny. She was in a spot; no doubt about that.

Evvie began to consider possible courses of action. What if she confessed to Kathy, handed the fossils over to her? The thought of Kathy sleeping right on top of the damn things brought on another fit of laughter, but Evvie fought it down. No, she couldn't return the fossils to Kathy without implicating her *and* Evvie herself; they'd both go to jail! Evvie had no illusions about the Kempetai, and no desire to gain personal knowledge of their judicial methods. Also, the confession would lead the Japs to Snyder, who, poor guy, was in enough trouble as it was. Besides, there was that drug business; that might come out too. No knowing what the Kempetai would make of that. For all she knew, they might shoot her after tortures that were best left unimagined.

Pablo would know what to do! She would go and call him right now. . . . No, she couldn't. If she told him, he would become an accessory in a crime of international ramifications. He would have to go to the Japanese authorities, or to the Chinese puppet regime, which amounted to the same thing. The scandal would ruin his diplomatic career. He could not possibly marry her in the circumstances. And the consequences for herself would be the same as if she told Kathy directly.

Evvie had no intention of ruining her own future for the sake of some old bones. She could definitely not tell Pablo.

What would Joe have told her to do? Evvie suddenly heard the rasping, painful croak: "Tell nobody. . . . Swear, Evvie!" Joe's dying words . . . and she had sworn. An oath was sacred! Evvie was intensely loyal—to the people she loved, not to abstract moral principles. She would keep her sacred promise. It would remain her secret and Joe's, and she'd hang on to the fossils at least until the end of the war. Then, perhaps, she would hand them over to the Americans, *if* the Americans came out on top. In that case she might even end up as a heroine who had saved a great national treasure from the grasp of the Japanese.

Evvie felt positively virtuous as she fell into an untroubled sleep. Knowledge that she had just shortened Captain Omura's life expectancy by some forty years would only have increased her feeling of righteousness.

Evvie was still asleep when Kathy left the house the next morning, unaware that she had spent the night just one floor removed from the objectives of the Kempetai's search.

Kathy arrived at the Swiss Warehouse office a little early, which gave her a feeling of having scored off Captain Omura and his cohorts, who showed up a few minutes later. Peter Rosanoff was as icy as the day before. He said that the supervisor at the warehouse was expecting them. He trusted that the search would be conducted with a minimum of disturbance, and that his company would hold the searchers responsible for damage. Peter winked at Kathy, who was the last to leave the office, while Captain Omura swore to himself that he'd get back at this arrogant White Russian swine as soon as his primary mission had been completed.

The floor and tiered wall shelves at the Swiss Warehouse were stacked with trunks, suitcases, footlockers and crates of all sizes and descriptions belonging to American military personnel.

Captain Omura said, "Miss Ewers, I want you to

look around carefully and point out any chest that resembles the one containing the fossils."

Kathy looked around. There was no sign of the well-remembered redwood chest. However, she felt that she owed Captain Omura a run for his money as well as a demonstration of cooperativeness. She pointed at several redwood boxes and wooden chests, selecting those that were located on top shelves, at the bottom of the stacks of luggage.

Captain Omura barked orders. The two Japanese privates scrambled up ladders and with much groaning managed to extract the boxes Kathy had indicated from the bottom of the piles, and then to maneuver them awkwardly down the ladders in an attempt to avoid bumping.

Captain Omura opened the dozen or so boxes with a chisel, revealing household effects, clothing, children's toys, souvenirs and other personal belongings, pitiful to contemplate in view of their owners' present plight.

Captain Omura swore. He resealed the chests, and under the watchful eye of the supervisor, they were restored to their exact former place, again with much groaning.

Ignoring Kathy, the captain now ordered inspection at random. Dozens of chests, packing cases and footlockers were opened, resealed and replaced, yielding nothing. The operation lasted all day. Lunch consisted of tea and Chinese cookies, which were gulped down hurriedly while the search continued.

At four-thirty the supervisor approached the captain and said it was closing time. The captain agreed grudgingly to stop the search and said in reply to the supervisor's question that there seemed to be no need to return tomorrow.

They left. The two privates saluted smartly, bowed and went off. The Peking party returned to the station. Dinner was not mentioned. Kathy asked and received permission to call her friends.

Evvie answered the phone. Knowing the answer only too well, she did not inquire as to the outcome of the search, but Kathy volunteered the information that it had been a failure all around.

"Oh, Kathy, that's too bad!" Then, somewhat anxiously, "I hope the Japs won't take it out on you. Punish you or something?"

Kathy assured her that there seemed to be little danger of reprisals against herself. "I've cooperated as best I could; what more can they want? Besides, I'm a neutral."

"I am so sorry that you can't stay at least another day! But you must come down for the wedding, at the latest."

The Peking train left on time. Kathy was starved, but dared not mention the subject of food to Captain Omura, who was obviously too preoccupied to feel hungry. He sat opposite her in the corner seat by the window, staring at nothing and chain smoking American cigarettes, of which he seemed to have an inexhaustible supply.

Kathy realized that the redoubtable captain was in trouble. Peter Rosanoff had got his wish; the captain had failed in an important mission. In the circles in which Captain Omura moved, failure was probably unforgivable. No wonder he appeared dejected! Kathy tried to rejoice, but unaccountably she suddenly felt sorry for the man.

"Captain," she said diplomatically, "you have not had lunch; you must be very hungry. At least I am," she added a little more boldly, "and there is a dining car on the train."

The captain was startled out of his contemplations. "Yes, dinner . . . of course, Miss Ewers; unforgivable of me."

He said something to Matsuhashi, apparently ordering him to stay behind, then rose courteously and ushered Kathy to the dining car.

"The condemned man ate a hearty dinner," he muttered after he had ordered a meal and, inexplicably, a bottle of wine.

"Captain," said Kathy timidly, "please believe me, I am very sorry. I am as concerned as you are about recovering the fossils."

He looked at her as though seeing her for the first time. The greenish glint in his eyes was very pronounced.

"That is very kind of you, Miss Kathy." (Miss

Kathy!) He crumbled a piece of bread and seemed to come to a decision. "Miss Kathy, have you formed any opinion, *any* opinion at all, as to where the fossils could be? I would truly appreciate your thoughts, even speculation, wild guesses—*anything.*"

When Kathy hesitated, he added, "Believe me, this is off the record, as the Americans say. . . . I am at my wits' end," he added suddenly, in a tone of despair.

Kathy had indeed formed an opinion. If the fossils had remained in their original redwood container, she would have hit the nail right on the head, envisaging the fate that had befallen the glassware Joe had substituted. She felt that the bones had either been reduced to dust under the regulation boots of some Japanese soldier, or had been dumped into the sea, in either case with the intent of inflicting a final insult on a dead American enemy by denying his remains a decent burial.

This opinion had to be expressed with utmost tact, since it reflected adversely upon the Imperial Japanese Army. Kathy was not sure how the captain would react to such a slur even in his present, mellowed mood.

She chose her words with care. "You understand that I have no firsthand knowledge about the movements of the fossils after they were packed and placed in the PMS vault. Whatever I may think about what might have happened after that is pure guesswork. Also, I do not know how far your own inquiries have progressed. . . ."

Captain Omura said impatiently, "Yes, yes, please continue."

"Well," said Kathy, "I have always assumed that the fossils were to be shipped to the United States—to the Professor in New York. I was not informed to that effect," she added hastily. "I was just the secretary; I was not in the confidence of the administration. . . ."

"Yes," said the captain with some exasperation. "I agree with you. Please do go on!"

"I suppose the redwood chest was no longer in the vault when you began your inquiries?"

"No; the vault was empty."

"In that case, the chest must have been removed either to the American Embassy or to the barracks, and from there to Chinwangtao."

Captain Omura shook his head. He then volunteered a piece of information that was news to Kathy although it wouldn't have been to Commissar Liu.

"Your reasoning is correct, Miss Kathy. But the fossils were not at the embassy, not at the barracks and not in Chinwangtao. Believe me, our search was *most* thorough. We questioned the American prisoners of war, and also our own troops who were in Chinwangtao on December 8 and took over from the Americans."

Kathy bristled inwardly at his euphemisms. "Took over," indeed! She could imagine the "takeover!" Her sympathy for the captain evaporated rapidly.

Captain Omura failed to notice. "If the redwood chest had been at any one of these places or at Camp Holcomb, we would have found it. Or at least someone would have noticed and informed us of its present whereabouts. You yourself were a witness to today's search in Tientsin. You must agree that if the chest had been there, we would have discovered it. That was the last possible location. Unless the chest was stolen by the Chinese somewhere along the way. But as we reconstruct it, the chest was never out of the sight of the American Marines, from the moment it left PMS. Moreover, *they* did not know what it contained. At least, no one has admitted to such knowledge, and believe me," he added grimly, "we would have got it out of them."

I'll bet you would, thought Kathy bitterly. She took another risk. "Do you think the fossils could have reached Japan?"

"No; we searched. Our scientists were most cooperative. They have acquired"—Acquired! You mean looted, Kathy exclaimed inwardly—"some fossil specimens for our collections, but Peking Man is not among them. Our scientists are as concerned about the loss as we are. There is concern in the highest places. . . . I am at my wits' end," he said again. "I have failed." He completed the sentence to himself: . . . failed in the mission entrusted to me by the Emperor himself.

Kathy digested this in silence. She had to agree with

the captain. Every possibility had been investigated efficiently. It did not occur to Kathy then or at any time that there was one footlocker that had been overlooked—the one that performed such a useful service as an end table in her living room. Nor that Evvie's vehement rejection of assistance while packing her belongings after Joe's death could have any bearing on the whereabouts of Peking Man.

They returned to their compartment. Omura and Matsuhashi exchanged an occasional remark in Japanese; otherwise the remainder of the journey passed in silence.

At Chien Men Station, Captain Omura said, "You will forgive us, Miss Ewers, if we do not see you home. We still have duties to attend to. Thank you for your cooperation. We shall not meet again. *Leben Sie wohl.*"

Unexpectedly he held out his hand. Kathy, bemused, shook it in a reflex action.

The captain directed the rickshaws to Colonel Kimura's house in the north city, where he and the lieutenant made their reports.

The colonel's reaction could be heard all over the house and apprised Moon, the houseboy, of the failure of the search for the fossils in Tientsin.

The colonel ended with a none too subtle, loudly expressed hint as to the obligations of a Japanese officer who has failed ignominiously in a sacred mission.

Captain Omura listened in respectful silence. Upon being dismissed, he bowed, saluted and returned to his own quarters.

He took off his custom-tailored uniform and the handmade oxfords. He put on a black silk kimono, white, mitten-like socks and thong sandals.

Kneeling by a low, lacquered table, he brushed a beautifully literary note to Colonel Kimura, folded the delicate rice paper, sealed and addressed it, and neatly cleaned the brush he had used.

After this he went into the bedroom and knelt in front of the mirror. He made an exceedingly odd gesture with his right middle finger, touching successively his forehead, his chest, the left and then the right shoulder—perhaps in memory of the late Maggie O'Brien and her teachings.

He then raised his service revolver and shot himself behind the right ear.

Kathy went to the institute early the next morning. Father Lorrain suggested she report in the presence of Dr. Detwyler, and they walked over to the one-room "Swiss Consulate" at the Wagons-Lits Hotel.

Both men listened attentively and were particularly interested in the information concerning the Kempetai's unsuccessful searches at Chinwangtao and in Japan.

Father Lorrain said, "There is no doubt that the Japanese have been most thorough. Me, I cannot think of any other place where the fossils might be. And I cannot think of any explanation for their disappearance. Even if they had been destroyed, they would have had to be *seen* by the one who destroyed them, and the Kempetai would have found out."

"Well," said Dr. Detwyler judiciously, "not necessarily. The culprit would have had to be some clod of a Japanese soldier, and he'd know better than to confess to the Kempetai."

Father Lorrain and Kathy concurred. Father Lorrain noticed Kathy's distress.

"Do not disturb yourself so much, *ma petite*," he said kindly. "It is true that the fossils are of great value, but their loss is not so tragic as all that."

Kathy stared at the priest in disbelief. Father Lorrain smiled. "It is true, Katee. The *Sinanthrope* has been dated, described, measured, x-rayed, drawn, photographed and cast in plaster down to the last fossa, crista and tubercle. Whatever information the fossils contained with regard to human evolution has been extracted. Besides, the casts are excellent, and so are the reconstructions of the other remains. The Professor has all these materials and will be able to carry on his work without the originals. The loss is more a matter of sentiment than a true tragedy for science. Besides, even if these specimens are lost, more will no doubt be found once the excavations can be resumed."

This was comforting. Kathy began to feel better.

Dr. Detwyler now began to question her closely

about the treatment she had received at the hands of the Japanese. He seemed disappointed when Kathy said that Captain Omura had been invariably courteous and his manners beyond reproach.

"That S.O.B.," said Dr. Detwyler darkly. "Others were not as fortunate as you. Omura is a dangerous man and a sadist. I have had reports about him and have complained to the Japanese authorities. I have quite a list on Captain Omura; after the war he will get what he has coming to him. You be careful in your dealings with him, Katrin, and don't be taken in by that Irish charm."

Kathy said that her dealings with Captain Omura seemed to have come to an end and described his solemn farewell and handshake, and his admission of failure. Dr. Detwyler grinned. "Maybe he'll commit harakiri," he said cheerfully. "In that case, good riddance, and may he rot in hell!"

16

The duties of Dr. Reinhard Detwyler, Acting Swiss Consul, were far removed from the happy hunting grounds of the pet species of Reinhard Detwyler, M.D., Ph.D., Professor of Dermatology and Syphilology. But the acting Swiss consul had little time to miss the gram stain, the culture tube and the dark-field microscope, and the fascinating life they revealed. He was responsible for a great deal more than the well-being of the six or seven Swiss nationals in Peking. Far more importantly and exactingly, he represented the interests of the Americans and the British and those of their allies who were not being looked after by the Swedish representative. Like his Swiss colleague, Mr. Sjoström was not a career diplomat. He was a postgraduate student from the University of Uppsala who had come to Peking to complete his doctoral dissertation on the literature of the Sung dynasty and, like Dr. Detwyler, had been promoted by exigency to his present diplomatic status.

With diplomacy, aggressiveness and persistence, Dr.

Detwyler wrested a variety of concessions from the Japanese authorities. One of the first was the institution of "Red Cross letters," twenty-five-word missives which, though heavily censored, permitted communication of a sort between individuals in Japanese-occupied territory and their friends and relatives in POW camps or in "enemy" country.

Shortly after her return from Tientsin, Kathy and Father Lorrain composed such a message to the Professor in New York, to the effect that Nellie was missing, "present whereabouts unknown; exhaustive search by all interested parties unsuccessful." Two months later they received a reply stating in twenty-five frantic words that Nellie had not arrived in New York as scheduled and to continue inquiries. There the matter of "Nellie" stopped for the time being.

Kathy was also able to exchange messages with Tom, who was still at Kiangwan POW camp near Shanghai. He wrote that he was well and happy, that food was plentiful and treatment excellent, and to "be sure to tell this to the Marines!"

The Japanese censor had let this pass, probably enraptured by the praise and unfamiliar with the subtler shades of American idiom.

The "civilian prisoners of war" remained out of bounds to Dr. Detwyler, despite his frequent, strongly worded protests. He was consistently refused access to the villa in the east city and learned of the inmates' plight, including the torturing of Mr. Mitchell at the hands of Captain Omura, only via the Chinese servant grapevine. He could not protest these inhumane procedures without giving his sources away, but the information was added to Dr. Detwyler's dossier on the captain. Dr. Detwyler kept this record on file even after learning, with a feeling of having been cheated, of Captain Omura's suicide, just in case this was a rumor deliberately spread by the Japanese.

The Japanese began to tighten the screws. Word went out that "enemy nationals," hitherto stigmatized only by red armbands and in some cases by house arrest, were to be interned, and were to prepare themselves accordingly. Only a limited amount of luggage would be permitted, subject to inspection. The aged and the sick would be exempted from internment upon certification by a Japanese army surgeon.

Preparations followed a basic pattern, with individual variations. Almost everybody concerned stored rugs, antique Chinese furniture and other valuables large and small with neutral friends. Canned food and heavily smoked, garlicky sausages were much in demand, and the Russian delicatessen store on Hatamen Street soon had sold out its stocks.

The Hickmans (New Jersey Oil Company) put up a false wall in front of their liquor cabinet (and were to rejoice to find the contents undisturbed upon their return almost three years later).

Mr. Horton-Smith, Peking manager of the Anglo-American Tobacco Syndicate, Ltd., prepared twelve Haig & Haig Pinch bottles. Six contained the authentic product. Six were filled with weak tea. Mr. Horton-Smith reasoned that the Japanese would confiscate at least half of the supply he proposed to take to camp. Which they did. Mr. Horton-Smith arrived in camp with six bottles of Haig & Haig "dimple" whisky, but was to derive little of the intended personal comfort from it. The whisky was immediately confiscated by the duly elected camp administration and rationed out sparsely to the internees upon demonstrated medical need only.

Mr. Robert Williams (First Manhattan Bank), twenty-six years old and unattached, as well as young Father Jenkins (Dominican Mission Society) notified the Swedish representative of their objections to internment, and suggested measures for its prevention. Young Mr. Sjoström talked to his houseboy. The houseboy went shopping and had a conversation with the shopowner.

Three days later, Mr. Williams and Father Jenkins took a picnic lunch to the wilderness-like grounds surrounding the Temple of Heaven, which adjoined the southernmost wall of the city. There they were suddenly set upon by masked bandits, bound, gagged and blindfolded, and abducted, unprotestingly, over a secluded, unpatrolled section of the wall.

The bandits took their captives to their village hideout several miles out in the countryside, which, being

Palou territory, was shunned by the Japanese. There the gags, blindfolds and fetters were removed. The kidnap victims were handed over to another group of bandits, who conveyed them to a village twenty miles farther west and passed them on to Chinese peasants, who supplied them with bicycles, route instructions and passwords. Traveling west by night, and handed on from one helpful group of peasants or bandits to the next, like buckets passed along by a bucket brigade, Mr. Williams finally made it to Chungking and from there eventually to Burma, where he joined Merrill's Marauders.

Father Jenkins turned south somewhere along the way toward an American mission station in northwestern Szechuan. Bishop Timothy Mulrooney, who headed the diocese in peacetime, had abandoned his spiritual duties for the time being and become a colonel in the OSS. He was happy to welcome his young Brother in Christ into the organization. Father Jenkins distinguished himself and by the end of the war had risen to the rank of major.

The kidnapping of two American citizens was reported to the Japanese authorities with indignant, strongly worded protests. The Japanese, knowing full well that both Dr. Detwyler and Mr. Sjöström knew that they knew the real story, apologized officially for the regrettable incident and privately gritted their teeth. They had no intention of pursuing two relatively unimportant enemy aliens into Palou territory, a fact that had figured significantly in Mr. Sjöström's arrangements for the abduction.

There was also Father Van Dekker of the Belgian Mission. Father Van Dekker was in the prime of his life and enjoyed the robust health of a Flemish peasant. By no stretch of the imagination could he be described as either aged or ill, and thus eligible for exemption from internment.

However, Father Van Dekker considered internment an intolerable interference with his life's work, the compilation of a French-Chinese-Mongolian dictionary. He therefore took counsel with his brethren as to how this nuisance could be avoided.

Six large, red-cheeked Flemish priests with enormous beards sat around a gallon-size ashtray smoking black, redolent tobacco in long-stemmed pipes and discussed Father Van Dekker's problem. Father Van Heeren found the solution. "You are going to be *very* sick when the Japanese inspection comes," he promised. "Just leave it to me."

Father Van Dekker's illness was reported to the Japanese, who announced the date and time of a medical examination.

Two hours before the appointed time, Father Van Heeren stood by while Father Van Dekker drank a quart of very hot coffee, as strong and black as the home-cured tobacco in his pipe. The results were beyond all expectations.

Father Van Dekker turned pale. His body, clammy with cold sweat, shook with tremors. He was racked with violent nausea, and his chest and heart seemed on the point of bursting with palpitations.

Father Van Heeren watched the agony with satisfaction and grinningly refused a feeble request for last rites.

When the Japanese sent a message that their visit would be postponed for twenty-four hours, Father Van Dekker was beyond caring. He resigned himself to internment, packed up the notes for his dictionary, and vowed to abstain from coffee for the rest of his life.

His confreres also prepared for internment. Informed that after their departure their mission compound would be occupied by an order of Italian monks, the Belgians looted their own richly appointed wine cellar and distributed the contents among their friends, rather than let them fall into the hands of the "Wops," hatred for the enemy outweighing love for the Brothers in Christ. Father Lorrain was the lucky recipient of a dozen bottles of hock and of a sweet, resinous Tunisian white wine, which he hoarded for special celebrations.

The aged and the sick, duly certified, were moved to the British Embassy compound, where they would spend the war years in relative comfort. One of their first actions was the removal of the Japanese seal from their shortwave radios and concealing the sets in the recesses of closets and cabinets, where for some reason they were never discovered, small long-wave sets being on hand for display to the Japanese when required.

As a result, the inmates of the British Embassy compound were always well informed of developments. News from this focus spread to the rest of the Allied sympathizers with such rapidity that the Allied invasion of North Africa was celebrated within twenty minutes of its reception in the British Embassy—in the case of the Geological Institute, with the first of Father Van Heeren's bottles of Tunisian wine.

Dissemination of intelligence was facilitated by the fact that the internees were granted passes to visit the two German-Jewish doctors and the Austrian dentist in the Legation Quarter. As a result, physical and dental health deteriorated precipitately among the internees and their friends in the city, and the waiting rooms of the three practitioners were always filled to bursting.

The rest of the prospective internees were ordered to assemble for departure to camp on a warm, sunny spring morning in 1943. All wearers of green armbands were on hand to see them off. The occasion was characterized by a display of stiff upper lips and much gallows humor, hiding the apprehension felt by everyone present, with the exception of the student body of the American School, who were rejoicing at the prospect of a prolonged vacation.

The loss of Father Van Dekker to linguistics and etymology was to be a gain for the internees. Father Van Dekker, discovering that he possessed hitherto unsuspected criminal tendencies, put his talents to good use in the smuggling of food into the camp. The procedure entailed lowering a basket with money over the barbed-wire-topped wall, in exchange for eggs and produce supplied by Chinese peasants waiting below. Anyone caught in the act was severely punished with solitary confinement and reduction of the rations, which were meager to begin with; furthermore, the Japanese were not averse to inflicting corporal punishment.

On one memorable morning Father Van Dekker had just hauled up a basket of eggs when the sentry hove into sight. With great presence of mind, Father Van Dekker squatted down, spreading the skirts of his cassock over the incriminating basket, and began to read his breviary until he and the sentry were out of each other's sight. He was rewarded with two eggs and a sip of Mr. Horton-Smith's whisky for his act of heroism.

Almost coinciding, but not correlated, with the departure of "enemy nationals" from Peking, Colonel Kimura lost his number one houseboy. The loss was abrupt and without the formality of notice being given. In the evening, Moon assisted at the preparation and serving of sukiyaki at the colonel's dinner table; in the morning he had vanished.

The colonel's fury knew no bounds. No fool, he summed up the situation correctly. He, the head of the Kempetai, had been beaten at his own game, had been taken in by cleverly faked credentials, and had harbored a Chinese agent in his own household. He could not even tell whether Moon's allegiance was to the Nationalists or the Communists—though more probably it was to the latter. Moon's description went on the Kempetai's equivalent of the Ten Most Wanted list, but searches and vigilance remained unrewarded. Moon had disappeared as though the earth had swallowed him up.

Moon's resignation from Colonel Kimura's service had not been as spontaneous as the manner of its execution implied. Many *shaoping* had been consumed during nocturnal chats with the owner of the stall. The last conversation, short and to the point, took place during the night after Colonel Kimura's sukiyaki dinner. A tall young Korean accepted a courteous invitation to take a cup of tea in the shopowner's "unworthy" premises behind the bakery.

Twenty minutes later, a middle-aged scholar in a blue silk robe topped by a black brocade vest joined the milling crowds in the aisle leading to the Morrison Street exit of the market. Blue silk trousers, neatly tied at the ankles, peeped out from under the robe and were tucked into hose that showed up snowy white against black silk slippers. The scholar's short, grizzled hair was hidden under a stiff, semi-spherical black silk cap. Drooping gray Fu Manchu mustaches bracketed the mouth. A large black mole sprouting two long hairs projected from the chin. The scholar was tall, but stooped; his near-sighted eyes peered over the brass rims of circular spectacles perched on the tip of the nose. In one hand the scholar carried a fan made from a dried lotus leaf; suspended from the index finger of the other was a small bamboo cage housing a noisily shrilling cricket.

The scholar shuffled to the exit and mounted a rickshaw, which carried him and his stridulating pet to the theater district outside Chien Men Gate. Impatiently pushing aside a jostling crowd of ragged beggars, he entered the theater.

The entertainment had reached its climax. The star, a famous female impersonator, had just minced gracefully onto the stage and was delivering himself of an aria in a shrill falsetto voice close in pitch and frequency to the ultrasonic range. The six-man orchestra, consisting of two-stringed violins, drums and cymbals, was accompanying the aria with ear-splitting clangor.

The audience, occupying seats both in the pit and on the stage, were sipping tea, or expertly cracking melon seeds with their teeth—the floor was slippery with the ejected shells—and carrying on conversations, hawking and spitting constantly and freely. Mothers nursed their infants. Vendors walked through the aisles and between the rows of seats, loudly advertising ice cream and melon seeds; attendants were serving tea or airmailing hot steaming towels over the audience's heads, to be fielded by the intended recipients and returnmailed with unerring aim.

The scholar ignored the heroine, who, weaving graceful arabesques with her floor-length gauze sleeves, was shrilly exhorting two warring armies to stop their fighting. The eight thousand men on the stage were "led" by two black-bearded, fierce-browed generals in resplendent martial costumes of scarlet, and gold. The "good guy"'s face was painted white, the "bad guy"'s red. Each commanded four thousand men, represented by four flags stuck into his topknot.

This was the moment for which the audience had been waiting patiently for five hours. The scholar remained unimpressed. He despised the classic opera, which, like all the rest of the repertoire, extolled a shameful feudal past. He also was disdainful of the "heroine," whose charcoal-rimmed almond eyes and pink-and-white face, suggesting a virgin of seventeen, concealed under the heavy makeup the raddled features of a middle-aged homosexual.

The scholar passed behind the propless stage, which was populated, in addition to the screeching heroine and her audience of eight thousand, by spectators, and by actors sipping tea and changing their costumes between scenes, assisted by blue-gowned attendants.

The aria came to a deafening end amid a crescendo of booming drums, screeching violins and clanging cymbals, amplified by the appreciative roar of *"Hao"* from the audience. The heroine and the two warring factions were refreshing themselves with tea and a smoke on stage when the scholar entered a dressing room.

There he proceeded to divest himself of the cricket, the owlish spectacles, the wispy mustaches, the hairy mole and his robes. He sat and stood naked while his head was being shaved and the smooth ivory-colored skin of his scalp and body was rubbed with grime, mud, soot and garlic juice. He sat in silence while the makeup artist applied lepromatous sores and crusts to scalp, face, body and limbs. These would not have fooled a dermatologist of, say, Dr. Detwyler's caliber for one minute in bright daylight, but were sufficiently realistic to shock a casual beholder into horrified recoil. He was then clad in filthy tatters; head and feet were swathed in dirt-encrusted rags, leaving an abundance of sores in view. Finally, furnished with a wooden clapper with which to proclaim his affliction, the leper left unobtrusively through the back door of the theater and joined the equally dirty, evil-smelling beggars in the street, jostling a blind old man with sunken shriveled eyes.

The blind beggar detached himself from the company, put his hand on the leper's shoulder and allowed himself to be led to the southernmost gate of the city.

Dawn was near; the gates were being opened. The two Japanese sentries shrank back in revulsion and could not pass the leper and his sightless companion out of the city fast enough, speeding the two derelicts through the gate with prods of their bayonets.

"What barbarians these Chinese are, to be sure," said one sentry.

"*Hai, sso-dessu,*" agreed the other.

The first sentry elaborated on the subject. "These lepers—they will try to smear their snot on you out of spite, to infect you. The women try to get you to sleep with them. Lepers think if they sleep with a healthy person, that one will get the disease and they will be cured. I say they should all be rounded up and shot."

"*Hai, sso-dessu,*" agreed the other again, shrugging disdainfully and spitting into the dust.

The leper slowly guided the blind beggar along the dusty country road to a mud-walled village some two miles farther south. Recognizing the authentic aroma, the village mongrels ignored their approach. The two men were given food and shelter in one of the huts, whose occupants did not seem to fear contagion.

The journey continued in similar stages for several days. An occasional Japanese patrol cursed them, but gave the leper a wide berth.

The journey ended in Commissar Liu's current headquarters, halfway between Peking and Tientsin.

Ch'en thankfully washed off the leper's identity in a hot bath and donned clean clothes with a feeling of sensual pleasure.

A conference followed.

"It is clear that our search for the Peking Man has come to an impasse," said Commissar Liu. "But at least the futile search has led to the self-liquidation of that Irish-Japanese turtle's egg Omura, which has saved us some trouble. Besides, negative information is also information. We must now await the end of the war and then concentrate on the American, Snyder. I have no doubt that he knows where the fossils are and will lead us to them. You, Comrade Ch'en, have done well. You are valuable to us because of your specialized knowledge. You will therefore be kept in reserve. We will utilize your qualifications as a theoretician, but you will be removed from exposure to physical danger."

Accordingly, Ch'en was sent on the long journey to Yenan, the Communist Chinese capital in faraway Shensi Province. There he spent the remainder of the war years in the company of Soviet Russian officers, teaching young comrades the skills of foreign languages, espionage and infiltration, and the deadly martial arts of unarmed combat, under the benevolent supervision of Party Chairman and Supreme Commander Mao Tse-tung.

The blind beggar, an extremely valuable prop, in due course escorted another agent back into Peking.

17

The departure of some one hundred fifty "enemy nationals" left the foreign community even more shrunken and bent inward upon itself than it had been that last year "before Pearl Harbor." Not only had the social life become constricted and narrow, but intellectual and scientific stimulation flowing from the West had become a trickle and then dried up altogether. Peking became a stagnant backwater, and scientists like Father Lorrain and Father Lautrec had to depend on limited local resources and rapidly outdated information to continue their work as best they could. Father Lorrain's manuscripts began to deal less and less with "hard" science and ascended more and more into the loftier realms of philosophy and theology. These papers, which were considered highly heretical, were published and distributed privately.

Father Lautrec was a zoologist. He was a dashing redhead, had been a captain in the *chasseurs alpins* before he took his vows, and neither his elegance nor his speech was marred by the stub of Gauloise that seemed to be a permanent outgrowth of his lower lip.

Both Father Lorrain and Father Lautrec were sociable individuals who now found themselves deprived of the American, British and Belgian drawing rooms where they had been welcome visitors before their hosts were sent off to internment camp.

Kathy benefited from this loss. A warm friendship developed between her and her two Jesuit employers. Her high school French expanded rapidly, enriched by songs and idioms that were clearly carry-overs from

Father Lautrec's military past—he had most certainly not acquired them in the seminary.

The work, too, was interesting enough and afforded an education of sorts, but it was also largely mechanical and did not seem to lead anywhere in particular, except to the monthly salary. Kathy felt vaguely dissatisfied with the prospect of being eternally doomed to typing up other people's ideas. The wish to utilize the war years to complete her education, and perhaps type her own manuscripts someday, recurred with increasing frequency and intensity, although she knew that Tom would not approve. He had objected loudly enough, clearly enough and often enough to a wife who was better educated than himself. But as Kathy began to rationalize her wish, it became increasingly obvious to her that Tom would *benefit* from a college-trained wife. She would be able to teach at whatever base Tom would be stationed in; there were always schools for dependents or American schools abroad like the one in Peking, enabling her to help out with the finances. How could Tom possibly object to that! She suppressed the thought that Tom was far away and their future uncertain, while her determination increased to the point that she discussed the problem with Father Lorrain. "I'd be more useful to Tom if I had my degree," she said. "I'm sure he'll see it that way too."

Father Lorrain doubted that but kep his doubts to himself, as he had done all along with regard to Kathy's engagement to the young Marine, whom he considered entirely unsuitable as a husband for his secretary. Now he expressed approval of her idea. "You 'ave made a very wise decision, my dear. Let us go out to St. Joseph's now and make arrangements for you to be admitted in the fall."

St. Joseph's University, built by the same White Russian architect in the same pseudo-Chinese style as PMS, was located in the north city, some thirty minutes' rickshaw ride from the Legation Quarter. The ride was definitely "scenic." It led along the moat which encircled the crimson-walled Forbidden City and was now glowing rosily with lotus blossoms. The rickshaws skirted Coal Hill to the north, an artificial elevation crested with turquoise-roofed pavilions. These afforded a breathtaking view over the crimson and gold of the city's palaces interspersed with the dark green of its parks, to the slate-blue silhouette of the Western Hills in the shimmering outer distance.

St. Joseph's was conducted by a religious society in which Germans predominated. American and Dutch priest-members of the faculty were kept out of sight in the adjoining monastery for the time being.

Father Müller, the jovial, red-jowled chairman of the Biology Department, received Kathy and Father Lorrain with pleasure. He refused a Gauloise—"Smoke Ve Don't"—but offered his visitors a glass of wine—"So Ve Drink"—he grinned, alluding to his society's initials. He saw no objections to Kathy's admission. "Fortunately, we are now admitting girls. You can probably enter as a junior, Fräulein Ewers," he continued. "You will take examinations in some of the courses you have already taken in Basel, so that you won't have to take them over again."

Accordingly, Kathy spent the summer of 1943 reviewing her rusty knowledge of physics and mathematics, tutored by Father Lorrain and Father Lautrec, and passed her examinations, partly as a just reward for her efforts and partly through the charity of her examiners, one of whom was Dr. Peters.

Kathy rediscovered the world of botany, zoology, genetics, chemistry—exacting, absorbing, and utterly remote from the war that was continuing its pitiless ravage of much of the world beyond the quiet, tree-lined campus in the north city of Peking.

She did not inform Tom of her new life as a third-year student of biology, reasoning that she would surprise him with her newly earned degree when they met again after the war, but admitting to herself that she found it impossible to share with him in writing what she felt and did in her new kind of life. She blamed this on the constraint of the permissible twenty-five-word message. But she also had increasing difficulty in finding anything at all to communicate to him, even within the twenty-five-word limit. However, the opportunities for these exchanges became rarer and rarer as the war dragged on. Kathy barely glanced at Tom's infrequent, scrawled messages, noting absent-mindedly only that they came from Hokkaido, Japan. Tom invariably described himself as "in good health, bearing up, hoping you are the same."

The gold ring with the Marine emblem had long since been returned to its small brocaded box, on the grounds that it might be ruined by the chemicals she had to handle in her laboratory work.

In the measure that Tom Aiken receded into a shadowy background of Kathy's thought and visual memory, Professor Peters gradually advanced into the foreground.

Martin Peters, Ph.D., was a tall, gangly man who looked much older than his thirty-five years. His mouse-colored hair was graying and receding at the temples. His movements as he lectured learnedly on "dominant" and "recessive" genes, "linkage" and "crossing over," were jerky and awkward. His eyes, very blue behind horn-rimmed glasses, were inclined to twinkle in unguarded moments. Kathy had taken a vague and quite unreasonable dislike to Dr. Peters in the old days when he had visited the Professor at PMS, a sentiment of which Dr. Peters had remained unaware but which would have left him supremely indifferent had he known about it. Perhaps Kathy's dislike of the man stemmed from the Professor's casual remark that Dr. Peters was "a devout Catholic." But her prejudice against "papists," nurtured in her Swiss Calvinist home, in the Methodist mission compound and at the predominantly Lutheran German school, had abated through her contact with Father Lorrain and Father Lautrec, and had subsided further when nobody at St. Joseph's seemed interested in making a convert of her.

At any rate, her dislike for Dr. Peters evaporated along with her anti-Catholicism, but inexplicably she began to feel a certain hostility toward a statuesque German lady who, gossip said, took care of Dr. Peters' periodic physical requirements but was disqualified from marrying him by being both a Protestant and a divorcee.

Kathy was one of the three "coeds" in the predominantly male biology class of 1945. She and her two female fellow students, whom she privately characterized as "amah types," stolid, compactly built and sexless in

123

their blue cotton gowns, were assigned to the front row in each lecture. Kathy's presence had at first aroused a great deal of mirth among her classmates, but soon the Chinese students recognized that "I-wu" was valuable. Being the only one in the class whose English was fluent, she had no difficulty taking notes in the tough courses taught with questionable pronunciation by two German and two Austrian instructors. Kathy's notes were circulated liberally among her classmates and formed the basis for cram sessions before examinations. The Chinese students reciprocated by coaching I-wu in the courses given in Chinese by Professor Yang, who hailed from an obscure northwestern province and whose dialect was practically unintelligible even to his Chinese audience.

However, all the Chinese faculty spoke some Western language, and Kathy took her examinations in English, German or French, depending on what country had granted the Chinese instructor his doctorate.

Winter approached. It became too cold for Kathy to spend time between classes on a bench in the campus grounds. Dr. Peters invited her to warm up and eat her lunch at his house near the university. Sometimes he was there, sometimes he was in class. At all times his elderly amah was present as a chaperone. Whether in the classroom or at his home, Dr. Peters' demeanor remained distant and formal, never letting Kathy forget that he was faculty and she was a student. His glances at her occasionally belied this circumspect attitude, especially when the conversation turned from term papers, grades and biological theory to more personal matters.

Kathy learned that Dr. Peters had been engaged to a Jewish girl (so he couldn't be as "Catholic" as all that), who with her parents and two young brothers had disappeared from her home in Vienna one night. "Transport to the East," the neighbors had said vaguely and with furtive glances over their shoulders. This had happened shortly after the Anschluss which had converted the Republic of Austria into a southeastern appendix of "Greater Germany."

For this, and for his personal loss, Dr. Peters hated the Nazis and all they stood for. This hatred had caused him to resign his assistant professorship at the University of Vienna and made him only too eager to accept the appointment at St. Joseph's when it was offered to him by a visiting faculty recruiter.

The stiff teacher-student relationship between Kathy and Dr. Peters relaxed further when—inevitably—they met socially at the gatherings of the small anti-Axis community. Dr. Peters took to seeing Kathy home and even to stopping for a cup of tea after these get-togethers, which always included the same people.

The year 1943 passed into history. With it went such turning points of the war as Hitler's defeat at Stalingrad and Italy's surrender. Also such minor events as the frustrated search for Peking Man, Captain Omura's suicide, Kathy's resumption of her studies, and Evamarie Zimmermann Cramer's marriage to Señor Pablo Álvarez.

This ceremony took place in the vestry of St. Ignatius' Church in the ex-French Concession of Tientsin, conducted by a broad-minded French Jesuit. Evvie wore champagne-colored silk and, for the second time, the family lace, and was radiant. She was also secretly relieved that Kathy had been refused a travel permit. The thought of Kathy in connection with the contents of the steamer trunk still made her feel slightly uneasy.

Mrs. Zimmermann deplored the "papist" ritual even in its watered-down form, but abandoned herself to the happy tears that the occasion demanded.

The news of the wedding, received circuitously in Havana via radiotelegram, was equally deplored by the senior Mrs. Álvarez, who disliked the thought of having a heretic, and a German to boot, as a daughter-in-law.

The two fathers were less concerned. Mr. Zimmermann cut short his wife's lamentations with, "Main thing is she's happy! Pablo is a nice boy, good family, fine career, well off. What more do you want for our girl?" Mrs. Zimmermann expresed her worries about religiously riven grandchildren. "She will have to bring up the children as *Catholics*," she wailed.

"Let's worry about that when the time comes, *if* there's something to worry about," admonished Mr. Zimmermann, and he poured himself a drink. Mrs.

Zimmermann confined herself to a last "I don't understand you, Oskar," but wisely left the argument at that.

In Havana, Mr. Álvarez interrupted his wife's protestations with, "Pablo is a good boy; he's got excellent taste in girls. Trust him to have made a wise choice. You can always try to convert her when they get back here . . . and we'll see about the children," he added hastily.

Neither the Zimmermanns nor the Álvarezes were aware that the problem of their grandchildren's religious upbringing was not going to arise in the foreseeable future. Evvie had seen to that as a routine procedure, although she had found it unnecessary to inform her Catholic husband concerning the equipment in a small watered-silk bag among her toiletries.

Untroubled by the respective parental misgivings, Señor and Señora Pablo Álvarez boarded the Blue Train for Shanghai, traveling in comfort and comparative luxury and with only one hour's delay due to guerrilla activity north of Nanking. Evvie's steamer trunk, sealed with a diplomatic seal, traveled with her over Mrs. Zimmermann's protests at its shabbiness, and found its third resting place in as many years in the basement of the small, tastefully furnished villa off Avenue Joffre which would be the Álvarezes' and the Peking Man's home till the end of the war.

Kathy completed her junior year with a B average computed from A's in biology and C's in chemistry. Her relationship with Dr. Peters had progressed to frequent cups of tea at her house, and to his addressing her as "Kathy" in private. In public she remained "Miss Ewers," and he avoided being seen alone with her.

Meanwhile Peking was beginning to feel the pinch of wartime. Food and fuel became so expensive that only people earning, for instance, reichsmarks or yen could afford to continue living in the prewar style to which all Westerners had been accustomed. Flour and sugar were rationed. Every resident of Peking received thirteen ounces of damp gray sugar per month, wrapped in soggy newsprint, water having been added to boost the weight. The flour was blackish and poorly milled, and anything prepared with it gritted sandily between one's

126

teeth. Steamed wheat bread had given way to large, indigestible lumps of yellow corn bread, which left a bitter aftertaste since the cornmeal was not refined. Millet replaced the rice that only the rich could now afford. Coal and wood were replaced by coal balls, and reports of carbon monoxide poisonings increased in frequency.

Señora Álvarez in Shanghai was warm, well-fed and elegantly clothed, thanks to her husband's diplomatic status and salary.

In the Peking winter Kathy rode her bicycle to school, mittened hands inside mufflike attachments to the handlebars, and dressed in woolen underwear, wool slacks and sweater underneath a silk-waste padded Chinese gown, as warm and light as an eiderdown. She wore two pairs of woolen socks and padded Chinese slippers, leather shoes being both too cold and too expensive. Even so, she and her fellow students shivered in the unheated university. Kathy's fingertips were numb in their mittens as she clumsily took notes or tried to do dissections or handle histology slides. Not only were the students cold; they were also perpetually hungry. The pigeons issued for dissection in comparative anatomy were plucked, boiled over Bunsen burners and devoured by the investigators immediately after they had served their pedagogic purpose.

St. Joseph's charged a bag of flour for a semester's tuition, and paid its faculty in flour, sugar and molasses, supplementing a cash salary which, as Dr. Peters calculated wryly, amounted to about fifteen U.S. dollars a month.

Professor Soong, head of the Chemistry Department, augmented this meager salary by selling ethyl alcohol, which was in short supply, to the French and German hospitals. This profitable reagent was the only outcome of two semesters' laboratory work performed by junior and senior chemistry majors. Professor Soong earned cash, and the students earned six credits in organic chemistry, and everybody was happy.

Social gatherings continued. Tea and peanuts had replaced the cocktails, dainty sandwiches, "smallchow" and rich pastries of better days, but moods and conversations had become more cheerful. The news emanating from the hidden shortwave sets in the British

Embassy compound indicated that the tides of war were turning, in Russia, in Africa, in the Pacific. It was no longer a matter of "*if* the invasion comes," but "*when* the invasion comes," the "when" and "where" being a subject of constant, impatient speculation.

Winter passed into spring and early summer. It was a pleasure to peel off the layers of padded clothing and substitute year-before-last's summer clothes for the innermost layer. For a short while it was even pleasant to swelter in the heat instead of shivering in the cold, although by early June that pleasure had worn off.

But on Tuesday, June 6, 1944, the ninety-five-degree heat remained unnoticed.

D-day had arrived at long last!

At a small, spontaneous gathering at the Geological Institute, Father Lorrain opened two of Father Van Heeren's remaining bottles of hock, and Dr. Peters kissed Kathy for the first time. It was a chaste peck on the forehead and highly unsatisfactory as kisses went, but at least it was a breakthrough and, perhaps, a portent of better things to come, like the invasion of Normandy which had occasioned the "kiss."

But Kathy's personal affairs progressed more slowly than the Allied advance through France and were still at an impasse when the liberation of Paris occasioned another celebration at the institute. There was no kiss this time, and Kathy reflected bitterly that she would probably have to wait until Vienna was liberated—and both the Russians and the Allies were still far from ex-Austria's capital!

Kathy was by now in a state of chronic emotional turmoil that she recognized as love, in which blackest despair alternated with feverish elation, depending on whether or not Dr. Peters had given indications of returning her sentiments. The signs were faint—a glance here, a touch of the hand there—and seemed to lead nowhere except to a welcome loss of weight.

Kathy's work began to suffer. Father Lorrain did not fail to notice the abundance of typographical errors and omission of whole sentences in his manuscripts, and the thin paleness of his secretary's face. He was quick to establish the causal relationship between the two phenomena.

"Are you ill, Katee? Or per'aps you are in love? I think per'aps with Dr. Peters, eh?"

In the face of this direct frontal attack Kathy was unable to simulate indignation at Father Lorrain's suggestion. Head bowed, her clasped hands dangling between her knees, she unburdened herself, first haltingly, then in a spate of words that wouldn't come fast enough. It was a relief; was this what a Catholic confession was like?

"Yes, Father, I love him; I never knew I could love anyone so much! And sometimes I think he loves me too, but then again he is so—so distant, and I think it is all in my imagination, that I am a fool and should stop loving him, but I can't. . . . And besides, he is still seeing that fat Mrs. Schultz. . . . Her amah knows my amah," she explained upon noticing that Father Lorrain had raised his eyebrows. Returning her gaze to the floor, she failed to see the twinkle with which her confessor was receiving this piece of gossip.

"I don't know what to do, Father," she continued. "It's making me sick, not knowing; I can't concentrate on my work and on my studies. If this goes on, I'm going to flunk all my courses next term. . . . And then there's Tom! I feel I should write to him and tell him that I love somebody else and that I can't marry him, but it seems so *cruel* to write a letter like that to a prisoner of war, and how can you tell *anyone* in twenty-five words that you no longer love him? What should I do, Father? Please tell me—what should I do?"

Father Lorrain gently touched the bent brown head. *Pauvre petite.* How difficult it was to be young!

"Look, *mon chou*," he said. "Let us take your problems one by one. You love *le docteur* Peters, *bon*; he is a chic type, you 'ave made a good choice. I 'ave observed the way he looks at you, and I am sure he loves you too. But do not forget, you are still a student and he is your teacher; his position requires discretion and prudence. He will not be free to declare himself until you 'ave finished your studies—unless you wish to give up now?"

Kathy shook her head no.

"Then you must be patient. I, too, feel you must finish what you started; you 'ave only one more year to go. I think if you asked Dr. Peters, he would tell you the same, and he would respect you less if you were to quit now. As to Madame Schultz, believe me, *ma petite*, it means nothing! He is a normal man, with normal needs, and Madame Schultz gives him what he cannot yet honorably ask from you. Believe me, he will forget all about Madame Schultz when that time comes. I know it will come," he answered the imploring question in the blue eyes.

"As to Tom," he continued, "I agree it would be honest to let him know that your feelings for him 'ave changed, but as you say, it would also be extremely cruel in his present situation. He must be suffering a great deal. . . . Go on writing to him as before, so that he knows he is not forgotten; this means more to a prisoner of war than anything you may say in the letter itself. Do not deprive him of this comfort. Consider it a patriotic duty, and suppress your honesty until the war is over."

Kathy got up. The relief was exquisite. "Thank you, Father," she said. "Thank you more than I can say!"

She went home and wolfed down the meal of millet and vegetables that Amah set before her, and despite the August heat fell into the first restful sleep she had had in weeks. The next day she composed a fairly cheerful twenty-five-word letter to Tom, which was acknowledged three months later with his usual "Am keeping well, hope you are the same, please write as often as you can."

After Kathy's departure Father Lorrain thoughtfully lit an extra Gauloise. (He and Father Lautrec had by now rationed themselves to three a day, and the rest of the time smoked Chinese cigarettes, which, smokers complained, were made of hutung sweepings.) The Japanese sulfur match head broke off and hurled itself like a vicious small projectile onto Father Lorrain's cassock, adding another small burn hole to the rest.

When Father Lorrain's Gauloise was half consumed, he came to a decision. Taking pen and paper, he wrote a note to Dr. Peters, asking him to call at his convenience to discuss a personal matter, and dispatched the institute coolie with it to the north city.

Dr. Peters called two days later and the "personal matter" was discussed at length. Father Lorrain's charm and tact easily overcame his visitor's initial resentment at having his private life dragged into the open. Father Lorrain pointed out, reasonably, that "You can hardly call it private if you cause unhappiness to another human being."

The conversation dwelt mainly on Kathy, touching only in passing on fat Mrs. Schultz. The outcome satisfied both Father Lorrain and Dr. Peters and would have enraptured Kathy. However, she was never told of Father Lorrain's role as a catalyst in her and Martin Peters' life.

The optimism generated by her talk with Father Lorrain sustained Kathy through the rest of the summer and into the fall term, enabling her to continue writing to Tom without feeling like a hypocrite, and to concentrate on the lectures rather than the lecturer in Dr. Peters' classes. Shortly after the midterm examinations she composed a Christmas letter to Tom.

"Dear Tom, again I pray that this will be the last Christmas in your present situation, and that you will celebrate next year's with your family. Love, Kathy."

It was twenty-seven words instead of twenty-five, but perhaps the censor would let it pass.

In the middle of January the letter was returned to Kathy unopened, with a notation: "Recipient deceased." At the same time she received a Red Cross message from Hokkaido POW camp.

"Dear Kathy, sorry to tell you Tom died of pneumonia early November; I did what I could for him. Regards, sympathies, William Snyder, Corporal, USMC."

Snyder had hesitated before including the self-praising bit of information. He decided to let it stand. It would make him look good with Kathy, whose good will he might need one of these days. He forbore to elaborate that doing what he could for the mortally ill Tom had involved a wadded-up pair of pants pressed over the patient's face for about thirty seconds in the middle of the night.

Tom's parents in Woodbury, Vermont, received a similar letter of sympathy from Corporal Snyder, and were also officially notified of their son's death. The conditions under which Tom had contracted pneumonia became known to a shocked world only after the war; Snyder's assistance in terminating Tom's illness remained known only to Snyder himself.

Kathy did not have to bear her grief alone. Martin Peters was on hand to comfort her. Martin knew all about Tom; in fact, he knew all there was to be known about Kathy and had known since Christmas Eve. Father Lorrain's meddling had borne fruit.

On the last day of school before Christmas recess, Kathy plucked up her courage and invited Dr. Peters for Christmas Eve dinner. He accepted with unconcealed pleasure.

Buoyed by his reaction, Kathy set about her preparations. She managed to obtain a small pine tree and decorated it lovingly with ornaments that had been brought from Switzerland more than twenty years before, and with Chinese candles fitted into the clip-on holders that had come from Switzerland along with the ornaments. The effect was almost authentically Swiss-German-Austrian.

The fruitcake, made with the gritty black flour, soggy gray sugar, shortened with peanut oil that never let you forget what it was made from, and sporting cut-up jujubes instead of raisins, was rather less authentic. Fortunately, the company, which also included Fathers Lorrain and Lautrec, was spared the necessity of sampling this concoction. The two priests had scrounged genuine butter cookies from the French Embassy cook, which they brought as a gift along with a bottle of wine. The fish dinner served with rice hoarded for such special occasions was a success, for Chinese food could never taste unpalatable, and Amah was a superb cook.

The two priests excused themselves soon after dinner. Dr. Peters stayed on. He and Kathy sat on the sofa, sipping the rest of the wine. In the soft glow of the candles and of the wine, one thing led to another. Dr. Peters put his arm first on the backrest behind Kathy, then around Kathy, as he began to talk softly about himself, about her, and about themselves. Kathy's glass stood forgotten on Snyder's footlocker.

By the time they rose to go to midnight mass, Kathy

had been kissed intensively and expertly, wore a jade ring on the fourth finger of her left hand, and was engaged to be married the day after her graduation in June 1945.

It was a joyous Christmas, not only in Kathy's personal life. News was received on Christmas Day that the Allies had finally broken the stubborn resistance of Hitler's armies in the Ardennes. There was increasing reason to hope that this would be the last Christmas of the Second World War.

18

Kathy floated into her last term of school on a cloud of euphoria. She and Martin had agreed to keep their engagement secret. The jade ring, transferred from Kathy's left hand to a gold chain, now hung cool and reassuring between her breasts. Since certain high-minded New Year's resolutions soon proved impossible to keep and graduation day was a long way off, Dr. Peters had frequent occasions to admire the green, translucent glow against the white skin. Fat Mrs. Schulz—*poor* fat Mrs. Schulz—had become a thing of the past. Kathy had taken over the lady's therapeutic functions and performed them joyfully.

In public and on campus they comported themselves with the utmost decorum. In her fiancé's classes Kathy sat in one corner of the room, while he steadfastly addressed the other. Personal interviews were kept to a minimum and conducted only and formally in the presence of other students.

In spite of this discretion, the secret leaked out in no time—how, neither Kathy nor Dr. Peters was ever able to discover. Father Müller smirked and winked benevolently at Kathy and threw out elephantine hints whenever he met her in the hallways. The Very Reverend Father Cremers, rector of St. Joseph's and known among students and lay faculty as "Father Creamass," went his way with his head piously slanted toward his left shoulder, choosing to ignore the potential scandal as long as there were no overt improprieties.

Kathy's classmates were delighted. The delight turned into dismay when it turned out that Kathy's new, privileged status did not bring with it a foreknowledge of exam questions. Reconciling themselves to this blow, the students tried to exploit the situation in other ways.

"Eh, I-wu, blessings on your house, tell that turtle's egg Pei Tu-szu—I mean, *Professor* Pei Tu-szu—that his last quiz was too hard."

"I-wu, blessings on your house, please explain to Pei Tu-szu that I couldn't hand in my term paper on time because my grandmother was sick."

"I-wu, blessings on your house, I need at least 80 to get into Chinghua graduate school. Ask Pei Tu-szu to raise my grade 10 points."

Professor Pei Tu-szu's intransigence to these requests—so properly presented via a go-between—remained incomprehensible to the Chinese students. Upon being turned down—"Pei Tu-szu says, if you want something from him, ask him yourself"—they shrugged philosophically. Aiyah! Who could ever hope to understand the inscrutable ways of these foreign devils?

Despite these setbacks, there was a certain amount of fun to be extracted from the situation. It was most rewarding to sit behind I-wu and speculate in whispers, audible to her but not to the professor up front, whether and how often Pei Tu-szu "ki-su"ed I-wu, whether they practiced this exotic Western custom in hidden corners of campus and what corners would be most suitable for the purpose, and to watch I-wu's neck and ears turn scarlet while she pretended not to hear.

Kathy finally put a stop to this. She buttonholed two of the worst whisperers in the hall, making sure that the rest of the class was in hearing distance. Addressing the two young men in her most exquisitely polite Mandarin, she asked if the elder brothers would do her miserable self a great service and talk more softly in class. She was so stupid and unworthy as to be easily distracted and thus wretchedly unable to take good notes.

Since the whole class depended on Kathy's notes,

the point was quickly taken. The "elder brothers"—both a good five years younger than Kathy—stood grinning sheepishly, well aware that they had lost, and I-wu had gained, a great deal of "face" in the eyes of their classmates. The whispers ceased.

Kathy's cup was overflowing, and she felt impelled to bring some happiness into the lives of people less fortunate than herself. Like poor Bill Snyder, languishing in POW camp in Hokkaido. She had acknowledged his note concerning Tom's death.

"Dear Bill, thanks for letting me know. How you, too, must miss him! Will write again; keep well and hoping. . . . Love, Kathy."

Snyder read this with a grimace on his emaciated face, but was touched and not a little gratified. Not only was it pleasant to receive a letter every now and then, but Kathy's initiative had relieved him of the necessity of finding a pretext for keeping in regular contact with her.

"Dear Kathy, thanks a million! Your letters mean a great deal. Keep them coming. How & where is Evvie? Yours, *always* hoping, Bill."

"Dear Bill, I am back in school. Bio major. Will graduate and get married in June. Evvie's remarried in Shanghai. Keep well and hoping. Love, Kathy."

"Dear Kathy, congratulations! Who's the lucky guy?"

Snyder hesitated. He was dying to inquire about his footlocker, but did not dare refer to it openly, and could not think of a way of hinting. Kathy must not guess at the importance of his property. Better not mention the footlocker at all. There was no reason why it shouldn't still be at her home. Though she'd probably move in with the guy, whoever he was—not that Snyder gave a damn, except about his footlocker's change of address, maybe even leaving Peking and perhaps being opened by the Japanese. It didn't bear thinking about!

"Will you remain in Peking?" He racked his brains for another thirteen words. "How are your grades in bio and chem? Love, Bill." Three words short; never mind.

"Dear Bill, thanks for your interest. Marrying bio

prof, staying in Peking, no other place to go, but keep hoping. A's bio; C's chem. Kathy."

Snyder read this and felt relieved. The footlocker would remain in Peking for the time being. He'd forgotten to ask the nationality of Kathy's prof. It couldn't be American. He had to be a neutral, like Kathy, or a German—though it wasn't like Kathy to marry a Kraut. Anyway, he must be someone whose effects weren't likely to be searched as long as they were moved only within Peking. Snyder relaxed and concentrated on the job of surviving, which required his full-time attention. Belatedly and fleetingly it occurred to him that Kathy might be marrying a Chink, but he was too weary to consider the implications of such a calamity.

Germany, having sown the wind, had reaped the whirlwind and lay crushed between the Allies and Soviet armies. But Japan was still fighting with her back to the wall when Kathy was graduated, capped and gowned but otherwise with a minimum of fanfare. St. Joseph's University considered it prudent to call as little Japanese attention as possible to its activities.

The next day Katrin Ewers, Bachelor of Science, became Frau Doktor Peters, painlessly acquiring her husband's title along with his name, as was the European custom.

Gentle hints from Martin and Father Müller, combined with her own sense of diplomacy, had led to Kathy's conversion to Catholicism following instruction from Father Lorrain. Father Lorrain's interpretation of the Faith would have scandalized his superior, but agreed suprisingly well with Kathy's own Calvinistic beliefs, although the Catholics seemed to be rather more broad-minded about sin and eternal damnation. Father Lorrain reduced the saints, archangels, the Virgin Mary and similar objectionable "idols" to utter insignificance, and even accepted Kathy's defiant declaration that she intended to practice birth control. As a result, Kathy had been salvaged from the heretic's fate of sizzling everlastingly in Purgatory, had been re-baptized conditionally, and she and Martin were married by Father Lorrain at a proper nuptial mass in the university chapel. After which she, Amah and most of her furniure, including Snyder's footlocker, took up residence in Martin Peters' gray Western-style house near St. Joseph's.

Two months later the Second World War ended abruptly underneath two mushroom-shaped clouds.

People took to casting their eyes skyward, hoping for the first glimpse of American planes. The Nationalist Chinese armies were awaited as eagerly. There were rumors that Russian troops, awaited far less eagerly, had been seen in the Western Hills. People spending summer vacations in temples in that area dropped everything and rushed back into the city.

The Japanese military recognized the handwriting on the wall and began to take out insurance.

One midmorning Amah brought a card to Mrs. Martin Peters. The card read:

> *Mr.*
> ~~Lieutenant~~ Yiro Matsuhashi
> ~~Imperial Japanese Army~~

Matsuhashi! Could it be . . . ? It was. Bowing, hissing and smiling as toothily as ever, the lieutenant (though now apparently retired) advanced into the room. His civilian clothes sagged and flopped as untidily about his person as his uniform had done. He had let his hair grow; it was now parted on one side and slicked down over the brachycephalic head.

He stood in front of Kathy, bowed again and sucked in his breath with a sibilant hiss. Kathy bowed slightly, smiled, indicated a chair and told Amah to bring tea.

The ex-lieutenant perched on the edge of the chair and hissed again. "Ah, Missus Peterssu. So grad to see you. Rooking so well and rovery."

Kathy hid her surprise. So he did speak English after all, did he! "How are you, Lieutenant?" she said politely.

"Missuter, prease. No ronger rootenant."

Amah served the tea. Kathy racked her brains for some topic of conversation. "How is Captain Omura?"

Mr. Matsuhashi bared all his teeth in a radiant smile. "So sorry. He is dead."

The conversation lagged. Mr. Matsuhashi sipped his tea, inhaled and exhaled audibly several times, then said, "Missus Peterssu, I have come to ask favor."

"Yes," said Kathy encouragingly.

"Missus Peterssu, you have known me for some time." Hiss. Pause.

"Yes?" encouraged Kathy again.

"Missus Peterssu, I have never been discourteous to you, isn't it?" Kathy agreed. Another pause. Then, addressing his pointed, somewhat cracked black patent leather shoes, the ex-lieutenant said, "Missus Peterssu, will you write me retter to who it may concern that I have always been respectful and courteous to you in interrogations about Peking Man?"

Ah, so—Kathy shook herself; this was contagious! So he was after insurance for the Americans. Well, it was true, he had never been discourteous. How could he have been? He'd never opened his mouth. Surely there was no harm . . . She said, "Certainly, Mr. Matsuhashi. I'll type it for you right now."

He smiled happily. "Thank you so much, Missus Peterssu. Maybe you have retterhead paper? Maybe PMS retterhead paper?"

Kathy regretted. "I am afraid I never had any at home, and I, ah, had no reason to take any with me when I, ah, left." She was quick to forestall his next suggestion. "I cannot use St. Joseph's stationery. I am not on the faculty." St. Joseph's, being German-run, would at this time hardly welcome an implied association with, let alone an endorsement of, a former Kempetai officer.

"And I am so recently married, I have no personal notepaper yet."

He hissed and managed to convey disappointment with the drawing in of his breath. "No matter, Missus Peterssu. I will be grateful."

Kathy typed a brief note informing To Whom It May Concern that Mr. Yiro Matsuhashi had been unfailingly courteous and correct in what contacts she had had with him, signed it and slipped it into an envelope.

The former Kempetai lieutenant received the envelope with a grateful hiss. He rose, hissed again, and bowed repeatedly and deeply from the waist, arms straight and hands sliding up and down his thighs with each bow and elevation. "Thank you so much, Missus Peterssu. I wish you much ruck and happiness."

Adhering to Oriental custom, Kathy refrained from shaking hands. She inclined her head, said, "I wish you the same, Mr. Matsuhashi," adding silently, "You'll sure need it," and saw him out.

She told Martin about the visit. "It was funny," she said, "but also pathetic. He practically *slunk*, and he was so—so *servile*."

"How the mighty have fallen," Martin said unsympathetically. "I'll bet he won't get many letters of recommendation from the other subjects of his interrogations."

This was true enough. Katrin Peters' letter for the defense was far outweighed by the unanimous testimony of numerous witnesses for the prosecution at Mr. Matsuhashi's subsequent war crimes trial.

These witnesses included, among many others, a beating-scarred Mr. Mitchell, former administrator of PMS and former "civilian prisoner of war," who with his colleagues and fellow witnesses against Mr. Matsuhashi had finally been liberated from the secluded villa in the east city. Similar testimony was given in similar trials by civilian and military ex-captives from camps all over China, Malaysia, the Philippines and Japan. The witnesses' physical condition spoke for itself. It was exemplified by two of three Doolittle fliers who had been shot down over and held captive in Peking for two years, and had to be nursed back from stark staring madness resulting from advanced beriberi and starvation before they were halfway fit for repatriation. The third flier had not survived captivity.

The liberators had taken their time in coming to Peking. During the interregnum the Japanese not only had nobody to surrender to, but were asked to carry on and police their former territory until the victors could get around to them. But finally they did come. Kathy had observed correctly. The Japanese *were* slinking and servile.

The arrogant swaggering and strutting was now done by the Chinese Nationalist soldiers, who were determined to impress upon everyone that they had won the war single-handedly.

The U.S. First Marines, sent straight to Peking from Okinawa for R&R, were too weary to strut and swagger. People like the Peterses, overwhelmed with gratitude, literally carried the heroes off the streets to ply them with hospitality. But there was no common topic of conversation. What was there to talk about with these old, old men of twenty whose empty eyes looked straight through you into some nameless, unfathomable outer darkness. It was like trying to make small talk with Christ after His descent into Hell and Resurrection.

One could, and did, of course ask about their homes. Alabama, Georgia, Massachusetts, Oregon, California, New York—all forty-eight states were represented. The home towns mentioned were for the most part unknown to the Peterses. Nearly all of the boys had enlisted immediately upon graduation from high school—some, lying about their age, had not even waited that long—so there were no academic subjects of mutual interest. Conversation with natives of Alabama, Georgia, the Carolinas, was further impeded by the total unintelligibility of their speech.

One boy came from Vermont. Kathy asked if he knew the Aikens in Woodbury. No, but Vermont was full of Aikens. He knew some in Bennington, but Woodbury was up north, "somewheres around Manpeelya"; he had never been that far north. (Upon consulting an atlas, the Peterses surmised that "Manpeelya" was probably the state capital, Montpelier.)

After these topics were exhausted, one could only sit and smile lovingly and urge the old-young veterans to eat—which they did, gorging themselves on fresh meat, fruit, vegetables, and most of all, milk.

The GI's reciprocated in kind. Peking became acquainted with K rations and Ten-in-ones, and fell to, ravenously devouring Spam, pork-and-egg and crackers, washed down with "battery acid," as the GI's inexplicably termed the delicious, vitamin C-fortified dehydrated lemon and grape juice. The canned butter—a porous yellow sponge floating in a sea of oil—and especially the sugar, the Milky Way candy bars, not to mention the powdered Nescafé in its little one-ounce tins, these transcended all epicurean delights! And the bread, baked by GI bakers, defied description.

These delicacies as well as American cigarettes soon became available in the black market which sprang up overnight on Tung Chang Ang Chieh. Chinese servants in the American barracks ran the market and kept supplies coming. The MP's did not seem to care.

A similar open-air market, but more of the "flea" variety, spread out over the Polo Grounds between Hatamen Street and the Legation Quarter. The Japanese, short of money and soon to be repatriated to their defeated country, were selling their effects. Neatly displayed on blue cloth, and presided over by their timidly smiling owners, were the pretty lacquer bowls and trays, the delicate china and earthenware, the batiqued silk kimonos and embroidered brocade obis, straw rugs and tatamis, at which the Japanese excelled, to be acquired for a song though a little shamefacedly by the victorious troops and the long-time civilian underdogs.

Peking got used to its second "occupation." The Americans quickly expanded the locals' vocabularies with new terms like "jeep" and "radar," the most useful and generally applicable being "snafu." The Chinese population had little or no objection to the Americans, who enriched the economy by way of a liberal inflow of cash and black-marketable goods. The Chinese Nationalists were something else again. The local inhabitants frequently expressed the opinion that "it was better under the Japanese." The puppet premier, now jailed, was reported to have deplored the fact that China had never been a British colony.

Lives that had long lain dormant began to resurface. Internment camp inmates returned to Peking, still lean and haggard but cheerful after two months' nurturing and "reorientation" by their American liberators. The Hickmans were joyously reunited with their walled-up liquor supplies. Mr. Horton-Smith lost no time in replenishing his stock while tax-free goods were available at the PX. Father Van Dekker resumed work on his dictionary where he had left off three years before, and also took to drinking coffee again.

Then the repatriations began, some nonstop, some in installments. The POW's from Hokkaido, all emaciated and chronically ill with dysentery and other debilitating diseases, were sent to a military hospital at Guam before moving on to various VA hospitals in the States.

Corporal Snyder wrote to Kathy from Guam, asking her to send his footlocker to his home address in Harlingen, Texas.

Immediately upon receipt of this letter, Kathy enlisted the help of the military in Peking in returning an ex-POW's property. The footlocker was carried from her house by two privates under the supervision of a Sergeant Scali from Brooklyn, New York. The two privates commented on the lightness of their burden— "Poor guy, he can't have much in there"—and promised that the locker would reach its owner without delay. "We'll send it on to Guam right away; he might need it." Sergeant Scali gravely thanked Mrs. Peters for looking after an American's interest during the war.

The footlocker did reach Snyder in Guam.

He sat looking at it.

Sweat broke out on his forehead and trickled clammily under his arms. His heart beat a tattoo against his ribs. He felt choked and barely able to breathe.

Here it was, at long last, after more than four years. . . .

His hands were shaking and so cold that he had trouble detaching the small key ring from the chain where it had dangled alongside his dog tag ever since it had been handed to him after his return from Chinwangtao on December 7, 1941.

He dropped the key three times before he finally managed to insert and turn it in each of the two locks.

With still shaking hands he lit a cigarette, inhaling deeply and staring at the footlocker without raising the lid.

He dropped the half-smoked Lucky on the floor, automatically stubbed it out, and opened the locker. He tossed aside the brightly colored rags with which Joe had covered the cartons—something wrong here, those colors—and he encountered no resistance as he dug frantically, like a terrier digging a hole, scattering limp cloth to the right and left until the locker was empty. No cartons . . . Where were the cartons?

Foolishly he rummaged through the softly yielding heaps, throwing clothing aside until the floor was covered with crumpled regulation underwear, tan and olive drab pants, blouses, fatigues, socks and multicolored pieces of women's apparel—but still there were no cartons.

He stood staring into the empty locker, then dealt it a sudden vicious kick. This time he did encounter resistance. Snyder let out a yell and clutched at his foot, which was practically bare in an open-toed shower sandal. The foot began to swell almost immediately.

Snyder's yell brought a medic, who took one look, then ran to fetch a basin of ice water, in which Snyder immersed the throbbing limb.

"I'll bring more ice water in a while," said the medic. "Toe may be fractured. No use putting it in a splint, though; it'll heal by itself. Just keep applying the ice water to keep the swelling down. And what the hell is going on here anyway? You holding a rummage sale or something?"

Snyder thought fast, despite the pain. "Goddamn broad I was shacked up with in Peking. Stole me blind! Took all my good stuff out and sent me her old clothes instead.'"

The medic suppressed a grin, commiserated, "Tough shit," and departed.

The ice water was beginning to numb the pain. Snyder lit another Lucky and cast his mind back to Sunday, December 7, 1941.

The locker had been at Joe's from December 4 to December 6 or 7. According to Kathy's note, delivered with the keys, Joe had died on the sixth. Meaning he could have removed the fossils on the fourth, when he had received them, or the next day. But would he have? It didn't make sense. Joe would never have been able to smuggle the fossils into the States. The whole scheme hinged on Snyder's ability to get them in undetected. No, not Joe. Anyway, Joe was dead.

That left Kathy or Evvie. Kathy had had the locker in her possession for four years and must have had the keys for at least a day before returning them to the barracks. But Kathy was dumb and honest. She wouldn't pry into other people's luggage. Moreover, if she had, she would have screamed blue murder at the contents and would have handed the footlocker over to the M.P.'s forthwith. He would have found a welcoming committee equipped with handcuffs waiting for him, instead of a friendly little note and the keys. Besides, the Japs would have discovered the fossils that very night when they searched the barracks. In which case those two Kempetai bastards wouldn't have come "questioning" him and his buddies at Kaingwan camp. Snyder grimaced. He remembered the "questioning" only too well; it had been the first and by no means the most brutal of many more such "questionings" during his four years as a POW. No, Kathy could be discounted too.

That left Evvie. . . . Snyder absent-mindedly picked up one of the crumpled rags and shook it out. It was a summer dress, orange linen; he remembered Evvie wearing it. It had to be Evvie. Joe certainly wouldn't have stowed his own or Evvie's belongings in Snyder's footlocker; Synder wouldn't have let him if Joe had been stupid enough to try, and Joe certainly hadn't been stupid. . . .

Evvie must have the fossils! Unless she had turned them in? Somehow such rectitude wasn't like Evvie. But he had to find out! First thing tomorrow he'd write to Kathy, thank her for returning the footlocker and ask for Evvie's new married name and address. He'd get the fossils back from her if it took the rest of his life!

That night Snyder drank himself into a stupor, which, boosted by the analgesic furnished by the medic, afforded a brief respite from the throbbing pain in his foot and his mental anguish. Before sinking into a coma, he thought dimly that he needn't have helped Aiken along into the Hereafter after all. . . . But remorse wasn't Snyder's long suit. The poor bastard would have died anyway. No POW in Hokkaido survived pneumonia on top of the general state of extreme malnutrition and vitamin deficiency from which he, Snyder, and his buddies were still trying to recover here on Guam. . . . That pair of pants pressed briefly but firmly over Aiken's face had simply saved the guy a lot of suffering . . . done him a favor, actually.

The combination of liquor and codeine took effect. Snyder sank into temporary oblivion.

Two days after Sergeant Scali and his aides had started Snyder's footlocker on its way to Guam, the sergeant appeared again at the Peters house. This time he was in a subordinate position to a Major O'Neill and a Lieutenant Weinstein, who flipped leather folders and asked courteously if they might ask Mrs. Peters a few questions.

The whole scene had an eerie flavor of *déjà vu*, from the leather folders to the content of the questions and Kathy's answers.

American military intelligence were searching for Peking Man, retreading the ground already trampled and meticulously dug over by the late Captain Omura and ex-Lieutenant Matsuhashi.

Mr. Mitchell had contacted G-2, giving them what information he had and urging the investigation, stressing its importance. As a result, Major O'Neill, Lieutenant Weinstein and Sergeant Scali were now solemnly taking notes as Kathy reiterated her account of the packing of the fossils.

The questions went into minute details. "Embedded in wood shavings, you say, Mrs. Peters? You're sure it wasn't absorbent cotton?"

They made her describe the cartons. "Cardboard? Grayish brown? About one cubic foot each? Taped down with surgical tape?"

Then the redwood chest, *ad infinitum* and *ad nauseam*.

"About eighteen by twenty by twenty-four—is that correct?"

It was, as far as Kathy could remember; the cartons had fitted very snugly between two thick protective layers of excelsior.

"These measurements refer to the *inside* of the chest? So the *outside* dimensions must have been a little more?"

Kathy supposed so.

"Now the lock. Please describe the lock."

"You say the redwood chest was taken to the PMS vault. Who was present? What was the name of the coolie who wheeled the dolly?"

Kathy had never known.

"That assistant, Ch'en. Where is he now?"

Kathy didn't know. She hadn't seen Ch'en since they had parted company on Hatamen Street on December 8, 1941.

"Can you give us a description?"

"About twenty-five, tall and thin, maybe five-eleven, kind of lanky, shaven head. He doesn't speak English."

The description fitted at least a third of some 150 million northern Chinese males, including certain members of the major's office staff. But they, of course, spoke English.

The major took Kathy over the search at the Swiss Warehouse in Tientsin.

"Did you notice any luggage—chests, suitcases, trunks—with the colonel's name on it?"

Kathy didn't remember. "I'm not sure, but I don't think so."

All this was noted down, adding nothing to what the two officers did not already know.

"Thank you so much, Mrs. Peters. May we contact you again if something comes up?"

Major O'Neill had set up headquarters in the German Embassy, whose former occupants were now lodged in "denazification camps" in their devastated homeland.

Major O'Neill liked Peking and he liked the Chinese, although his contact with the "natives" was limited to his houseboy and to the office staff, who handled nonclassified material. He felt fortunate in having secured the services of a very well-qualified clerk by the name of Wu, a tall (about five feet eleven), bespectacled young college graduate of about twenty-five, who spoke excellent English. Wu frequently expressed the desire to go to the United States

146

to pursue graduate studies in economics. Wu had been thoroughly screened, and his antecedents, his politics and his pro-American sentiments were impeccable.

Major O'Neill, who held a master's degree in psychology and in civilian life had been a guidance counselor at a boys' college in New Jersey, recognized "motivation" and "potential" when he saw it. He promised himself that he would do all he could to help Wu obtain a student visa.

In the meantime, the major and Lieutenant Weinstein did a lot of traveling, retracing the steps of Captain Omura and Lieutenant Matsuhashi in Tientsin, Fengtai and Chinwangtao, and coming up as empty-handed as their Kempetai predecessors.

The team flew to Guam, where they questioned those of the China Marines who had survived Hokkaido. None of them, including their former commanding officer, was able to shed light on the mystery. The colonel had not inspected, let alone opened, the PMS cases that were to travel under his name. A Corporal Snyder, limping slightly and displaying a swollen and discolored right foot, remembered a redwood chest with the colonel's name stenciled on it among the crates and boxes that he had guarded on the train to Chinwangtao. "I guess maybe I even *sat* on it." There had been a similar box among the stuff he'd picked up at PMS the day before; "might have been the same, even." He had helped unload the boxcar and store the stuff in the godown at Chinwangtao to await the *Harrison*, but he had returned to Peking the next morning, "or tried to; we didn't make it back till Sunday, and that night the sky fell in. *You* remember, sir."

Major O'Neill needed no reminder. On that day of infamy the sky had caved in also on Rahway, New Jersey. "Who was on that train with you, Snyder?"

"Pfc. Aiken, sir. But he died in Hokkaido. Of pneumonia, sir. He didn't know any more than I did, sir."

Questioning of the Chinwangtao Marines elicited descriptions of the Japanese looting on December 8: "They broke open *everything* and just trampled on what they didn't like; they just left a pile of garbage."

No, nobody had noticed any old bones among the loot. And nobody remembered what specifically had

147

happened to the colonel's redwood box, or remembered its contents. The consensus was, "If there'd been bones, *somebody* would have noticed."

Major O'Neill and Lieutenant Weinstein returned to Peking with a briefcase full of depositions, both convinced that the Peking Man had either never reached Chinwangtao or, if it had, had been reduced to rubble under some Japanese soldier's boots.

In Guam, Corporal Snyder was more determined than ever to latch on to Evvie, who obviously had *not* handed the fossils over to the American authorities.

In Peking, the clerk Wu filed the Guam depositions and notes, which were not considered classified. He noted with satisfaction that Corporal William Snyder had survived prison camp and made a note of the corporal's home address in Harlingen, Texas. There must be universities in Texas. He'd find out as soon as he could and then go to work on Major O'Neill for a student visa.

Within two weeks after dispatching the footlocker, Kathy received a letter from Snyder.

"Dear Kathy, thanks for looking after my footlocker for me. I just received it in good condition. Will be staying on at the hospital here for a while yet before I get sent back Stateside. It sure beats POW camp; plenty of chow, hot showers and loafing. And no Nips! Kathy, would you send me Evvie's new name and address? I never had a chance to write her after Joe's death to tell her how sorry I was. Me and Joe were good buddies. And Evvie was always nice to me, having me to the house and all. Hope you are keeping well. Let me hear from you soon. Your friend, Bill."

"Dear Bill, I am so glad your ordeal is over at long last and that you are recovering and going home soon. How I wish poor Tom could have lived to see the day." Yeah, too bad about poor Tom, especially since he'd have sung like a canary to those two G-2 officers! "Evvie is now Señora Pablo Álvarez, c/o Cuban Consulate, Shanghai. I don't know if she is still there; she doesn't write very often. In her last letter she said she and Pablo would be going home soon; I suppose that means Havana. They may already have left Shanghai. I'll send you her Havana address as soon as I have it. I am sure she'll write to me from there. Kindest regards, Kathy."

Snyder had no intention of writing to Evvie, condolences or otherwise. He'd wait for the Havana address and then take it from there, but he'd certainly remain in touch with Kathy and keep track of Evvie through her.

By that time, Señor and Señora Álvarez, and Señora Álvarez's steamer trunk (under diplomatic seal), had already arrived in Havana, theirs having been among the first departures from Shanghai. It was considered that after bravely enduring the hardships of wartime China, Vice Consul Álvarez deserved a promotion and a prolonged rest before his next posting. The vacation was spent at the Álvarez family home in Havana.

Interlude

———

125 Calle Garcia
Havana, Cuba
June 19, 1946

Dearest Kathy:

It still seems strange to be out of China after all
these years and to see so many white faces and no rickshaws in the streets!

Havana is *fabulous*—you can't imagine the night
life! It beats even prewar Shanghai, not to mention
Tientsin. Both were missionary compounds compared
to this!

We are living with Pablo's people—that's less fabulous. Papa Álvarez is okay, a real old-world *hidalgo*.
He and I don't have much to talk about, but he goes
out of his way to be nice. But Mamacita! Ugh! She dis-
approves of me so, you can *taste* it! And every day she
looks me over, and you can *smell* her disappointment
because I'm not bulging!

But we'll be out of her clutches pretty soon, thank
God. Pablo has been posted to Buenos Aires and has
been promoted to Third Secretary. We'll be leaving in
a couple of weeks. Funny to think that I'll need *winter*
clothes there in *July!*

Write me, and write soon, c/o Cuban Legation,
Buenos Aires, Argentina. Tell me about Peking!

Love,
"Evita"

Dearest "Evita":

I knew you'd enjoy yourself in Buenos Aires! Very interesting about hearing so much German spoken in the streets. I just hope you're not hearing it at your parties!

I bet you get along a lot better with your mamacita now that she isn't around to spoil your fun! I am getting along just great with *my* mother-in-law, as long as she is in Bregenz and I'm in Peking, but I am afraid that beautiful friendship isn't going to last very much longer.

Things are changing here and not for the better either. Prices are terrible, and there are actual shortages because the Palou are blockading the city at least once a week and food can't come in from the country. The inflation is getting so that you need a shoe box to carry five U.S. dollars' worth of Chinese money! Fortunately, Martin somehow qualified for UNRRA packages and they really keep us going. I think of you every time I open a can of beef from Argentina!

The Communists here are really *busy*, and Martin is sure they'll take over sooner or later, despite the efforts of General Marshall to get the Nationalists and the Reds to work together. They call the building where the Americans and the Chinese are negotiating the Temple of the Ten Thousand Sleeping Colonels. But the Nationalists seem to be doing all they can to help the Reds get to power. There was a drought in Honan last summer and UNRRA sent relief supplies, and, can you imagine, the Nationalist government seized the supplies for taxes!

Martin is putting out feelers to go back to Austria; he is trying to get a teaching job in Vienna or Innsbruck. Of course, things are still *chaotic* in Austria, but I guess I wouldn't mind living there, though not as long as the Russians are around! And just so it isn't Bregenz!

Guess you are still not bulging, neither am I . . .

154

yet. Martin and I are going to wait until things settle down and we know where we are going. Has Bill Snyder written to you? He was going to. He writes me once in a while, which is nice of him. We never were very good friends, really, so I am a little surprised that he keeps up the contact. Maybe he is lonely, poor guy. He must have gone through a terrible time as a POW. His health must have suffered too; he is still at a Veterans' Hospital in the States. He said something about going back to school in Texas when he is well again.

Love,
Kathy

Winzergasse 12
Innsbruck, Austria (British Zone)
September 15, 1948

Dear Bill:

I am really running out of words trying to keep thanking you for the CARE packages! [*Think nothing of it, babe; they're worth every dime of the ten bucks a month.*] You can't begin to know how much they mean—though on second thoughts, having been a POW, I guess you can, better than most! We hoard that wonderful Nescafé and stretch it with chicory—awful bitter stuff, but it makes the coffee last longer and the flavor does come through! Martin and I are managing to stay in good health, and he is happy back teaching. They gave him a full professorship at the university with a fairly decent salary, except it won't buy very much because there isn't very much *to* buy. I have started to work for a British relief mission—at least we are spared the Russians here in Innsbruck. That means some extra rations, but the work is terribly depressing. We are trying to reunite and relocate displaced persons, like former concentration camp inmates who are looking for their families. The suffering these people have gone through defies description, and I feel ashamed and guilty when I gripe about not having a cup of coffee! But no more of this—you've had your fill of this kind of misery yourself.

I was so glad to hear that you are back in school. That GI Bill certainly sounds like a marvelous invention! I sometimes wish Martin had gone to the States instead of back to Austria; Texas must be nice, even if 120° in the shade in summer is hard to imagine. Though it sounds good when I think of the coming winter here with coal and firewood at a premium. Sorry, here I go again, griping! So you have switched to political science! Now I can't even ask about *your* chem grades; no more chem for you, I guess.

Don't be annoyed with Evvie for not answering your letters. You know how she is—she's always been a poor correspondent. She does ask me to send her regards every time I hear from her. [*This was a barefaced lie. Evvie did nothing of the kind, but it would make Bill feel better.*] Last time she mentioned that Pablo would soon be transferred with another promotion; again some South American country—Chile or Peru, she wasn't sure. I'll keep you informed. All good wishes and thanks again for the package, from Martin and me.

Kathy

Houston, Texas
June 26, 1956

Dear Kathy:

Well, congratulate me, I finally got that M.A. Just in time too—my GI Bill was running out. It was a long grind, what with having to start all over again as a freshman and that M.A. thesis taking *ages*, but it looks like it's going to pay off. I have a job lined up with the U.S. Delegation to the U.N., just a glorified office boy, but it'll be a start. Pay is good, and the job is more or less permanent, with civil service status and a pension, at least as long as there is a United Nations. I am going up to New York in a few days for an interview. So Evvie is still in Colombia; well, maybe someday she'll end up in New York too. Wouldn't that be some re-union! Will write as soon as the job is clinched and I have an address in New York. Keep your fingers crossed and keep in touch!

Regards,
Bill

[No return address; postmarked Hong Kong, September 18, 1956. Received Peking, People's Republic of China, October 12, 1956]

Venerable Elder Brother Liu:

Your inferior servant Wu Hsien-lu hopes that this reaches you as intended and finds you in good health.

Permit your inferior servant to reassure you again that the recurrent reports in the *People's Daily* are *false!* The East German Comrade was mistaken in reporting that the Peking Skull had been seen in the Professor's hands at the museum here in New York! The object seen must have been a *cast!*

Your servant personally made and shipped the Peking Man casts to New York before the war, and has frequently inspected them since arriving in this city.

As Venerable Elder Brother well knows, the fossils remained in Peking after the Professor's departure, and your servant handled them many times until they were packed and removed from PMS.

The continued vilification of the Professor as a thief is therefore not only devoid of a basis in fact, but in your inferior servant's humble opinion also *most unwise.* The Professor has been dead for several years. The continued besmirching of his name cannot but make a laughing stock of our Glorious Revolution and thus of Comrade Mao, since this and similar errors are avidly seized upon and sneered at by such Imperialist publications as the *New York Times* and *Lives & Times* magazine, thus making us lose face with our sympathizers in the West.

Your servant is still convinced that Szu Nai-du will eventually lead us to the fossils.

Due to Venerable Elder Brother's most wise and provident arrangements, your servant is fortunate in having Szu Nai-du under constant observation, since his office is near that of the Taiwan Turtles. Your inferior servant regrets that Szu Nai-du has made no move so far, but will keep him under surveillance.

With the most respectful greetings,
Elder Brother's humble and inferior servant,

Wu Hsien-lu

Former Commissar, now General, Liu frowned. Ch'en, alias Wu Hsien-lu, should not have referred to his current employers, the U.N. delegation from the Republic of China, as the "Taiwan Turtles." It was apt, but it was also imprudent, and so were his open allusions to the "Glorious Revolution" and "Comrade Mao." It was true that in their incomprehensible disregard for security the American Imperialists did not censor the mails. Still, he would have to rebuke Ch'en, perhaps even arrange for surveillance?

But Ch'en was right in what he was saying. General Liu would stop those ridiculous reports in the *People's Daily* today!

201 East End Avenue
New York City, N.Y.
March 26, 1957

Dearest Kathy:

Well, we finally got out of South America! Argentina, Peru, Chile, Brazil, Colombia—I was really getting fed up, not to mention the vacations with Mamacita between postings! Now we are here, the most fabulous place in the world! You should see those shops on Fifth Avenue!

Pablo has been appointed Consul General, and I think and hope we'll be here for a while. Just keep your fingers crossed that Mamacita doesn't suddenly decide she wants to come and live with us now that Papa is gone. . . .

We meet a lot of interesting people, and it is nice to speak English again. I was getting quite rusty! But my Spanish is now so authentic, I am always taken for South American, or even real Spanish Spanish, but sometimes for Puerto Rican, which is no compliment here in New York!

I am sending you a parcel with some cute pregnancy and baby clothes; the first set must be worn out! Congratulations! Sweet of you to say you'll call it Eva if it is a *niña*. I am so glad that things have been getting better in Austria and hope they are really back to normal now that the Russians are out of there.

So you still hear from Bill Snyder! That creep! You've really got a long-lasting friendship going there, haven't you? Well, at least he has stopped writing to me. I guess he finally got the message.

Keep well, write again soon.

Love,
Evvie

PART III

The Payoff

New York: Summer 1957 to January 1960

19

Snyder prepared to make his first move on a hot day at the end of June, a few days after receiving a letter from Kathy Peters which dealt mainly with the beauty and exceptional intelligence of her new daughter, Eva, and of Eva's older brother, Franzl. These effusions left Snyder with a slight feeling of nausea, but the one nugget he had been hoping for was there. Evvie was in New York, her husband with the Cuban Consulate General. Although Kathy, in her raptures about her brats, had forgotten to give Snyder Evvie's address.

Snyder was sitting at his desk in his mercifully air-conditioned office. Stacked at his elbow were the telephone books of Queens, Brooklyn, the Bronx and Staten Island. Westchester and Nassau lay on the floor just in case they were needed.

Snyder had the Manhattan directory open at the A's and was going through the Álvarezes. There were dozens of them, but only five Pablos. Snyder ruled out a grocery on East Fourteenth, and a luncheonette on West Twenty-fifth. That left three listings, which he jotted down. One gave an address in Greenwich Village, the second was on East End Avenue, and the third on West 110th Street.

Snyder went down to the public phone booth in the lobby, took three dimes from his pocket and lined them up neatly on the ledge under the phone. He had second thoughts; he rummaged in his pocket and added three more dimes, just in case he struck pay dirt and the conversation exceeded three minutes.

He dialed the first number. A child answered in staccato Spanish reminiscent of the cadences of Japanese. Snyder hung up in the middle of the chatter.

He rang the East End Avenue number. A tinny soprano chanted, "The number you are calling is temporarily disconnected. This is a recorded announcement. The number you are calling is tem—"

"Fuck you," retorted Snyder automatically, and called the third number. A raucous baritone informed him in heavily accented English, "Ain't no Eva Álvarez here; you gotta wrong number. Drop dead!"

Snyder repocketed the three surplus dimes and returned to his office. He'd go through the rest of the directories, but would keep calling the East End Avenue number until he got a connection and would know for sure one way or the other.

On the way back to his office he met one of the Chinese from the Taiwan delegation across the hall, who gave him a courteous little bow. Snyder acknowledged the greeting with a nonchalant flip of his right forefinger. The Chinese, tall, lanky and bespectacled, looked vaguely familiar; there'd been a student at Baylor, could have been this guy's brother . . . but then these Chinks all looked alike, he couldn't tell them apart; hadn't been able to even back in China!

Two dollars and eighty cents' worth of phone calls to Brooklyn, the Bronx, Queens, Staten Island, Westchester and Nassau remained unproductive except for repeated exhortations to "drop dead" from respondents in Brooklyn and the Bronx.

The East End Avenue number remained "temporarily disconnected" until a week after Labor Day. The Álvarezes then returned from a summer vacation at Martha's Vineyard.

After three rings a woman's voice answered. "Hello?"

"Is Mrs. Álvarez home?"

"I will go and see. Please wait. Whom shall I say is calling?"

"Tell Mrs. Álvarez it's an old friend. I want to surprise her."

"Yes, sir. One moment, please."

A second female voice. "Hullo, yes?" The British, China Coast English inflection was still there.

"Evvie?"

"Yes; who *is* this?"

"Well, Evvie, how nice to hear your voice after all these years."

A pause. Then a hesitant, "Bill Snyder?"

"None other. . . . Now don't hang up, Evvie, unless you'd like me to come calling and meet your husband."

"How did you know I was in New York?"

164

"Kathy's been a good friend, Evvie; better'n you."

Another pause.

"Evvie?"

"What—what do you want, Bill?"

"You know damn well what I want, Evvie! You've got something that belongs to me."

Evvie started to say, "I don't know what you are talking about," but Snyder cut her short.

"Now you listen to me! You can keep my property, at least for a while, but I am going to charge you storage fees, know what I mean? Starting today it's going to cost you three hundred bucks a month rental fee to keep you know what!"

Evvie started to say something; again he cut her short.

"Starting this morning, you will deposit three hundred dollars every month to the account of Richard Myers; that's *M-y-e-r-s*—got that? Number 178–324; take that down—got it? Yorkville Savings Bank, First Avenue and Ninety-sixth Street branch. Got that? Read it back to me!"

Evvie began to bluster. "First of all, I don't have that kind of money. Second, even if I did, I wouldn't dream of giving it to you, you dirty blackmailer! I'll go to the police!"

The operator interrupted the conversation. "Deposit another dime, please."

"Oh, so you'll go to the police! With what? Let me lay it on the line, Evvie, and listen good! You've got stolen property in your possession, and there is no way you can connect *me* with it! But *I* can connect *you,* all right, and don't think I won't! Now don't give me that crap about diplomatic immunity! One phone call from me will bring the FBI running, and they'll have you deported before you can say Peking Man. And you'll probably go to jail in Cuba. And it takes just one more phone call to get your name splashed all over the front page of the *Times*. 'Cuban Diplomat's Wife Arrested for Theft of Peking Fossils!' I can just *see* the headlines! That would *really* help your husband's career, wouldn't it? No, Evvie, you be a good girl and start depositing that money—today, y'hear? If that dough hasn't been credited to Myers' account by ten o'clock

165

tomorrow morning, you can expect a visit from the FBI, plus an interesting article in the *Times* . . . *and* the *News* . . . *and* the *Post*," he added for good measure. "And your husband will be an *ex*-Cuban diplomat. Just remember, you've got everything to lose . . . and you can't pin a thing on me!"

Evvie stammered, "B-Bill, listen, don't ring off. How can I get in touch with you if—if something comes up . . . if there is a delay before I can deposit the money?"

"You can't. Don't try; I have an unlisted number. I'll be in touch with you."

"Bill, listen—"

Snyder rang off. He returned to his office, satisfied with the results of his first move. He had no doubt but that "Richard Myers" would be richer by three hundred dollars by ten o'clock the next morning, and every month thereafter. It wasn't a million, but better than nothing for the time being. He'd get that million yet, but now wasn't the time, not while Evvie was around to point the finger at him.

There was one of those Chinks again, or was it The Chink? "Hiya," said Snyder, waggling his forefinger in response to the man's bow.

After Snyder had rung off, Evvie did two things that were quite out of character. She poured herself a shot of brandy and she lit a cigarette. Taking drink and cigarette to the bedroom, she sat down on the unmade bed from which she had arisen when Gloria had called her to the phone.

She downed the brandy, choked and sputtered, and puffed on the cigarette. She began to cough. When the irritation in her throat subsided she began to think.

She had done this kind of thinking once before, in Tientsin, while Kathy was sleeping practically on top of the fossils she had come to search for. But this time there was nothing funny about the situation, nothing at all!

So Kathy had informed Snyder that Evvie was in New York, had probably even given him the address. Dear, naïve, loyal Kathy, never suspecting that that bastard had been *using* her all these years, sending

CARE packages and all, just to keep tabs on Evvie's whereabouts. Evvie could cheerfully have wrung dear, loyal Kathy's neck! Why hadn't Kathy let her know that Snyder was in New York? Well, it was her own fault; Kathy had tactfully stopped mentioning Snyder after Evvie had referred to him as "that creep." If she'd known, perhaps she could have talked Pablo out of accepting the New York appointment, asking instead for a posting in Europe or South America or wherever. Well, no use iffing; the harm was done and she'd have to cope with it.

Evvie considered the angles, but whichever way she figured, Snyder held the aces. She could not possibly confess to Pablo, for the same reasons still as long ago in Tientsin. Nor could she persuade him to resign his post, or even move from the apartment on East End Avenue, or at least get an unlisted phone number. Although that last could be managed—she could plead receiving obscene calls—but it would not solve her problem. Snyder would simply make good his threats and show up at the house. . . . That was unthinkable!

She could go to the FBI and ask for immunity . . . but Snyder was right. The story could not be kept out of the papers and would make *headlines*. The "Mystery of the Missing Fossils" kept popping up in the *Times* and in *Lives & Times* magazine. The search for Peking Man had by no means been abandoned.

How about dropping the trunk someplace, perhaps in Central Park? She could then call the museum and tip them off anonymously.

It seemed a great idea . . . in theory. The practical difficulties immediately became apparent. She couldn't get the trunk up from the basement without the doorman noticing. If Briant didn't think the incident memorable then, he would as soon as the story of the recovery of the fossils hit the headlines—provided they weren't swiped before the museum could pick them up, which, in New York City, was more than likely! In either case the papers would have a heyday, and Snyder, just out of spite, would sic the FBI on her. Evvie had great faith in the interrogative powers of the FBI and was sure she'd break down under their questioning.

The scandal and Pablo's ruin seemed unavoidable, no matter what.

There was one final reason for rejecting the idea of returning the fossils, none the less compelling because it remained unacknowledged: Evvie did not *want* to return them, neither to whoever the rightful owners were, nor to Bill Snyder. The memory of Joe's dying words referring to the value of the fossils had always been at the back of her mind. Evvie knew very well that Joe had not meant the "scientific" value. She was reluctant to part with something that might come in very handy someday, you never knew. It was true that Pablo received a good salary and that his family were wealthy, but it would be just like Mamacita to cut Pablo out of her will because she hated Evvie. Also, there was that business with Castro. . . . A little insurance in the background was always useful!

Evvie, knowing herself to be beaten for the time being, recognized that she would have to pay up, starting that morning. Her thoughts turned to the problem of how to meet Snyder's demands without Pablo suspecting. The first three and one third of the payments would present no major difficulty, but she'd have to start planning ahead right away, even though a lot could happen in three months.

Evvie got dressed, took three of the ten hundred-dollar bills from the envelope that Hans von Albers had given her after Joe's funeral, and reinserted the envelope in a sheaf of old letters, where nobody would think of looking for money. She called for Gloria to come and straighten up the bedroom, told her she was going out for some air, and walked the five blocks to First Avenue and Ninety-sixth Street to make her first payment to the account of "Richard Myers."

The "Chink" had returned to his office. The several little encounters with Snyder that Ch'en, taking a calculated risk, had engineered at the U.N. and at Baylor University had confirmed the fact that the son of a turtle didn't know him from Adam (although Ch'en did not phrase it quite that way).

Ch'en was sure that Snyder did not have the fossils

in his possession. If he had had them, he would have collected the ransom long ago (Ch'en was convinced that this had been the purpose of the theft) and would be enjoying the money somewhere abroad, in a country that had no extradition treaty with the United States— except that Ch'en would have prevented the transaction; there would have been no ransom money, Snyder would be dead, and Ch'en and the Peking Man would be back in their home town. None of this had happened. The fossils certainly were not at Snyder's apartment in Brooklyn Heights; a little breaking and entering by a helpful "Brooklyn connection" had established that conclusively.

The footlocker was there in full sight, and unlocked. It contained a folder with Snyder's birth and baptismal certificates, his high school diploma, some college transcripts of prewar vintage, textbooks, lecture notes, a copy of his master's dissertation and his Master of Arts diploma from Baylor University, his discharge papers from the Marine Corps and correspondence with the Veterans Administration. Bankbooks and bank statements revealed that William Snyder had a checking account and a modest savings account at the Yorkville Savings Bank, Montague Street, Brooklyn, had made no large deposits or withdrawals since his arrival in New York, and was still making payments on the 1956 Chevy Bel Air of whose pink-and-gray existence and license number Ch'en was well aware.

Snyder's life was an open book, and one that made dull reading. Any lurid elements that would have qualified it for publication in paperback form were conspicuously lacking. There was no personal correspondence of any kind, no photographs, no address book, not even the "little black" kind that one might expect to find in a bachelor's apartment. Snyder had no permanent attachments. His needs for love, friendship and companionship were apparently satisfied by occasional visits to Times Square. . . .

But the very blandness of Snyder's life was in itself suspect. Snyder was up to something. Ch'en had not failed to notice the stack of telephone books on Snyder's desk. Snyder's apparent success with the front section of the Manhattan directory (A? B? C?) had not remained a secret to the observant Ch'en. Neither had Snyder's frequent trips to the public phone in the lobby during the summer. Ch'en had passed by the phone booth whenever he could do so inconspicuously and tried to discern what number Snyder was dialing, but he had been unsuccessful. Snyder had shielded the dial with his back.

The *A–C* section in Snyder's Manhattan directory had not been annotated. Ch'en had established that by the simple expedient of sending his office boy over to the U.S. delegation's office with the courteous request for the loan of the Manhattan phone book for a few minutes while the Chinese delegation's was in use elsewhere. The directory fell open at Altman—Amalgamated, but there were no marks on this, nor on the preceding or following pages, and none in the *B,* the *C,* and for good measure, the *D* sections. Snyder was too smart to leave a clue of this kind.

From the smug look on Snyder's face that morning, Ch'en had deduced that he had finally made his connection. This subjective evidence was reinforced by the subsequent observation that Snyder ceased his daily trips to the public phone and did not use it again until a month later to the day . . . and the next month . . . and the next.

Ch'en was by now fully convinced that Snyder knew, and was blackmailing, the person who had the fossils. They were therefore not accomplices. If they had been, they would have acted in concert a long time ago. They hadn't. The Unknown obviously could not dispose of the fossils without risking immediate exposure by Snyder. He in turn could not expose Snyder without exposing himself. (Ch'en was by tradition what, a decade later, would be called a "male chauvinist pig"; the thought that the Unknown might be a woman never entered his head.) Therefore, neither man could make a move.

But the stalemate could be broken . . . by money, the only thing that was valued by these capitalist-imperialist American turtles!

Ch'en outlined his premise in his next report to General Liu via one of the numerous cover addresses in Hong Kong. He ventured to add certain suggestions.

These were discussed at length and at the highest levels in Peking and Hangchow, and resulted in directives being sent to the editor of the *People's Daily,* and to the embassy of the People's Republic of China at Ottawa. Ch'en in New York received instructions whose implementation would require the utmost delicacy, discretion and finesse.

20

Upon returning from the First Avenue and Ninety-sixth Street branch of the Yorkville Savings Bank, Evvie settled down at her desk and began to devise measures by which to increase her cash reserves without having to withdraw suspiciously large amounts from her and Pablo's joint checking account, and without touching the joint savings account or her jewelry. This left chiefly the generous check that Pablo gave her every month for household expenses, including Gloria's full-time wages.

She began by reducing Gloria to three mornings a week. Pablo did not suspect since Gloria usually arrived after he had left for the office, blaming her habitual lateness on the vagaries of the downtown IRT. By the time Pablo returned home, Gloria had left unless there was a dinner party. For such occasions Gloria was now hired for a few extra hours.

Evvie did the shopping and cooking on the Gloria-less days. She soon discovered that the A & P on 103rd Street was cheaper than Gristede's on Eighty-sixth, and that economies could be effected by looking in the *Daily News* for "specials" and coupons. It also turned out that Pablo could not tell the difference between imported and domestic Swiss cheese, was unable to distinguish between a mixture of butter and margarine and pure butter and could not tell half-and-half from cream.

She even got away with a deception that had caused her initial misgivings. Pablo did not seem to mind when she usurped his prerogative of opening the wine bottles, and once a bottle was opened his palate was

171

apparently not sensitive enough to detect the gradual replacement of Harvey's Bristol Cream with a product from upstate New York so long as it was poured from the Harvey's bottle. The same proved true for California wines now served in bottles bearing French and German labels but long since drained of the original Beaujolais or liebfraumilch or whatever they had contained. Pablo was absent-minded these days, seemingly uninterested in what he ate or drank, and not even complaining when hamburger began to appear on the dinner table with increasing frequency.

Still, Pablo was a wonderful, generous husband. He paid the substantial monthly charges from Lord & Taylor's, Bergdorf's and Saks' without once rebuking Evvie for her extravagance, even complimenting her on her elegance and chic. Pablo never suspected that Evvie timed her shopping trips on Fifth Avenue so that they fell within a week before the charge payments were due, then returned the merchandise for a cash refund two days after Pablo had sent the check. Her continued elegance and chic were due to the fact that Evvie still managed to look like a *Vogue* cover girl in a $12.99 creation from Klein's on Union Square.

Pablo Álvarez failed to notice the gradual deterioration of his life style, but he also failed to notice that Evvie was losing weight, was using makeup lavishly to cover up paleness and shadows under her eyes, and was alternating tranquilizers with pep-up pills. He did notice that she had developed a tendency to drop things, for which he blamed her recent acquisition of the smoking habit. "How come you have suddenly started to smoke? You never did before. You should quit. It's making you nervous, and you look haggard—it's taking away your appetite." But he accepted the lame explanation that Evvie had started to smoke in self-defense. "They keep blowing their smoke in my face at those bridge parties; these women *all* smoke. If I smoke, too, it's less irritating."

Evvie, on the other hand, was too preoccupied with being a blackmail victim to become aware that Pablo, too, seemed to have his troubles. True, his appetite appeared to have suffered, but Evvie put that down to the quality of her cooking, which left much to be desired.

But Pablo never complained while he picked at what she served him, and she couldn't blame him; it really did taste pretty awful!

It never dawned on Evvie that Pablo did not complain because he did not *notice* what he was eating, and that he did not notice because he was too deeply preoccupied with very real and serious worries about their future.

Evvie didn't listen to the news on the radio; she watched chiefly the soap operas on the newly acquired television set (the problems on the screen could momentarily take her mind off her own), and concentrated on the society and entertainment sections of the *Times.*

She knew dimly that there was that repulsive-looking, bearded guy Castro making trouble in Cuba, but assumed, equally vaguely, that things would work out somehow.

Pablo Álvarez was all too aware of the trouble Castro was making, and it kept him awake nights. Batista's days seemed to be numbered. Pablo made frantic phone calls to his mother, imploring her to leave Havana and join him and Evvie in New York while there was still time. But Señora Álvarez refused stubbornly, making the flimsiest of excuses, and Pablo suspected that his mamacita preferred living with Castro to living with Evita.

The time came when Pablo could no longer conceal his worries from his equally troubled wife. Fidel Castro in Cuba and William Snyder in New York between them were rapidly destroying the Álvarez marriage.

Pablo became short-tempered and extremely irritable.

"I don't know how much longer I will have my job. You *have* to economize! I have to cut the household allowance! Do you really need Gloria every day?"

He blew his top one morning when the charge account bills were presented.

"You have to give up those charge accounts! You are *much* too extravagant! Surely there are cheaper stores than Lord & Taylor's! You've got two closets full of clothes and shoes; in *my* country they would last

173

a woman ten years! I am not going to pay another bill."

Evvie's stomach was a hard, painful knot while she promised meekly to close out the charge accounts, to destroy all her credit cards, to dismiss Gloria (who was already reduced to one half day a week), to economize on food and wines and on her personal expenses.

"We'll manage, Pablo," she lied. "I'll do my best, I promise."

Pablo, mollified, kissed his wife and left for the office. He walked the distance twice a day now; it cleared his mind. He had put the Lincoln up for sale; he hoped it would go through soon. Any extra bit of cash would be needed. One did not really need a car in New York City. One could always take a taxi or even a bus; Pablo still balked at the subway.

Evvie tried to vacuum the apartment, but was too upset by Pablo's outburst and by the problem of raising the next installment for Snyder. He was keeping up his demands relentlessly, calling and threatening her regularly every month a day or so before a payment was due; he'd probably call today. Evvie felt she could not face it. She had managed to scrape up the three hundred dollars thus far, but from now on her sources of cash would be severely curtailed. She would have to start on the jewelry.

The phone rang. Evvie let it ring. But Snyder was fully capable of coming to the house. . . . She picked up the phone.

"Well, Evvie, taking your time, aren't you? Better be a little snappier next time. I haven't got all day to wait for your ladyship to answer the telephone. I won't take up much of your *valuable* time; I know how *busy* you are, Mrs. Álvarez. Just a little reminder—you won't forget what date it is, will you, Evvie? You'd *better* not!"

Evvie tried to plead. "Bill, listen, please. I can't go on paying that much. Pablo said he was going to lose his job; he isn't giving me enough money; we have to economize. *Please*, Bill, I *have* to make it less . . . maybe a hundred. *Please*, Bill!"

"Why, Evvie, my heart bleeds for you. Don't tell me you haven't got reserves. Like jewelry? Nothing doing,

Evvie. You pay the full three hundred, or else. Your Pablo hasn't lost his job *yet*, but he will, sure as God made little apples, if there's a dime less than three hundred paid into that account day after tomorrow."

For the first time since Snyder had started to blackmail her, Evvie felt *terrible* about getting a refund on her most recent purchases which Pablo had just paid for—for the last time. She clung to that thought; it was the last time she had to cheat Pablo in this really *despicable* manner, but what choice did she have! She was sure Pablo would understand, even in his present disturbed state of mind, if she could only explain her situation to him . . . but that was just it, she couldn't; not now, not ever. The refund from Bergdorf's, together with what she had managed to squeeze out of last month's household allowance, would be just enough to pacify Snyder this time. After that . . . yes, she would have to start selling her jewelry. She'd take Grandmother Zimmermann's pearls to Cartier's tomorrow. They should be good for at least ten installments, with perhaps something left over. Maybe she wouldn't even need it all for the blackmail payments. Maybe that bastard Snyder would drop dead, get run over or get mugged—or something!

Evvie finished vacuuming the living room, picked up the unopened cartons from Bergdorf's and set out for Fifth Avenue by taxi.

Pablo immediately regretted losing his temper. He loved Evvie dearly and would not have hurt her feelings for the world. True, she was extravagant, but that was part of her charm. She had no conception of what was at stake for both of them, and that was *his* fault. He had not wished to burden her with his worries; she seemed so trusting and defenseless in her sleep while he tossed around most of the night in a torment of indecision. Pablo was quite unaware that Evvie owed her enviable deep sleep to a nightly Seconal taken to counteract the daytime buoyancy induced by a little green-and-white capsule.

Pablo could not decide whether or not to resign his position, return to Cuba and join Castro's guerrillas in the mountains. He sympathized with Castro's movement and detested the Batista regime, which he

175

represented in New York and which paid his salary. He hated the blatant corruption, the political persecutions; he hated to see Havana wide open and practically run by the American syndicate. On the other hand, he deeply disliked and distrusted Castro's associates and what they stood for, particularly that hothead Guevara. Pablo Álvarez was not, and never could be, a communist, which was clearly what Castro was headed for once he came to power. Pablo Álvarez abhorred violence of any kind, no matter how noble the end to which it was the means. He was essentially a gentle man, gently reared, pampered and fastidious. He could not see himself, bearded and unwashed, wielding a rifle or a machine gun in the company of Ché Guevara and killing his fellow Cubans. But neither could he continue to serve Batista's Cuba with the loyalty his position demanded. . . .

Deeply torn and tormented, he was still vacillating when the decision was made for him, finally and irrevocably, one week before another payment for Snyder fell due.

CASTRO PROCLAIMS REPUBLIC IN CUBA, announced the *Times* in a sedate headline. "Dr. Fidel Castro today proclaimed himself Premier of the Cuban Republic. He pledged free elections, a democratic government and freedom of the press as well as freedom and prosperity for the Cuban people, as soon as the revolutionary takeover was completed. . . ."

The *News* screamed, CUBAN DIPLOMAT SLAIN. Underneath this headline was a smaller one: CASTRO TAKES OVER.

The body of Cuban Consul General Pablo Álvarez, 46, was found late last night in an alley off First Avenue near 72nd Street. (See pictures in center fold.) Pending an autopsy, the medical examiner estimates that Mr. Álvarez had been dead several hours. Death is attributed to internal bleeding from multiple stab wounds to the chest and abdomen. The victim's wallet was missing, and the body appears to have been stripped of valuables, including a wristwatch and several rings. A description of these items, whose value is estimated at several thousand dollars, is being circulated in the city's pawnshops.

The body was taken to the morgue, where it was formally identified by the victim's attractive wife, Mrs. Evamarie Álvarez, 42, of 201 East End Avenue. The widow, in shock and under a physician's care at her home, could not be interviewed by reporters at this time. However, Mrs. Álvarez told police that her husband had been working late at the Consulate for the past several weeks including Christmas Eve, frequently returning after she herself had retired, so that she had not been unduly alarmed by his lateness last night, even though it was New Year's Eve.

Police believe that Mr. Álvarez was the victim of a mugging and are conducting a search for clues and witnesses in the area where the crime was committed. However, this newspaper is investigating the possibility that Mr. Álvarez may have been assassinated by Castro agents. (See today's editorial, p. 56.)

The *Times* reported the mugging of a Cuban diplomat on page 32 in its second section, confining itself to the bare facts.

Snyder read the article and editorial in the news and frowned. He called the East End Avenue number and was informed curtly that Mrs. Álvarez was in strict seclusion and was not accepting any calls. If the caller cared to leave his number . . . Snyder rang off.

He tried again the next day and the day after that, with the same results. Evvie was still in seclusion and would remain thus for an unspecified period of time. The man who answered the phone was beginning to show signs of irritation, implying strongly that he would inform police if these nuisance calls didn't stop.

Three days after the report of the mugging, both the *Times* and the *News* carried a brief follow-up. The body of Pablo Álvarez, slain Cuban diplomat, had been released for burial. Funeral services would be held at the graveside at 10 A.M. the following day at Lilyvale Cemetery on Long Island. The police were following up a promising clue.

This was the last public reference to Pablo Álvarez. The killers, whether sinister Castro agents or ordinary New York City junkies, were never apprehended, and Pablo's jewelry was not recovered.

Snyder drove all the way out to Long Island on a freezing cold day to attend the funeral. But there were at least thirty cars, each carrying at least four mourners, all of whom clustered around the widow during the service. Snyder could not get near Evvie, who, huddled in a black fur coat and deeply veiled, was supported by two women and conveyed an impression of shock and prostration even from a distance.

Snyder phoned again three days after the funeral, gambling that the irritable watchdog had finally left Evvie's apartment. He had.

"The number you are calling is no longer in service. This is a recorded announcement. The number you are calling . . ."

Snyder drove to 201 East End Avenue, where the doorman informed him that Mrs. Álvarez had moved out.

"Poor lady, can't blame her for wanting to get away, with her husband killed and all. I'm telling youse, it ain't safe no more walking the streets in this town. Where's the cops when you need them? Too busy writing parking tickets or busting hookers to protect a citizen in the streets—know what I mean?"

Snyder made the appropriate response to the New Yorker's litany, and tried, gently, to guide the conversation back to the one piece of information he had come to seek.

"Did Mrs. Álvarez leave a forwarding address?"

"Youse a reporter? There was lots of them around, I'm telling youse! Even took my picture; maybe you seen it in the *News?* 'Cept the joiks spelled my name wrong; called me *Ryan.* Name's Briant, *B-r-i-a-n-t,* Briant!"

Snyder took out his wallet, slowly removed a five-dollar bill and kept it folded between index and middle finger.

"Yes, Mr. Ryan—I mean, *Briant,* I saw your picture. . . . Now, did Mrs. Álvarez leave a forwarding address?"

178

Mr. Briant hungrily eyed the five-dollar bill.

"No, she didn't leave no address. Believe me, mister, I'd tell youse if I knew."

"Did she leave by taxi? Did she take a lot of luggage?"

"Yeah, she left by cab. Well, she took a couple suitcases and that old steamer trunk she had in the basement; I helped carry it up for her. Real old-fashioned; haven't seen a trunk like that must be twenty years or more. People don't use them no more now that they all travel by plane . . . and *shabby* like you wouldn't believe." Snyder swallowed. So she kept them in a steamer trunk! "You'd never believe a classy lady like Mrs. Álvarez would be seen *dead* with a piece of junk like that."

"Mr. Briant, you say she took just two suitcases and that trunk. What about the rest of her things, like furniture—know what I mean?"

"Yeah, I guess they didn't have that much; apartment comes furnished. I guess she put most of her belongings in storage; van came day before yesterday. Acme Moving and Storage; warehouse is someplace on Tenth Avenue."

"Did you call the cab for Mrs. Álvarez, Mr. Ry— Briant?"

"Yeah, I did, from the rank down at the corner."

"Then you must have given the driver an address, or heard Mrs. Álvarez give it?"

"Well, yeah. I hoid her say Idlewild Airport. She probably left the country. She didn't leave no address in *New York* is what I mean."

Snyder handed over the five-dollar bill, which was gratefully accepted, and a slip of paper.

"Mr. Briant, will you call me at this number, evenings, if something comes up? There'll be another fin in it for you, maybe more."

"Sure, mister. Thanks a lot! Sure I'll call youse. I'll talk to the driver; his stand is just down the block. Or if I hear from the poor lady . . ."

Snyder escaped and drove home, mechanically dodging the buses, cabs and jaywalkers that were cluttering up the stop-and-go, downtown-bound traffic. He was deep in thought.

Evie had to have the fossils in the old steamer trunk; no other reason for lugging that kind of antique around. Those things were just the right size; the cartons were too big to fit into a suitcase.

Idlewild Airport . . . Snyder was sure that this was pure eyewash, intended specifically for him, to throw him off her trail. Where could Evvie go? Certainly not back to Cuba; she was a refugee now. Another South American country? Europe? Very unlikely. No more diplomatic immunity now for little Señora Álvarez; she'd never get those fossils through customs anywhere in the world. Except maybe Red China. Snyder grinned. No, Evvie was still in the U.S., probably hadn't even left New York. He'd find her again, and this time he'd get the fossils—choke them out of her if necessary!

Briant called the next day. Could the mister come over? He had some news.

"Can't you tell me over the phone?"

"No; better you come over, see what I mean?"

Snyder saw. A five-dollar bill couldn't be transmitted over the phone. . . . He went back to East End Avenue.

The fin changed hands, followed by another. Mr. Briant had had "expenses."

The cabdriver had taken the fare to Idlewild, had dropped her at the Avianca departures terminal and immediately returned to Manhattan with another fare.

This was bad news. So Evvie had left for South America after all; perhaps she still had a diplomatic passport and diplomatic immunity. She'd gotten away from him for good now, the bitch! He was right back where he had been in that hospital on Guam when Kathy had sent him his footlocker full of Evvie's old clothes. Kathy . . . He'd write to Kathy again; Evvie was sure to remain in touch with her old friend. He'd get back on Evvie's trail as he had before with Kathy's unwitting help. He'd catch up with Evvie if she went to the end of the world.

Snyder was astute, but he had underestimated Evvie.

Upon dismissing her cab at the Avianca terminal and watching it take off and out of her sight carrying her replacement, Evvie had hailed another cab. She gave an address in Spanish Harlem. The driver looked dubious, suspicious of the discrepancy between the elegant lady and the crummy address. He started to say, "Sorry, lady, I don't take no fares uptown, I'm from Brooklyn," but changed his mind when he saw the ten-dollar bill in the lady's hand. Threading his way out of the airport, up the Van Wyck Expressway, he told himself philosophically, "Just another nut; this town is full of nuts. Or maybe she's a madam looking for merchandise up there among the Spic girls. No skin off my ass, so long as she pays the fare."

He deposited Evvie and her luggage on the sidewalk among the overflowing garbage cans in front of a run-down tenement, accepted a two-dollar tip in return for the change from the ten-dollar bill, and drove off.

The tenement sported a sign in a first-floor window: HABITACIONES AMEUBLADAS. INFORMACION M. RAMIREZ, APT. 109."

Evvie had located Señora Ramirez' establishment through a classified ad in *El Diario*. After a telephone conversation with the Señora, she had taken a surreptitious trip uptown the day after Pablo's funeral, had inspected the *habitaciones*, which were spotlessly clean, and had made the necessary arrangements with Señora Ramirez, which consisted simply in paying a month's rent, forty-five dollars, in advance.

Evvie now pressed the button for apartment 109. Señora Ramirez came out, gave a startled glance at Evvie's black seal coat—last time the lady had worn a cloth coat, estimated price $39.99 at Klein's—and helped her new roomer carry the luggage in.

The steamer trunk was taken to the basement and stored out of sight in a dark recess behind a gleaming new garbage compactor. Señora Ramirez piled some cartons on top of the trunk, covered the small mound with an old tarpaulin, and assured Evvie that her trunk would be quite safe. There was so little to steal here that regular thieves wouldn't even *bother*, and the trunk was well out of sight of the junkies who came into the basement to shoot up.

Señora Ramirez then conducted Señora Elena Acevedo to the sixth-floor back room that would be Evvie's hideout until she was able to decide about the future. The room, though clean, certainly wasn't comparable to the *habitaciones* Evvie had been accustomed to, from the worn linoleum to the cracked stuccoed ceiling and the painted-over wallpaper which showed through in patches where the paint had flaked off.

Evvie hung the seal coat in the closet, kicked off her shoes and stretched out on the bed, which, acquired at a Salvation Army furniture outlet, was surprisingly comfortable. Evvie sighed, relaxed. She was out of Snyder's clutches at last! Tomorrow she would go to the nearest bank and open an account in the name of Elena Acevedo with the certified check for $3,523.27 that was now tucked into her brassiere and represented what was left of her and Pablo's joint savings and checking accounts. This and the pearl money would keep her going for a while. Then there was the rest of the jewelry; she'd rent a safety deposit box. Evvie, despite her grief for Pablo, slept that night without Seconal for the first time in many months.

21

Obedient to high-level directives, the *People's Daily* had run an illustrated article reporting the opening of the Peking Man Museum at the site of the original excavations, some forty miles west of Peking. The ceremonies were attended by the highest dignitaries, including the deputy premier of the People's Republic of China, the ambassadors of the People's Democracies of Albania, North Korea and North Vietnam, and three "world-renowned" paleontologists representing these same countries. The article was illustrated with group photographs of the dignitaries and pictures of the displays, which seemed to consist chiefly of paintings, models and reconstructions, and of a few shapeless lumps described as artifacts fashioned and used by Peking Man. However, the article explained the absence of genuine relics from the museum's exhibits.

"The actual remains of the venerable remote ancestor of the toiling masses of China disappeared at the outbreak of the war. They were probably stolen by the American capitalist-imperialists, or by the Japanese aggressors. The workers, peasants and soldiers of China, under the leadership of Comrade Mao Tse-tung, will not rest until our National Treasure is recovered and the despicable robbers have been brought to justice."

The mute "dog" radical still accompanied the ideogram *mei,* which stood for "America."

The article, pictures and all, was duly reprinted in Hong Kong (omitting the "dog" radical), and was then translated into English.

The English version was picked up by the wire services.

In North America the story was carried by the New York and the Los Angeles *Times,* the Washington *Post* and the Toronto *Star.*

The editors commented briefly on the conspicuous absence from the ceremonies of the Soviet ambassador and of world-renowned Soviet scientists, and noted with some astonishment the positively affectionate references to the United States. "Capitalist-imperialists" and "robbers" were endearments compared to the usual epithets!

Lives & Times magazine dug through its morgue and also sent a reporter and a photographer to the museum on Central Park in New York. The outcome was a special issue devoted to the Mystery of the Missing Fossils.

The cover showed the curator of the museum gazing pensively at the bust of "Nellie," who gazed back at him enigmatically like a Pleistocene Mona Lisa. The caption read: "Where Is Nellie? (See Cover Story)."

The cover story had a picture of the same two subjects, shot from a slightly different angle. The caption repeated the question asked on the cover, but this time supplied the answer: " 'Where is Nellie? Your guess is as good as mine,' says world-renowned paleontologist Edward Bernstein, 61, museum curator."

The story was richly illustrated with photographs of the fossils with the late Professor and the late Father Lorrain, taken at PMS before the war, and of the casts, with and without Dr. Bernstein, newly taken at the museum. The text included interviews with various experts.

Timothy O'Neill, Ph.D., M.A., head of the Guidance Department at Rahway College (formerly Major O'Neill, U.S.A.), stated that G-2 had left no stone unturned and no avenue unexplored, and that he doubted the fossils would ever turn up again, considering that G-2 had failed to find a trace of them. Despite the failure of his mission, Dr. O'Neill expressed pleasure at having met so many worthy, *motivated* young Chinese in the course of his work in Peking, and was happy in the thought of having successfully sponsored at least one of them for study in the United States. Unfortunately, the student, Wu by name, had not kept in touch. . . .

The first secretary of the embassy of the Republic of China, contacted by phone in Washington, said, "No comment," in tones implying, at least to his interviewer, that he knew where the fossils were but wasn't going to tell.

Dr. Robin Running, interviewed by *Lives & Times*' South African correspondent, stated that the loss of the Peking fossils was a blow to science, although of course their significance was now secondary to that of the Australopithecineae, Zinjanthropus in particular. A picture showed Dr. Running smiling fondly at the newly discovered skull of Zinjanthropus.

Lives & Times enjoyed a worldwide circulation, with foreign-language editions tailored to the national interests of practically every country in the Free World.

The special issue's cover story appeared in every one of these, being deemed of "general human interest." The story was a success, eliciting reader response on the local, national and international levels.

Some of the more original letters to the editor were published under suitable headings. Like "Knows but Won't Tell," from a New York obstetrician, one-time resident of Nanking, China, who had personally entrusted the fossils to Chinese friends before being sent to internment camp; his friends still had the fossils, but of course he could not divulge their names and address lest he bring down the wrath of the communists on these anonymous custodians of the National Treasure.

184

(An editor's note stated that the doctor was not available for comment.)

Another letter, headed "Peking Man A Fake?" came from a Father Seamus Mulligan in Lafayette, Indiana. It stated that the Peking fossils had been cleverly manufactured by that heretic Lorrain, who had foisted them on a credulous scientific world. In support of this remarkable assertion Father Mulligan cited an anonymous article in a Midwestern Catholic journal, which had reprinted it from a South American journal, which had reprinted it from an East Indian journal.

Many of the correspondents suggested that the search for Nellie be resumed; a number of these proposed that *Lives & Times* should sponsor such a search, and two of the latter felt that the search might be successful if the magazine offered a reward. One of these was signed "L. L. Ling, Hong Kong."

Ch'en read the cover story and the ensuing correspondence with satisfaction. He smiled at the motivated student Wu; he was pleased that L. L. Ling's letter to the editor had been published, and wondered briefly as to the identity of one C. S. Young of Dayton, Ohio, who had expressed similar sentiments. No matter. The important thing was that the American press had swallowed the bait cast by the *People's Daily*.

Ch'en prepared for the follow-up.

Unknowingly, Ch'en had missed the chance of obtaining a clue to the fossils' present guardian, having been out of town and thus unable to tail Snyder to East End Avenue.

His employers, the Taiwan Turtles, had sent him to Washington two days before Comrade Castro's takeover. Ch'en was frequently required to act as a courier and liaison officer between the U.N. delegation and the embassy of the Republic of China. This was a bonus in a number of ways, since it enabled him to send valuable information, not necessarily connected with Peking Man, to General Liu. Also, Ch'en had been able to ascertain that the Taiwan Turtles had no immediate or long-range interest in the recovery of their, and his, remote ancestor. It was useful to know that there would be no competition or interference from Taipei. The

Nationalists were too busy right now worrying over Quemoy and Matsu.

This was very important at that time, because Ch'en had been devising strategy which would be put into action immediately upon his return to New York.

Ch'en went to his superior and requested a week's leave of absence.

"Elder Brother's inferior servant's unworthy uncle is dying in Toronto and has expressed the desire to see your inferior servant. Your unworthy servant's uncle was so fortunate as to escape from the Reds, leaving his considerable property behind. His sons and daughters were unable to escape and their fate is unknown. His nephew, your unworthy servant, is the closest relative left to Venerable Uncle."

Ch'en's superior fully appreciated this oldest of all Chinese ruses to "goof off" and the leave of absence was granted without question.

Ch'en boarded a Transcanada flight, not to his dying uncle's bedside in Toronto, but to Montreal. At Dorval Airport, Lionel Ling, British subject, resident of Hong Kong, passed quickly through Canadian immigration. The airport limousine deposited him in front of the Queen Elizabeth Hotel. There, in his seventh-floor room, Mr. Ling had several meetings with a man from Ottawa, who brought with him an overflowing briefcase. It took several days to screen the contents of the briefcase, but Ch'en found what he wanted and returned to New York within the week, this time using his U.N. passport in the name of Wu. Wu's return greatly surprised his superior, who had fully expected "dying uncle" to be synonymous with "better job."

On a mild March morning, the managing editor of *Lives & Times* magazine was buzzed by his secretary. "Yes, Sandra?"

"Mr. Weitzman, there's a Mr. Lynn on the line. He says he wants to talk to you, it's important, but he won't state his business."

"Put him on, Sandra. . . . Weitzman here."

"Good morning, Mr. Weitzman."

"Good morning, Mr. Lynn?"

"The name is *Ling,* Mr. Weitzman, but you may call

me Lynn if you find it more convenient; it makes very little difference."

"Thank you, Mr. Ling. What can I do for you?"

"I wish to compliment you on the excellent article on Peking Man in one of your recent editions. I assume that your esteemed magazine might be interested in sending a correspondent to the People's Republic of China for some firsthand information?"

"Keep talking, Mr. Ling."

"Mr. Weitzman, it is in the interest of the People's Republic of China that the West learn more about conditions there in a fair, unbiased manner."

"That would be in *our* interest too, Mr. Ling. Unfortunately, as you must know, our State Department forbids travel by American citizens to Mainland China." A slight cough on the other end of the line. "I mean, the *People's Republic* of China," amended Mr. Weitzman. "Further, even if the State Department issued a passport for such a visit, the People's Republic would not issue a visa or entry permit."

"I am, as you say, fully aware of these difficulties, Mr. Weitzman. However, there are ways of circumventing them. If *Lives & Times* magazine were to choose an accredited correspondent who was *not* an American citizen, but a citizen of a country with which the People's Republic has diplomatic relations—let us say, a Canadian?—the difficulties of which you spoke would be greatly minimized."

"Mr. Ling, you are quite correct in saying that the Canadian government would have no objection, but what about the Chinese government? I understand that *all* Western correspondents have great difficulty in obtaining permits to enter Main—the People's Republic."

"Not to worry, Mr. Weitzman. These obstacles are slight and can be overcome easily. I suggest that *should* you receive an inquiry from a Canadian journalist regarding a series of articles on the *cultural achievements* of the People's Republic of China, you consider it favorably."

"Thank you, Mr. Ling. I think I know just the man. . . . Where can I get in touch with you?"

"I regret, Mr. Weitzman, I travel a great deal"—I bet you do, thought Weitzman—"but I will be in touch with *you* should the need arise. Goodbye, Mr. Weitzman."

Mr. Ling rang off before Weitzman was able to ask the questions that were crowding his mind. What an intriguing call! Seymour Weitzman smiled to himself. The mysterious Mr. Ling—the name was obviously phony, but then phony names were not an exclusive perquisite of Red Chinese agents.

He now buzzed Sandra (metamorphosed from Shirley). "Sandra, see if you can locate the present whereabouts of Ken MacMillan. Try his home in Hamilton first."

Kenneth M. (MacDougal) MacMillan had been born and raised in Glasgow. He had served in the Royal Navy before and during the war, beginning his naval career as an ensign on H.M.S. *Mayfly*, one of the gunboats patrolling the Yangtze River between Shanghai and Hankow. In 1937 he and *Mayfly* had been instrumental in rescuing some DBS (Distressed British Subjects) after their floating shelter had been demolished by a squad of Japanese planes assigned specifically to take care of all shipping on the Yangtze River while their comrades were freely bombing Nanking, some three miles away. In fact, *Mayfly* had opened fire and driven off the attackers, saving the DBS from the fate of the U.S.S. *Panay,* which was sunk on that same day five miles farther upriver.

After his promotion to sublieutenant, Kenneth MacMillan had been transferred to one of His Majesty's sloops that periodically visited Tientsin, and had been able to spend several memorable weekends in Peking.

Unlike his brother officers, who were content to oscillate between the ship and "The Club"—which was the same with regard to membership, amusements, bar and tennis courts whether located in Shanghai, Nanking, Wusi or Hankow, and had the individuality of, say, a service area on the New Jersey Turnpike—Kenneth MacMillan developed a keen interest in China and its people. He read and loved Waley's translations of Chinese poetry; he was awed by the paintings of the Sung dynasty, and tried to collect Tang pottery and

Shang bronzes within the limits of his income. Peking got under his skin as it had got under that of many another, who came for a week and remained a lifetime. Sublieutenant MacMillan had been sorely tempted to do likewise, but the war interfered.

During the war he had seen service in the Atlantic, and had been demobbed in 1946 with the rank of lieutenant commander.

Like a large number of his brother officers, Lieutenant Commander MacMillan had found it impossible to obtain either gainful or congenial employment, let alone both, in postwar England, and had emigrated to Canada at the first opportunity. He had taken out Canadian citizenship as soon as the law permitted, dropping his naval title along with his native nationality, but retaining his small pension. This was paid, further reduced by the taxes imposed by H.M. Government, to his account at the Royal Bank of Canada, Hamilton, Ontario, branch.

Hamilton, Ontario, was Kenneth MacMillan's legal residence, but he was rarely there. His widowed sister Allyson looked after his small apartment and forwarded the mail.

Kenneth MacMillan had discovered that he possessed an unsuspected flair for writing, a keen imagination and a gift for observation. This threefold endowment had led to his marked success as a free-lance journalist, attested to by numerous by-lined feature articles and wire service dispatches that had appeared with regularity in the American and Canadian press, originating from a variety of countries. Even the Iron Curtain had proved penetrable, but the Bamboo Curtain had been an implacable barrier. His repeated applications for a visa had not even been considered worthy of an acknowledgment by the embassy of the People's Republic of China at Ottawa. His latest attempt had been prompted by the articles in the *Toronto Star* and the *New York Times,* and particularly by the spread in the special issue of *Lives & Times.* What a mystery! What a challenge!

In view of the past frustrations, Kenneth MacMillan could not now believe his eyes. He was sitting at a standard-type desk by the window in his room on the twelfth floor of the Hotel Bossert in Brooklyn Heights, reading and rereading the letter in his hand.

MacMillan always stayed at the Bossert when he was in New York and always occupied room 1219. He preferred the staid Bossert to the more fashionable hotels in midtown Manhattan because of the spectacular view from 1219 of the Manhattan skyline across Upper New York Bay and the mouth of the East River. If he craned his neck a little to the left, he could even see the Statue of Liberty.

Dusk had fallen and the view was at its most breathtaking. Lights were blossoming into brilliance in the slate-blue silhouettes of the skyscrapers of Lower Manhattan, stark against the turquoise and orange western sky. Tugboat and ferry lights scurried like fireflies across the bay, their reflections tracing wavy green, red and gold trails through the darkening waters. To his right, on the Brooklyn side, the floodlit Squibb Building had been transformed into a shimmering Taj Mahal; beyond it, red and yellow car lights streamed endlessly under the glowing green necklaces of lights outlining the span of the Brooklyn Bridge.

But for once Kenneth MacMillan was oblivious to the magic that was unfolding beyond his unseeing eyes.

He reread the letter.

EMBASSY OF THE PEOPLE'S REPUBLIC OF CHINA
Ottawa, Ontario, Canada

Kenneth M. MacMillan, Esq.
315 Mayfield Drive
Hamilton, Ontario

Dear Mr. MacMillan:

Your interest in visiting the People's Republic of China for cultural purposes is noted.

It is noted that your particular expressed desire to visit the Peking Man Museum is motivated by the recent article in the *People's Daily,* and by the publicity this article received in the North American press.

It is against the policy of the People's Republic of

China to issue a visitor's visa to private individuals at this time.

Should you care to reapply, presenting evidence that you are an accredited correspondent of, preferably, a magazine of international stature, your application will receive speedy and favorable consideration.

Yours very truly,
Han Lin-yu
Second Secretary

Kenneth MacMillan did not fail to do a spot of "noting" himself. First, the sudden reversal: a comparatively speedy reply to his last application, after the preceding ones had been consistently ignored for several years. Second, the reference to the "North American," *not* the Canadian, press. "North American" included the U.S.A., the People's Republic's archenemy. Finally, the preference for accreditation to a "magazine of international stature"—this quite obviously meant *Lives & Times,* certainly not the German *Spiegel* or the French *VU.*

MacMillan had the distinct impression that they *wanted* him to come, and they wanted him to be backed by *Lives & Times*—why, he could not at the moment imagine. But it was certainly intriguing, and he wanted so badly to see Peking again that he would have gone as an accredited correspondent for *Mechanix Illustrated* if there was no other way.

He'd call Seymour Weitzman first thing tomorrow morning.

MacMillan had finished the breakfast of bagels, cream cheese and lox to which he always treated himself when in New York, and was now on his fourth cup of coffee and sixth cigarette, as he watched the electric travel alarm clock on his bed table. It was nine-fifteen; no use calling Weitzman before nine-thirty. The next fifteen minutes passed slowly, but they passed. At nine-thirty sharp, MacMillan reached out to lift the receiver when the phone rang. "Hullo?"

"Mr. MacMillan?"

"Speaking."

"*Lives & Times* magazine here. Mr. Weitzman would like to speak to you."

"Ken?"

"Seymour! This must be mental telepathy. I was just about to call *you*. What a coincidence!"

"Yeah; how are you, Ken? Good to hear your voice. Say, I'd like to see you. How about lunch?"

"Fine. I want to see you, too."

"Okay, meet you at George's Steakhouse, Forty-eighth and Madison, at twelve-thirty. See you then."

MacMillan killed the next hour and forty-five minutes by walking up and down the promenade on top of the Brooklyn-Queens Expressway between Montague and Cranberry streets. He glanced absently at the skyline across the East River, fuzzy in a gray haze of smog. The Squibb Building, at the Cranberry Street end of the promenade, stood revealed in all its grime and discoloration, as unlike the Taj Mahal as possible in the cruel daylight. Traffic was whooshing and rumbling on the expressway underneath his feet. The forsythias were in golden bloom in little green islands bordering the promenade, and ailanthus trees were displaying fat buds in the adjoining backyards of Brooklyn Heights.

MacMillan was still amazed at the coincidence of Weitzman's calling him at the very moment when he was about to call Weitzman.

He remarked on that an hour or so later when he and Weitzman sat facing each other across the table in a booth at George's Steakhouse, waiting for their drinks and lunches to be served. Weitzman put down the letter from Second Secretary Han Lin-yu. "You know, Ken," he said thoughtfully, "I don't think this is *coincidence!* Looks more like a *plan* to me, you being offered a visa if you work for me, and me being offered a chance at a firsthand series on Red China if I send a Canadian—*you*. All within a week, and with a mystery man calling me about it yet."

MacMillan agreed. "They want something from us. They want *me* to come, and *you*, Mr. *Lives & Times*, to back me. What do you think it's all about?"

"No idea, Ken. Let's eat. We'll find out soon

enough. You come back to the office with me afterwards; Sandra can type out the contract for you, and we'll arrange for funds. I suppose you'll want to take off for Ottawa as soon as you can."

Weitzman began to eat his cottage cheese and green salad, casting wistful glances at MacMillan's steak—New York cut, medium rare, with French fries and green peas. MacMillan wondered why Weitzman made lunch dates at a steak house if he was going to eat rabbit chow. Weitzman answered the unasked question. "Diet. Doctor's orders," he said curtly. "You don't know how lucky you are."

They began to discuss the series of articles that MacMillan was to send in, "Exclusive, by our Special Correspondent Kenneth M. MacMillan"—but they immediately realized that the discussion was futile. The choice of topics would be entirely up to MacMillan's hosts. "They keep emphasizing 'cultural,'" said MacMillan gloomily. "I bet that means anything interesting, like the shenanigans of the Red Guards, is going to be off limits."

"Well, sure. But it doesn't really matter what kind of crap you file, although we'll have to run it, just to show them we are in good faith, 'sincere,' you know. Send it to Bob Richardson in the Hong Kong office; he'll forward it. He'll also keep you in funds if you need more. The main thing is to find out what they are after and to keep your eyes open when you are there. You can write up the really interesting stuff after you get back to Hong Kong. Maybe you'll even get a book out of it—first serialized by *Lives & Times*, of course. . . . Let's get back to the office if you've finished."

MacMillan caught the 4:50 P.M. flight to Montreal. There he made the connection to Ottawa. He had decided not to write any more letters, but to call on Mr. Han Lin-yu in person, and complete the formalities on the spot. If the People's Republic was as keen on his visit as it seemed to be, they'd be eager to speed him on his way. MacMillan was not disappointed. He was admitted into Mr. Han's presence after a wait of only fifteen minutes, and the meeting was extremely cordial. Mr. Han inspected the *Lives & Times* contract only cursorily and nodded with approval.

"There will be no delay validating your passport, Mr. MacMillan. We have all the information we require on file from your previous applications." You bastards, thought MacMillan. "We suggest that you proceed to Hong Kong and put up at the Peninsula Hotel. You will be contacted there and be informed of the arrangements for your itinerary. I am looking forward to reading your impressions in *Lives & Times*. Bon voyage, Mr. MacMillan."

Thirty minutes later MacMillan walked out of the embassy of the People's Republic of China with the visa, "good for 21 days," stamped in his passport. Smallpox vaccination was valid from his last trip abroad. It was still required by the People's Republic, although officially the "flower sickness" no longer bloomed among Chairman Mao's Thousand Flowers, having been eradicated along with flies, leprosy and beggars. . . .

Allyson met him at Toronto Airport and drove him home to Hamilton.

Two days later, Kenneth MacMillan, his two suitcases, typewriter and Leica camera were on a BOAC flight bound for Hong Kong.

22

This was MacMillan's third day in Hong Kong, and nothing had happened. He was spending a great deal of his time in the bar of the Peninsula Hotel, considering this the most logical place for being "contacted." But his only contacts thus far had been his colleagues of the press, led by Bob Richardson, who was basking in reflected glory, while the rest were green with envy.

"How come *Lives & Times* gets to visit the mainland? What have they got that we haven't got?"

"Well, they've got a Canadian correspondent"— MacMillan grinned—"and don't forget *Lives & Times'* international stature."

"So has the *Reader's Digest* got international stature."

But they didn't hold *Lives & Times'* privileged status

against him. They kept him company while he consumed Pink Ladies and gimlets, and invited him to the nonstop poker game in room 505. Occasionally they commiserated with him, hoping hypocritically that he wasn't being stood up.

It was as good a way to pass the time as any. It was too hot and humid to leave the air-conditioned Peninsula; besides, MacMillan didn't like the noise, stench and overcrowding of Hong Kong's narrow, climbing streets, worse than it had ever been before the war, when it had been bad enough. Of course, one couldn't blame the poor beggars who had fled the mainland by the thousands at the risk of their lives and forsaking what property they had owned, crowding into Hong Kong until the crown colony threatened to burst at the seams from the population pressure.

The Peak bored him; anyway, he could not accept cocktail and dinner invitations to his friends' homes on this privileged elevation for fear of missing his "contact" at the hotel.

By the end of his third day he had ordered two suits from a bespoke tailor and won thirty-five dollars at poker, and was beginning to feel that these would be the only positive achievements of his mission.

Returning from dinner on the fourth evening, he found that the "contact" had been made.

A Manila envelope, addressed and obviously delivered by hand, lay on his bedside table.

The envelope contained train tickets to Canton and Peking. A typed, unsigned note informed him that a berth had been reserved for him on the Peking train, departing Canton at 6:03 P.M. the following evening.

It appeared that the mainland were not interested in MacMillan's impressions of the cultural achievements of Canton. He hadn't even had time to leave the station between trains.

He was alone in the two-berth compartment on the Peking train. Nobody in particular seemed to be interested in him; he was probably imagining the feeling that his every move was being observed and recorded. A tall man, wearing the traditional long silk gown, occupied the compartment next to his. He nodded occasionally when he and MacMillan met in the corridor or in the dining car, but he never spoke. The tall man got off at Nanking and was replaced by a shorter, fatter one, who turned out to be equally uncommunicative.

The train crossed the Yangtze River at Nanking, still on the old train ferry. The river hadn't changed. It flowed quietly and majestically, wider than the St. Lawrence, giving no hint of its swift, treacherous current. It teemed with junks and sampans, just as it had in the old days. There were even one or two gunboats, but of course they no longer flew the White Ensign or the Stars and Stripes.

The train roared on through Kiangsu Province. Blue-clad men and women stooped in the rice paddies, planting seedlings in the almost knee-high water, as they had done for centuries. At dusk the water buffaloes returned from pasture, their horns resembling arms opened for an embrace. They lumbered docilely in single file, following the lead buffalo, from whose back a whip-wielding urchin sprouted like a mushroom under his enormous circular straw hat.

The hustle and bustle in the stations had changed little. The simple folk still wore their blue cotton jackets and trousers, carried wicker suitcases, baskets and bundles. The hawkers still passed buns, sesamum cakes, fruit and soft drinks to the hands reaching out from the third-class windows. Except that there were a lot of shapeless, olive-drab cotton uniforms, and the train was guarded. MacMillan was free to visit the dining car two carriages ahead, but passage to the third-class carriages in the rear was barred silently but eloquently by a uniformed guard with a fixed bayonet.

MacMillan's short, fat neighbor got off at Ch'ü-foo in Shantung, the birthplace of Confucius. Another anonymous individual moved into the next-door compartment.

In the hazy outer distance a purplish mountain rose steeply and abruptly from the plain. Tai Shan Mountain. MacMillan had always wanted to visit Confucius's tomb on the K'ung family estate at the foot of Tai Shan, and the temples sacred to the Sage along its ascent and on the summit, but there had never been time. . . .

Rice paddies gave way to spring wheat, corn and sorghum.

After three days, the Temple of Heaven soared on the left, rotated out of sight, the Fox Tower reared up on the right, and one minute later the train pulled into Chien Men Station, bringing MacMillan's solitude to an end.

Two individuals entered the compartment, dressed in identical gray cotton "Mao" uniforms and wearing gray caps. Ear-length hair hanging limply from underneath the cap, and a slight build, implied that one of them was female. They introduced themselves as Mr. Feng and Miss Yang, and welcomed him to Peking.

"We will be your guides and interpreters, Mr. MacMillan. Please to follow us. We will take you to your hotel."

Each grasped one of MacMillan's suitcases and struggled politely with him over the typewriter, which he was finally allowed to carry himself.

A small car which looked like a Fiat but was a Soviet-made Moskvich was waiting. MacMillan was ushered into the back seat; Mr. Feng drove, and Miss Yang, beside him, pointed out the sights to MacMillan. Chien Men, Tung An Men, Tung Chang Ang Chieh. The majestic gates and the boulevard had not changed, but the plaza in front of Wu Men, the entrance to the Forbidden City, seemed uncommonly bare. MacMillan realized that the evergreens that had studded the plaza and bordered the towering red walls had been cut down. Also, the enormous posters interspersed with portraits of Chairman Mao, Marx and Lenin, which were strung along the façade of the Midday Gate, did nothing to improve Kublai Khan's architecture.

The Moskvich drew up in front of a large, nondescript gray box. "The Nationalities Hotel," said Mr. Feng proudly. He and Miss Yang ushered MacMillan to a small, sparsely furnished but spotlessly clean room that had apparently been reserved for him. MacMillan's dream of putting up at the Wagons-Lits faded rapidly. That symbol of Western decadence probably no longer existed or had been converted into a hostel, or school, or orphanage, or something equally utilitarian for the benefit of the toiling masses. . . .

MacMillan never did find out.

Mr. Feng and Miss Yang left. "We will pick you up at eight-thirty tomorrow morning. Please to be ready. You will find dinner in the hotel dining room satisfactory, Mr. MacMillan. Good evening."

MacMillan unpacked. He found that the management had provided Uplift—not a Gideon Bible but its equivalent, an English translation of Comrade Mao's "Thoughts," was lying on the bedside table.

In the course of his first week MacMillan learned that when the Chinese had said "cultural," they did mean *cultural!*

Nursery schools—almond-eyed cherubs with black Dutch boy bobs, neatly dressed and aproned, parading around the room waving tiny flags and chanting martial-sounding songs, no doubt composed by or extolling Chairman Mao, whose portrait presided benevolently over playroom and dining room. After the third nursery school MacMillan could cheerfully have strangled the younger generation of the People's Republic.

Middle schools—uniformed striplings of indeterminate sex, bowing to him in unison, marching, parading, exercising, waving flags, studying. . . .

Peking University—uniformed students of indeterminate sex talking determinedly about "self-reliance," "the Struggle," "the Revolution," in the same stilted English used by Mr. Feng and Miss Yang. "The young comrades spend the spring and summer in the communes with the farmers; we train them to work with their hands as well as with their heads," explained Mr. Feng, or was it Miss Yang—MacMillan was no longer sure which was which.

The opera, the ballet—uniformed actors, uniformed dancers, the stages draped in red and supervised by backdrops depicting Chairman Mao. The music was still strident, but gone were the slender, undulating female impersonators and the fierce, bearded, beetle-browed war lords of the classic theater.

An art exhibit—four hundred paintings, like monstrously enlarged color photographs, showing the toiling masses toiling in the field or in the factory or waving guns under the guidance of Chairman Mao, not to mention the hundreds of portraits of the Chairman by himself. . . .

MacMillan dutifully took notes and pictures and asked questions. What courses were studied at the different levels, what textbooks were used? Marxism-Leninism, dialectic materialism, chemistry, physics, engineering. Some of the names of textbook authors were familiar: Marx, Engels, Lenin, Mao Tse-tung, Ho Chi Minh, Lin Piao (this one was to be dropped soon after MacMillan's visit), Darwin, Liebknecht, Russell.

Every morning MacMillan was provided with several typed sheets of information concerning the nature and purpose of the cultural establishments to be visited that day. Polite hints on his part expressing the wish to interview this or that government official, to visit the Summer Palace or the Peking Man Museum, were either ignored altogether or answered with a brief, "Please to be patient, Mr. MacMillan. Arrangements will be made."

A respite came at the end of the first week. "You will require time to write your article, Mr. MacMillan," suggested Mr. Feng. "We have nothing scheduled for two days, but we will be in the hotel lobby, should you wish to avail yourself of our services."

MacMillan stared at the typewriter. The sheet said, in caps: "A WESTERN CORRESPONDENT LOOKS AT PEKING, by Kenneth M. MacMillan," and was otherwise blank.

If the hotel room had been in Hong Kong, MacMillan would have had no difficulty in dashing off a description of what the Western Correspondent had "looked" at in Peking. Late-afternoon and evening walks in the streets, without his two companions, had enabled him to fill three notebooks with impressions, jotted down in a shorthand of his own devising and intelligible only to himself—very useful behind the Iron and now the Bamboo Curtain.

An opening sentence kept suggesting itself: "Peking is functioning with all the charm and exuberance of a well-organized ant heap." The temptation to put this on paper had to be firmly suppressed.

His chief impression had been the *drabness*, the lack of joy and spontaneity. It was reflected in the non-

199

descript gray boxlike buildings like the Nationalities Hotel which had sprung up all over Peking and were choking, almost symbolically, the crimson and gold of the ancient imperial splendor. Just as sex had been choked. MacMillan thought wistfully of the girls he had seen in Hong Kong a week ago, and in Hankow, Tientsin and Shanghai before the war—like ivory figurines, their long, high-collared silk sheaths split artfully and tantalizingly to the hip, the faces made up subtly, the hair shining like black lacquer and dressed with deceptive simplicity. No mistaking *their* sex.

Contrast this with that gray, shapeless sexual isomorphism here. Boys and girls looking equally unattractive in their Mao uniforms and you couldn't tell which was which—although presumably *they* could, perhaps by some invisible hormonal emanation; otherwise where did all those chubby infants in those maddening nursery schools come from?

Of course, everything was very *clean;* cleanliness was enforced. MacMillan had seen two uniformed youths cuffing an old man around for spitting on the sidewalk in the time-honored tradition of dust-laden Peking. Gone were the flies, and the beggars with their oozing or crusting sores, representing every skin disease in the book from scabies to favus. These dermatologists' delights no longer crowded shop entrances, threatening to bar customers from entering unless the shopkeeper and the customer paid them *cumsha.* The *cumsha* tradition had gone too—no more haggling, no more tips—gone with the rickshaw coolies who had exacted *cumsha* from the shops to which they steered their passengers. Well, perhaps that was no loss. But laughter and gaiety seemed to have vanished too, along with the more unsanitary but somehow charming aspects of Peking street life.

MacMillan wondered why zealotry always seemed to be correlated with the lack of a sense of humor. Perhaps one had to live in a free democracy to be able to laugh at oneself. Political and religious fanatics always took themselves so damn seriously.

Like Mr. Feng and Miss Yang. How solemn they were. He and these two had practically lived in each other's pockets for a week, but he couldn't remember either of them ever smiling. And it had been impossible to develop any kind of personal relationship with them; they remained forever correct, distant and formal. They ignored attempts at personal questions: are you married, where did you go to school, where do your parents live? The answer was invariably some cliché like "We are married to the Revolution"; "Chairman Mao is our father and mother."

How would you like to let powder and rouge bring a glow to your sallow complexion, Miss Yang, brush that limp, dull hair of yours until it gleams, put on a peacock-blue silk gown slit at the sides to reveal your legs in sheer nylons, exchange those splay-toed sneakers for high-heeled pumps and go dancing? Do you *have* legs under those baggy gray pants, and little ivory-colored, tawny-tipped breasts under that unspeakable jacket? Do you sleep with Comrade Feng, Miss Yang? Maybe one of those chubby, hand-clapping, flag-waving brats in one of those nursery schools is yours, Miss Yang? Conceived and birthed in the line of duty to Chairman Mao?

MacMillan shook his head to free it of these entertaining but fruitless speculations.

He could write none of these "impressions." So what *was* he to write?

He finally decided to write up his observations simply and objectively. The editor and readers of *Lives & Times* could conclude for themselves that if you'd seen one nursery school, one middle school, one opera, one painting, you'd seen them all, and if you'd heard one student's clichés you'd heard the speech of millions. He faithfully described the exercising workers on the rooftops, the cleanliness, the people in the streets, who looked healthy and well-fed, the absence of rickshaws, flies, beggars and skin diseases, the presence of thousands of bicycles, and the honesty. No more tips and gratuities, no more petty theft; you could drop your wallet on the sidewalk, and half an hour later it would be returned to you, contents intact, by a smiling citizen.

He shamelessly copied whole sections from the typed handouts that were so liberally provided every morning, larding them here and there with appropriate quotations from Chairman Mao's "Little Red Book" on his bedside table.

He read through the finished product.

Communist Peking was speaking for itself.

It made unutterably dull reading.

MacMillan wondered if Weitzman would print this cliché-riddled effusion or drop it immediately into the wastebasket, where it belonged.

He went down to the lobby, where he found Mr. Feng and Miss Yang sitting stiffly in the same chairs and attitudes in which he had left them that morning, each engrossed in a little red book.

MacMillan announced that he had finished the article. Mr. Feng stretched out his hand. "Is it permitted?" MacMillan handed over the typescript. Feng began to read.

MacMillan watched incredulously as a smile began to spread over Mr. Feng's face. At the end he was beaming. "This is excellent, Mr. MacMillan! Please to leave the manuscript with us. We shall see that it is dispatched with the greatest possible speed."

MacMillan handed over three exposed rolls of color film and left his companions. Miss Yang was now reading the article with a similar expression of pleasure on her face.

MacMillan had dinner and began to resign himself to a second week of unmitigated "culture."

Strangely enough, however, there was no more "culture" for him during the second week.

"Now we will have enjoyment," announced Mr. Feng the next morning when he and Miss Yang came to fetch him for the day's rounds. Both were smiling, Miss Yang revealing an unexpected dimple in her cheek.

The mileage on the Moskvich began to pile up. There were outings to the Temple of Heaven, and to the Lama and Confucius temples. MacMillan was taken on day excursions to the Summer Palace, the Jade Fountain Pagoda, to the Ming Tombs and even to the Great Wall. It really was "enjoyment" for him; the ancient grounds and palaces had not changed, and he had discovered an ability to tune out the droning voices of his companions. He only half listened when they praised the wisdom and leadership of Comrade Mao for the fine, waist-high stands or corn and sorghum in the countryside—both would reach well above a man's head at harvest time—and drowned out their endless denunciations of the decadence of Imperial China at their destinations. Although he did have to agree with them in condemning the barbarism of the British troops who had looted the Old Summer Palace after the Boxer Rebellion and reduced its splendid pavilions to the rubble that was now crunching under their feet.

Between Old and New Summer Palace he even discovered the priceless sign that he remembered from previous visits to Peking. SUB LAPICINUM, it said, and only a non-scholar of Latin would be ingenious enough to read it backward.

The period of "enjoyment" lasted for more than a week.

MacMillan had less than a week left before his visa expired, and still he had not found out just what was behind the invitation to Peking that had been practically forced on him and *Lives & Times* magazine.

Weitzman published "A Foreign Correspondent Looks at Peking" in the very next issue of *Lives & Times*. The magazine was brought to MacMillan by a broadly beaming Mr. Feng, accompanied by Miss Yang, whose dimple was very much in evidence. "It is excellent, Mr. MacMillan! The pictures are excellent too!"

Not only had Weitzman accepted the article; he had refrained from having it translated into the snide, smart-alecky style for which *Lives & Times* was famous. It was there in all its pedestrian dullness, though somewhat enlivened by the photographs.

Weitzman had done him proud. The cover showed Wu Men scarlet and golden against a bright blue sky, and did full justice to the garish posters and portraits of Chairman Mao and colleagues adorning the gate. The text was illustrated with color pictures of nursery schools, middle schools and universities and their wholesome scholars. There were quite a few street scenes, but none that showed posters of Uncle Sam in various stages of dismemberment by outraged workers and peasants; either Weitzman had been smart enough not to print these, or the censors had been too smart to let them leave Peking in the first place.

"Very good. Very fine," said Mr. Feng again. "Please to come with us. Today is special surprise."

The Moskvich headed out of the city in the direction of the Western Hills. It was stopped at a bridge. Uniformed guards appeared to object to further progress. Mr. Feng and Miss Yang got out of the car and apparently won the ensuing argument. The journey continued, covering some forty miles in all.

The Moskvich stopped in front of an L-shaped building near a small village in hilly country. A tall, thin man with grizzled hair and a lined face, dressed in the inevitable Mao uniform, came out of the building to meet the car.

He bowed to MacMillan. "Welcome to the Peking Man Museum, Mr. MacMillan. I am Dr. Ma Hsu-wei, director of the museum. It is a great pleasure to meet you." Dr. Ma bowed MacMillan into the museum; Feng and Yang followed at a respectful distance. MacMillan had recognized Dr. Ma from one of the group pictures in the special issue of *Lives & Times*, and was beginning to wonder whether that issue had anything to do with his being here today.

Tea was served in a small anteroom, then MacMillan was treated to a personal guided tour of the museum and, behind it, of the cave in which Peking Man had been discovered, which was reached through a communicating doorway. Dr. Ma took great trouble to explain the exhibits—charts, paintings, plaster casts and models—and pointed out the exact spots where the fossils had been found in the rock-strewn and wholly uninspiring cave. But at least the cave was cool. MacMillan shot three rolls of Kodachrome and took notes.

The tour took two hours, and MacMillan was grateful when it ended in a sort of conference room where lunch for two was awaiting them. Mr. Feng and Miss Yang apparently were not invited.

Dr. Ma personally served MacMillan with tidbits from the various dishes that were set before them, and poured warm *huang chiu* into tiny cups. But the rice wine, looking and tasting like sherry, was served and consumed in moderation by both host and guest. MacMillan was grateful to Dr. Ma for not starting a *kan pei*—bottoms up—contest, which was a traditional feature of Chinese feasts and usually ended with the host triumphant and the guest under the table. Although this was not a feast; it was more like a business luncheon. Dr. Ma made small talk in his literate English while they ate.

Bowls of plain rice were served to signify the end of the meal. MacMillan was familiar enough with custom not to eat of this. Only a boor would do so, implying insultingly that he was still hungry after a succession of fine dishes.

Dr. Ma poured fragrant jasmine tea and accepted a Players and light from MacMillan. The two men sat smoking in silence. Then Dr. Ma gave a slight cough and said:

"Mr. MacMillan, you have seen the Peking Man Museum and the paintings and models that represent the life and form of our remote ancestor. But the true glory of this museum, the fossils themselves, is missing. As you know, they disappeared at the beginning of the war. . . ."

MacMillan, spellbound, listened and scribbled notes as Dr. Ma told the detailed story of the search: the efforts of the Japanese, which had been ordered by the Emperor himself and had led nowhere, causing one of the investigators to commit suicide in disgrace and costing his commanding officer a promotion; the equally futile investigations of the Americans, and of the Chinese themselves—although Dr. Ma did not go into detail regarding the latter.

The narrator stopped. He sipped tea and accepted another cigarette from MacMillan. Then he looked straight at MacMillan and said, "Mr. MacMillan, I have read your article in the current issue of *Lives & Times* magazine. You are a fair and unbiased observer. One might almost say that you are sympathetic to our Revolution. We have strong reason to believe that the fossils are in the United States. Will you help us to recover them and return them to the people of China, who are their rightful owners?"

Enlightenment came in a flash. Dr. Ma's request explained everything—the ease with which MacMillan had obtained the visa, the contrived association with *Lives & Times*. He had been on probation while they were force-feeding him with "culture" during the first week. During last week's "enjoyment" they had simply been marking time until his article was published. They didn't give a damn *what* he wrote; they were only interested in *how* it was written, and how it was presented by *Lives & Times*.

MacMillan suddenly remembered Second Secretary Han in Ottawa. "I am looking forward to reading your impressions. . . ." It had not been a polite phrase, as MacMillan had assumed at the time; it had been a pointed, meaningful hint! And he had apparently written just the way they were hoping he would, and Weitzman, that smart cookie, had printed it verbatim instead of throwing the article out or at least jazzing it up.

MacMillan and *Lives & Times* magazine had passed the test, and as a result "they" had decided to make the proposition that Dr. Ma had just put to him.

MacMillan looked at Dr. Ma and said, "Dr. Ma, I shall be glad to do all I can to help your people recover their national treasure. But I do not know how to set about it."

"My main suggestion would be, Mr. MacMillan, that you write an article covering as fully as possible every aspect of the subject as we discussed it today. I have taken the liberty of preparing some reference material for you, and photographs."

Dr. Ma withdrew a bulky folder from his desk drawer and handed it to MacMillan.

"This contains all the information you may need. Write an article that will arouse sympathy in the United States, strong enough to overcome the hostility between our two countries. . . . Oh, excuse me, I forgot for a moment that you are a Canadian. Were you aware that it was a Canadian who directed the first excavations and described the first skull?

"The American people have a great sense of fair play," conceded Dr. Ma surprisingly. "If they learn that the fossils were stolen by Americans—there is no doubt about that, Mr. MacMillan; they *were* stolen by Americans—well, the American people will want to see justice done, even if it was one of their own who robbed the enemy."

This was quite a speech. MacMillan felt that Dr. Ma had a point.

"I will do the best I can, Dr. Ma. I will start writing as soon as I return to Peking and will send you a copy. The rest is of course up to the editor of *Lives & Times*."

"Do not worry about that, Mr. MacMillan. I shall look forward to reading your *manuscript*. Perhaps we can meet again when it is finished. if you will let me know through Mr. Feng or Miss Yang, so that I may have the pleasure of your company while we go over it together."

MacMillan agreed solemnly. The word "censorship" was not used. "I shall appreciate your suggestions, Dr. Ma."

They returned to Peking. Mr. Feng and Miss Yang seemed aware that something momentous had happened. For once they did not inflict their speeches on him, but left him to his thoughts, conversing softly with each other in Mandarin.

This time MacMillan had no difficulty writing his copy. The article composed itself in his head with such rapidity that his fingers lagged behind as they transferred his thoughts to paper. Meals were brought to his room, and he ate absent-mindedly, reading over and correcting what he had written while mechanically putting untasted food in his mouth. But he spared a thought of gratitude for the unknown who was thoughtfully providing unlimited amounts of surprisingly good coffee.

Once in a while he referred to the notes that Dr. Ma had given him. He was amazed at their completeness. The Chinese had apparently been aware of every step the Kempetai had taken in their intensive and futile search both in China and in Japan. MacMillan felt a twinge of compassion for the unfortunate Captain Omura; what a fascinating, complex and, yes. tragic man. MacMillan. having fought the war in the Atlantic, thus lacking firsthand experience with the Kempetai, was capable of judging the Japanese with some fairness.

And how had the Chinese got hold of the transcripts of the American interrogations after the war, containing verbatim interviews with Mr. Mitchell, Father Lorrain and Mrs. Peters in Peking, and the statements of every U.S. Marine who had been stationed in Peking, Tientsin, Fengtai, Chinwangtao and Camp Holcomb at the outbreak of the Pacific war? The Japanese and Americans had done the spade work; the Chinese apparently had sat back, not lifting a finger except to obtain the fruits of these painstaking labors! How they had managed to do so was not mentioned. . . .

The references were nothing if not thorough. They included every red herring that had popped up over the years, including the one that had come out of the German Democratic Republic. All the more surprising, therefore, that there was not a single hint to substantiate Dr. Ma's assertion that the fossils had been stolen by Americans and were now in the United States. Dr. Ma, unlike the *People's Daily,* was unlikely to fabricate unfounded accusations, at least not in a private interview that had no propaganda value. Dr. Ma must possess the necessary information, but it was obviously "classified." This deliberate gap only added suspense to the story.

MacMillan's fingers flew over the keyboard. Three days later he pulled the last page out of the typewriter and reread the article.

This time there was nothing dull and pedestrian about his report. "The Mystery of the Missing Link"—MacMillan x-ed out "Link" and substituted "Ancestor"—"by Kenneth M. MacMillan" read like one of the better Crime Club novels.

MacMillan shaved for the first time in three days, then descended to the lobby. Mr. Feng and Miss Yang were there, in their usual chairs, and as usual engrossed in the "Thoughts" of Chairman Mao. They were delighted to hear that he had finished his article. Miss Yang disappeared briefly. She and Mr. Feng had a rapid conversation when she returned. Mr. Feng then turned to MacMillan. "Please to be ready eight A.M.

tomorrow morning. We go to visit Dr. Ma at Peking Man Museum."

Dr. Ma read the article in silence, smoking three of MacMillan's Players, and nodding from time to time. He put down the last page and smiled at MacMillan. "An outstanding piece of work, Mr. MacMillan. I congratulate you!"

"Thank you, Dr. Ma. You are an author's dream of an editor—not a single change."

Dr. Ma let that pass. "If you will be so good as to leave the manuscript with me, Mr. MacMillan; it will be returned to you in one or two days' time." The session seemed at an end. MacMillan rose and prepared to take his leave for good—his time would be up in two days. Dr. Ma forestalled him. "We shall see each other again before you return to America, Mr. MacMillan," he said with a courteous bow.

Back in the Moskvich, something unheard-of happened. "What would you like to do today and tomorrow?" asked Mr. Feng. This was unprecedented. No *fait accompli*—enjoyment or culture—had been scheduled. He was actually given a choice! MacMillan realized that this sudden turnabout had a reason; his mission was accomplished, "they" had what they wanted and therefore no longer cared what he did during his last two days.

Perversely, he couldn't think of a suggestion. It was so damn hot! He wanted more than anything to get back to the hotel, turn on the electric fan and lie naked on his bed and sleep. The heat and the exertion of creativity had taken it out of him; he began to realize how tired he was. A swimming pool would be the next best thing. . . . He timidly suggested as much to his companions. They were unexpectedly sympathetic. "To be sure, Mr. MacMillan. Today you rest. Tomorrow we go swimming at Jade Fountain pool, but come back early so you can rest again. Perhaps tomorrow evening you will go out to dinner. . . ."

That last morning really was "enjoyment." The spring-fed Jade Fountain pool's translucent green and golden sparkle fully justified its name. MacMillan gasped at the water's icy coldness and stood shivering. Not only was he chilled, but he was also acutely and embarrassingly conscious of his freckled, goose-pimpled skin and the coarse hairiness of his chest and legs, which he felt compared most unfavorably with the hairless, ivory smoothness of the Chinese bathers around him. Miss Yang glanced at him and turned her head to hide a giggle. Her chaste black one-piece bathing suit revealed that she did indeed possess legs, smooth and straight if rather short, like all her countrymen's. MacMillan noted that she was also endowed with breasts. She giggled and squealed when a playful, muscular Mr. Feng splashed the icy water on her. These two dedicated servants of the Revolution thoroughly relished the outing, behaving in every way like their capitalist-imperialist counterparts at Brighton or Coney Island.

With obvious regret, Mr. Feng announced that they had to return to the city. Handing MacMillan out of the Moskvich at the Nationalities Hotel, he said importantly, "You are invited to a dinner party. I will pick you up at five-thirty sharp."

He would not say who had issued the invitation. "Very important," he said enigmatically. "Please to be ready at five-thirty sharp."

At five-thirty sharp, Mr. Feng headed the Moskvich for Nan Hai Park and conducted MacMillan to one of the imperial pavilions. Preceding him up the stairway, he then ushered MacMillan onto a terrace overlooking the Southern Lake, on which the lotus were in bloom. Four men rose politely to greet MacMillan. Mr. Feng bowed to them and faded discreetly.

Dr. Ma was there, dressed in his Mao uniform. He introduced his companions as Mr. Chin, Dr. Liu and Mr. Wei. No "Comrade," no titles. Unofficial anonymity was obviously the order of the day. Equally obviously, the three gentlemen were high in the governmental or party hierarchy. No one in the lower echelons would have dared appear in public dressed in the traditional long silk gown and satin slippers instead of in the party uniform. Mr. Chin and Mr. Wei wore white; the short, stocky Dr. Liu, who had a faintly military bearing, was in light blue.

Tea was poured; polite small talk was made. The small talk continued through a sumptuous Peking duck dinner, further enriched by grass carp that was crisply brown on the outside and flaked snow-white, moist and sweet on the inside; there was shrimp, prawn, chicken and beef, with green peas, pea pods, bamboo shoots, bean sprouts and water chestnuts, all cooked to perfection. The dishes kept coming, each more succulent and delicious than the last. Mr. Chin and Mr. Wei placed choice morsels in MacMillan's bowl in the age-old tradition of the attentive host honoring his guest. Just as several days ago at the Peking Man Museum, no attempt was made to drink MacMillan under the table. This was as well, for *pei ku'erh* was served instead of rice wine, a clear, colorless distillate of sorghum, which packed three times the wallop of vodka and tasted of fusel oil even when it was of the finest quality, like the present offering. MacMillan got away with one tiny cup of the brew, just sufficient for a sip in answer to a toast from each of his four hosts.

The last course, shark's fin soup, was brought in, followed by the bowl of rice that signaled the end of the banquet. A waiter brought hot, steaming towels.

The party adjourned to another table. Tea was poured, cigarettes and Cuban cigars were offered. The evening breeze blew in gently and refreshingly from the lake, which was becoming shrouded in dusk. The party got down to business.

Mr. Wei (or was it Mr. Chin?) fired the opening round. "Mr. MacMillan, my friends and I have read your article on the loss of Peking Man with the greatest interest and wish to compliment you on your excellent writing." Four heads bowed in unison. Mr. Chin (Mr. Wei?) took up the thread. "Dr. Ma informs us that you have generously agreed to help in the recovery of our National Treasure?"

MacMillan assented. The white-gowned speaker continued. "Dr. Ma informs us further that you are somewhat uncertain as to what method of recovery to use?" MacMillan assented again. The military Dr. Liu picked up the ball.

"We have some suggestions, Mr. MacMillan, if you care to hear them?" The tone implied that MacMillan had *better* care to hear them. He got the message.

"I shall be most eager to listen, Dr. Liu."

211

"We feel that the best and most discreet way would be for *Lives & Times* magazine to offer a reward for information leading to the recovery of the fossils. This reward should be substantial, and it should be offered in conjunction with your article, both to appear in the same issue of the magazine."

MacMillan nodded. "That is an excellent suggestion, Dr. Liu, gentlemen," he said. "However, you understand that I am not in a position to answer for *Lives & Times* magazine. The decision to commit what you call a 'substantial' sum of money would not even be up to the managing editor. It would have to be made by the publishers or the board of directors of the magazine."

"Quite so, Mr. MacMillan. We are fully aware of this. Now, *you* are fully aware that due to political considerations, the government of the People's Republic of China cannot offer such a reward through an American magazine. The State Department would object," said Dr. Liu with an unexpected grin. MacMillan grinned back.

"However," continued Dr. Liu, who now seemed to be the spokesman for the group, "there can be no objection if the reward is offered by *private* citizens who wish to remain *anonymous*. . . . Fifty thousand dollars have been made available in this manner for the use of *Lives and Times* magazine, under certain *strict* conditions." Dr. Liu counted them off his fingers:

"No names are to be mentioned.

"Tonight's meeting never happened.

"The reward offer must appear to originate entirely and spontaneously with *Lives & Times* magazine. Can you guarantee us this absolute secrecy on your word of honor, Mr. MacMillan?" Again there seemed to be a threatening undertone to the polite words.

MacMillan thought for a moment. "I think I can guarantee this, Dr. Liu," he said finally. "Of course, I will have to take Mr. Weitzman, the managing editor, into my confidence, and the chairman of the board of directors will have to be informed. But I think I can speak for both these men."

Dr. Liu nodded. "The funds will be made available in New York." He withdrew from a briefcase the folder containing MacMillan's manuscript. "We suggest that you take your manuscript with you and hand it to your editor in person. You may wish to retire early and get a good night's sleep before your departure for Hong Kong. There will be no need to undertake the tiring journey by train. It has been arranged for you to be flown to Canton. Comrade Feng has instructions and will pick you up at nine-thirty A.M. tomorrow morning."

The four men rose and bowed, thanking him and wishing him a peaceful journey home. MacMillan was dismissed.

He returned for his last night at the Nationalities Hotel, his stomach full of Peking duck, his mind bemused by the *pei ku'erh* and by the fantastic, dreamlike meeting with Dr. Ma and his three mysterious friends.

The plane was a DC-3, perhaps captured or bought from the Nationalists during the Revolution and paid for with "silver bullets," like most of the American matériel with which Comrade Mao had defeated Chiang Kai-shek's generals.

Five Mao-uniformed fellow passengers took no notice of MacMillan, who sat looking out and trying to identify landmarks as the plane circled over Peking before heading south.

Seen from the air, the reds and golds and turquoise of walls and roofs, and the dark green of the parks, won out over the drab grays of the newly added "people's architecture." The three artificial lakes glinted in the sun; the bottle-shaped Great White Dagoba that dominated the Northern Lake poked its gold-tipped neck into the blue sky. In the hazy, luminous distance the main pavilion of the Summer Palace pointed upward like a raised finger. Beyond stretched the brown vastness of the North China plain, limned by the scalloped blue silhouette of the Western Hills on the horizon. Chien Men, Hatamen, Fox Tower and the Temple of Heaven disappeared beneath him.

MacMillan felt pangs of farewell at leaving the city he had always loved, and his two companions. He realized that he had become fond of these two dedicated children of the Revolution, and they of him. Miss Yang had wiped away a furtive tear, and Mr. Feng's handshake had been uncharacteristically firm and lingering. They had even given him farewell presents—a portrait of Chairman Mao in primary colors and a copy of the Chairman's "Thoughts" in English. MacMillan had had to improvise, but had been able to reciprocate with an electric razor for Mr. Feng and a bottle of Yardley aftershave (in lieu of cologne) for Miss Yang. He had purchased both items in Hong Kong in case he needed spares.

The landscape below turned from brown and bare to green and lush, and from sparsely to densely populated as North China gave way to Central, and Central to South China.

A car with a nameless, taciturn driver met MacMillan in Canton and took him to the station in total silence. Fare and tip were rejected.

Late that night MacMillan fell asleep in his room at the Peninsula Hotel, having declined nightcaps and invitations to the poker game in room 505.

The next morning he picked up his two suits at the bespoke tailor's. By midmorning a BOAC Viscount was carrying him back to New York.

23

During the week that Kenneth MacMillan was experiencing "enjoyment" in Peking, Seymour Weitzman received a phone call, and the Republic of China's delegation to the United Nations lost a competent employee.

"That Mr. Lynn is on the phone, Mr. Weitzman."

"Put him on, Sandra."

The amenities were exchanged. Then Mr. Ling said, "You will shortly receive Mr. MacMillan's first article on his impressions of Peking. It is an excellent article, and it is suggested that you publish it exactly as written. without any editorial changes. This is very important!"

Before Weitzman could begin to discuss the matter, Mr. Ling said, "I will be in touch with you again, Mr. Weitzman," and rang off.

Weitzman was intrigued by the cloak-and-dagger atmosphere surrounding MacMillan's visit to Peking. How did the mysterious Mr. Ling know his correspondent's name, and, moreover, how had he managed to become familiar with the qualities of MacMillan's article before it had reached New York?

The article arrived a day later, and Weitzman did publish it verbatim, although as MacMillan had surmised, his first impulse was to file it in the wastebasket. But Ling seemed to know what he wanted, and the un-MacMillan-like dullness of the article just added to the mystery. No doubt there would be further developments.

On a Monday morning, Wu did not turn up at his office at 9 A.M. sharp, as he had done with such exemplary punctuality five times a week for the past several years. Instead his superior received a letter postmarked and airmailed from Toronto the day before.

With many flourishes and regrets expressed in the most exquisitely literary language, Wu informed his employers that his uncle had died, leaving him a house and a profitable Szechuan restaurant, with the express wish that both remain in the family. Since Wu *was* the family, Wu was compelled to resign his position, with the greatest regret and with heartfelt apologies for having to do so so abruptly. Although he did have a vacation coming that might be used as terminal leave in lieu of notice . . .

The ensuing correspondence for Mr. Wu Hsien-lu, addressed to the Four Rivers Restaurant on Bloor Street in Toronto, was duly forwarded to Mr. Lionel Ling at the Pierrepont Hotel in Brooklyn Heights.

Wu Hsien-lu had ceased to exist. Ch'en viewed his demise without regret and settled down into the identity of Mr. Lionel Ling, British subject, resident of Hong Kong.

Like Kenneth MacMillan, Ch'en had selected the hotel in Brooklyn Heights for the view it afforded. Not of Upper New York Bay and the skyline, which, though every bit as spectacular from the upper floors of the Pierrepont as from the Bossert one block over, were invisible from Ch'en's second-floor window. The spurious splendor of the Manhattan skyline at dusk left

Ch'en entirely cold. The view he was interested in was that of Snyder's apartment in an old brownstone on Hicks Street, diagonally across the street. An added bonus was the convenience of having a karate establishment near Borough Hall, only a short walk away, where he could continue his custom of working out two or three nights a week. He had managed to keep in excellent shape over the years. It was part of the job.

A cable from the Hong Kong office informed Weitzman that MacMillan would arrive at Idlewild that evening. He had just put the cable down when the phone rang. Mr. Ling was on the line.

"Mr. Weitzman, I would like to meet with you to discuss a matter of great importance."

Weitzman suggested lunch at George's Steakhouse, greatly surprised that the mysterious Mr. Ling was suddenly willing to materialize from his anonymity, and finding himself looking frequently at his watch until it was time to leave for the appointment.

A tall, bespectacled Chinese in well-cut Western dress rose and bowed politely when Weitzman approached the bar at George's Steakhouse. They chose a secluded corner booth and gave their orders. Mr. Ling refused the offer of a cocktail, asking for tomato juice instead, and coming to the point immediately after their orders had been served.

"Your correspondent will arrive tonight with an extremely well written, detailed article on the loss of the Peking Man fossils. My people are naturally most anxious to recover this priceless treasure. A group of wealthy Chinese in San Francisco who wish to remain anonymous are offering a reward for information leading to the recovery of the fossils.

"The sum of fifty thousand dollars will be put at your disposal, Mr. Weitzman. The reward offer is to be published simultaneously with the article. It is to be displayed *prominently*. The wording is to suggest that the reward is offered by *Lives & Times* magazine. The true source of the money is not to be revealed under any circumstances, now or in the future."

Mr. Ling sat back and addressed himself to his Kentucky-fried chicken.

Weitzman was momentarily speechless.

"Mr. Ling," he said after recovering. "How do I know that this money is available? How will I receive it? If the fossils are recovered, to whom will they be handed over? To Taipei? To Peking? To your friends in . . . uh . . . San Francisco?

"As you know very well, we do not have diplomatic relations with the People's Republic. Furthermore, a crime is obviously involved. In order to claim the reward, the criminal must reveal himself. How will I handle that situation? I will have the FBI on my neck right away, not to mention the State Department.

"Moreover, any leads that may turn up will have to be followed up and investigated carefully. I do not have the staff or the funds to support what may well necessitate extensive travel in this country and abroad."

Ling put down his fork. "Your arguments are of course valid, Mr. Weitzman. But the problems that occur to you are in fact minor and certainly not insurmountable. First, the money is ready and available, in cash. It is in a safety deposit box at the Eastside Savings Bank around the corner from here. If you wish, we can go there after lunch; I will open the box and you can inspect and count it."

Weitzman nodded thoughtfully. "That might be a good idea, Mr. Ling. Although I am inclined to take your word for it. Better to make sure, though."

"To take your other objections, Mr. Weitzman. I see no international complications, at least not at this time. The reward offer is made by *private* individuals. You have no way of knowing to which China the group offering the reward owes allegiance. Neither the FBI nor your State Department has any grounds to enter the discussion at this time."

Weitzman nodded again. "You may have a point. But what about leads, Mr. Ling? What about expenses for travel and for trained investigators? What if the fossils are found or at least traced? What about payment of the reward?"

"All this is not of immediate concern, Mr.

217

Weitzman. We shall deal with these problems if and when they arise. Travel may not be required. . . . As regards additional staff, I should like to offer my services as a dollar-a-year man, as you say in this country. I am in a position to recognize a true lead if one should turn up. The responses will be treated *confidentially;* this must be emphasized in the wording of the reward offer. I will help you screen whatever replies come in; there will be very few. Any overt dealing with the respondents will be left to you. It is my desire to remain entirely in the background.

"I believe that this arrangement will work out satisfactorily and arouse a minimum of diplomatic suspicion. However, if you cannot accept this proposal, Mr. Weitzman, you have only to say so. In that case, steps will be taken. . . ."

Mr. Ling did not specify what steps would be taken and by whom, but Weitzman had a feeling that he would never see the article that was even now on its way to Idlewild Airport, and that *Lives & Times* magazine would lose out on what might well be the most sensational scoop of the decade. The newsman in him won out.

"We will take the hurdles one by one, as you suggest, Mr. Ling. I will give you a desk in my private office and introduce you as a journalist from . . . where shall we say—Hong Kong? Manila? Singapore?—who is interested in studying the management of a major weekly magazine."

"That will be most satisfactory, Mr. Weitzman. Now, if you would like to accompany me to the bank?"

The new issue of *Lives & Times* magazine hit the newsstands on a brisk Tuesday morning in October.

Snyder, stopping for his morning paper, blinked when his vision was assailed by the magazine's glaring cover, which showed the reconstructed Peking skull floating golden yellow in a sea of turquoise. Blood-red capitals marched across the cover, asking: WHERE IS PEKING MAN? and underneath: $50,000 REWARD FOR ITS RECOVERY (SEE P. 5).

"The Mystery of the Missing Ancestor," by Kenneth

M. MacMillan, spread over eight consecutive double-columned pages and was fully illustrated.

Snyder, reading with fascination, almost missed his subway stop. He recognized himself and his buddies—most of them long dead, including Tom Aiken next to himself—being marched off to Chien Men Station under Japanese guard, on their way to Kiangwan POW camp. He had not even been aware that their ignominy was being preserved for posterity. There was a picture of the Japanese captain who had questioned him and worked him over. For the first time Snyder learned the man's name and that he had died by his own hand—served the bastard right.

Reading, Snyder had an eerie feeling of being transported back in time. Mr. K. M. MacMillan had certainly done his homework. The story was there far more fully than Snyder had known it from his own personal experience. Except that *he* knew the one detail that was missing!

He turned to page 5. There, heavily boxed in black and printed in red, was the inset: *"Lives & Times* magazine will pay a reward of $50,000 for information leading to the recovery of the Peking Fossils. Write *confidentially* to Fossils, P.O. Box 1239, Grand Central Station, New York City, N.Y. Do not call the magazine."

At his office, Snyder made coffee, lit a cigarette and reread the article. He leaned back in his chair to think. . . .

He had to locate Evvie! He had to locate her before she contacted *Lives & Times* and claimed the reward, as he had no doubt she would.

His attempt to con Evvie's address out of Kathy had not worked. The first of two carefully worded letters claiming that he had "lost" Evvie's current address had remained unanswered. The second had elicited a postcard depicting improbably snowy Alpine peaks soaring into an improbably azure sky, and the information that all four Peterses were fine, and that Kathy had not heard from Evvie since Pablo's death. "She was going to leave New York but didn't say where she was going. I am sure she'll let you know."

So how was he going to reach Evvie and the fossils?

She was going to have trouble claiming the reward. She would have to reveal herself. That would lay her open to prosecution. On the face of the evidence, Evvie had committed grand larceny at least, while he was in the clear.

Furthermore, fifty thousand dollars was peanuts. If he could lay his hands on the fossils now, or if he at least knew where they were—it might be better not to have them in his possession, leave Evvie stuck with them for the time being—he could easily hold out for the million for which he had waited so many years. But not without Evvie . . .

Now, Evvie. Item: Evvie was vulnerable, in danger of going to jail as soon as she made a move. Item: Evvie had a large share of cupidity and greed, otherwise she would long ago have found a way of getting rid of the fossils without incriminating herself. Evvie and Joe had been two of a kind, birds of a feather. Evvie had known and approved of the goings-on in Peking, knowing damn well where the money came from that she was so fond of spending. . . . She'd been working for von Albers long before she had ever met Joe.

Snyder became increasingly convinced that Evvie would prefer half a million dollars to a measly tenth of that sum.

He called in succession the *New York Times*, the *Daily News*, the *Post* and the *Miami Herald*—a lot of Cuban exiles lived in Miami—placing the same personal ad in each:

"Evvie! Please forgive me! Will return your money with interest. Let's stick together for Joe's sake. Million at stake. Call Richard M." And he gave the phone number of his Brooklyn apartment. He then mailed a five-dollar bill to each of the papers to cover the cost of the ad.

A fact of which Snyder was unaware but which played into his hands was that Evvie, out of sheer boredom, read each of the New York papers from cover to cover, including every item in the classifieds. She therefore hit upon Snyder's ad without fail. Staring at it, she began to think. She didn't trust Bill Snyder one inch. She had read *Lives & Times* and had in fact begun to plan on claiming the reward. But she hadn't got very far, since the problems that had occurred to Snyder had also occurred to her. She was in a jam! Snyder must have been planning for a long time. . . . He would know what to do every step of the way, from claiming the reward to the moment of truth when the fossils had to be handed over. Also, half a million was certainly better than fifty thousand dollars. Evvie knew herself well enough to realize that she herself was not capable of what amounted to extortion. Bill, on the other hand, had the necessary ruthlessness to hold out for that much. He was certainly able to do the dirty work that was involved, meaning Bill, not she, would be taking the risks. And she would end up free and clear, rid of the fossils at last, and half a million richer. She would be able to live on that for the rest of her life, leave this crummy hideout, leave the country, maybe go live in Europe, perhaps in Innsbruck near Kathy. What did she have to risk? Just a phone call; Bill couldn't trace her through a phone call. . . .

Evvie went to the nearest public phone booth and called the number that "Myers" had given in his ad. There was no answer. Evvie guessed that this was Bill's home number; he'd be at his office at this time of day. She looked up and dialed United Nations, asked for the U.S. delegation and then for Mr. William Snyder, counting out and lining up dimes while waiting for the connection.

"U.S. delegation. Snyder. Can I help you?"

"Bill?"

"Yes . . . Evvie?"

"I saw your ad. How come the sudden change of heart?"

"Look, Evvie, this is too big a deal. Believe me, I am truly sorry for what I did to you. Please forgive me! After all, Joe was my best friend," said Snyder piously. "We planned this together, and you are Joe's wife. You've always been a good friend too. Believe me, I want to make it up to you."

"Okay, Bill; I'm willing to forgive and forget, for Joe's sake. But I want you to show your good faith."

"Sure, Evvie; anything you say."

"I want you to transfer the contents of Richard Myers' account to the account of Elena Acevedo." She gave the account number and the address of the bank. "That will be $3,900 plus interest. Let's figure 6 percent of $4,000—that's $240. That will be $4,140. I'll call you again as soon as I have notice from the bank that that money has been paid in."

Evvie rang off without waiting for a reply.

Snyder could not believe his ears. She had handed everything to him on a platter, for $4,140! Talk of greed!

He drove to Ninety-sixth Street and First Avenue, closed out the account of Richard Myers and headed uptown. He thought better of it, purchased a money order and mailed it to Evvie's bank on West 125th Street for the account of Elena Acevedo.

Two days later Evvie called him at home.

"Okay, Bill, I got the money. Now what?"

"All right. Do you have a camera?"

"Yes; I have Joe's Rolleiflex."

"Do you know how to use it?"

"Of course," said Evvie indignantly. "Joe showed me."

"Good. Go out and buy a flash attachment and a dozen flashbulbs. Now, here is what *you* do, and here is what *we*'ll do. . . ."

Evvie listened, then said admiringly, "You really are smart, Bill. I would never have thought of all this myself. . . ."

Snyder was still shaking his head in disbelief at Evvie's stupidity as he was heading for West 125th Street the next morning. It took less than five minutes, and the flimsiest of pretexts, to get Señora Acevedo's address out of the little Spic teller. . . .

Snyder drove past Señora Ramirez's establishment, wrinkling his nose at its crumminess and the crumminess of the neighborhood, then grinning at the thought of how the elegant Evamarie Cramer-Álvarez had come down in the world.

To Ch'en's dismay, "Fossils" was flooded with letters. A number of them, though originating from different parts of the country, were variations on the same theme: "If you want old fossils, I'll be happy to sell you my mother-in-law [my wife; my husband; my wife *and* my mother-in-law] for $50,000."

One offer, in the ill-formed handwriting and doubtful spelling characterizing the average American high school student, said: "You can have my parents! Yours truly, Sharon Polacek. P.S. You can have them for free."

There was another letter from Father Seamus Mulligan from Lafayette, Indiana. It accused *Lives & Times* magazine in the strongest possible language of perpetrating a fraud on the American public by offering a reward for recovery of a *fake*, and that he would take the matter up with the authorities—he did not mention what authorities. He enclosed a photocopy of the anonymous article that he had quoted once before, which made, and purported to substantiate, the accusations against Father Lorrain.

A Mr. Hsiao wrote from Washington, D.C. A friend of his, a highly placed government official in Taipei, had the fossils and was prepared to talk business to the tune of $150,000. Mr. Hsiao would be happy to act as a go-between for a 25 percent commission.

A Miss May had absolute evidence that the fossils were in Manila. She would divulge their whereabouts for a finder's fee of $75,000, payable in advance.

Lady Zoroastra, from Sausalito, California, would be delighted to consult the stars for a donation of $10,-000, balance to be paid as soon as the stars had revealed the location of the fossils.

Madame Estrella, San Clemente, California, was deeply perturbed. She had had exceedingly strong vibrations during a séance while holding *Lives & Times* magazine in her hand. Peking Man had communicated with her and confided (no doubt in faultless English) that he could not rest in peace until his remains were restored to their native soil. She had been chosen to communicate this desire to "Fossils," and he had promised to reveal his present whereabouts as soon as *Lives & Times* had sent a check for fifty thousand dollars to his authorized representative, Madame Estrella.

Not all correspondents were as helpful as Lady Zoroastra and Madame Estrella. A goodly number denounced, in more or less violent language, *Lives &*

Times' intention of paying out fifty thousand dollars for "some old bones" as long as: the Palestinian Arabs were persecuted by the Jews; the Soviet Jews were persecuted by the Soviets; itinerant farm workers in California were exploited by the fruit growers; there were segregated schools and neighborhoods in Detroit, Rochester, Newark; the streets of New York (Chicago, Detroit, Newark) were unsafe.

One correspondent had gone to some trouble and expense. The red envelope, postmarked Kissimmee, Florida, bore the gold-embossed return address "The Golden Triangle," with a writhing dragon underneath; this motif recurred on the note, which said in gold writing: "I have masterminded the removal of my Ancestor's hallowed remains to a secret burial ground where no Barbarian shall ever desecrate them again. Death and Peril will befall you if you persist in your foolish search. The Dragon Lady."

The Dragon Lady's letter was probably unrelated to two bomb threats *Lives & Times* received during that same week. Both necessitated alerting the N.Y.P.D. Bomb Squad and evacuating the Lives & Times Building—needlessly, as it turned out—but the unexpected break in the routine was enjoyed by everyone, and delighted the press, who had been calling incessantly from the moment the reward offer had appeared.

The austere Ch'en was appalled at the levity, the misplaced social awareness and the lack of rational thought processes of the American public as reflected in this deluge of letters. He marveled at Seymour Weitzman, who was roaring with laughter and actually seemed to enjoy this total waste of time. Weitzman noticed his guest's discomfiture and said kindly, "Look, Mr. Ling, this kind of offer is an open invitation to every nut and joker in this country to let himself go on paper. It's a kind of compulsion they can't resist, like the compulsion some people have to confess to a crime they didn't commit. I assure you that these letters are not a random sample of the American people. The great majority won't write unless they have something constructive to contribute."

Ch'en nodded, only half convinced. He picked up the next letter. This one was totally incomprehensible

224

to him. It stated laconically: "I have them. Sincerely, Judge Crater." Ch'en passed the letter to Weitzman and stared uncomprehending as the managing editor went into convulsions of laughter. Weitzman recovered and explained; Ch'en smiled politely, but still failed to see the joke.

There were responses from Washington, D.C., which tried neither to be funny nor to con *Lives & Times* magazine out of the reward money.

Among these was a stiffly worded letter signed with the name of the ambassador of the Republic of China. It pointed out that the fossils were the property of the Chinese people, represented legitimately and *exclusively* by the Nationalist government in Taipei, to whom the fossils were to be handed over *immediately* upon recovery. Otherwise there would be *dire* consequences for Sino-American relations, adversely affecting the presence of the U.S. on Taiwan. Carbon copy to Secretary of State.

The Secretary had not needed the reminder. The State Department called. The Secretary was extremely displeased about the irresponsibility of *Lives & Times* in opening this diplomatic can of worms! Weitzman was expressly forbidden to take any steps whatsoever without the Secretary's approval, or else. . . . This conversation was subsequently confirmed in writing.

Weitzman took these admonitions and threats in his stride. He dictated soothing, diplomatically worded letters assuring both excellencies of utmost tact and discretion in handling this extremely delicate matter, and returned to the business at hand.

A week after the article and reward offer had been published, "Fossils" received a small package. It contained an exposed but undeveloped roll of black-and-white number 120 film and a typed note: "Please have this film developed. It contains proof that we have what you are looking for. If you are satisfied, place a Personal ad in the *New York Times,* saying, 'Nellie, let's talk it over.' You will then be contacted." The note was unsigned.

Weitzman took the film to the photo lab himself and stood waiting impatiently while it was being developed.

In the meantime, Ch'en examined the note. It was

typed on cheap paper, probably torn from a five-by-seven pad that could be purchased in any candy or dime store. The typewriter, pica size, was obviously old and had not been cleaned in a long time; the letters were out of alignment, and *o*'s, *e*'s, *p*'s and *a*'s were solid with accumulated ink. The small Manila envelope, addressed in the same smudged typescript, had been mailed uptown the day before. All this of course meant nothing. But Ch'en noted the "we." So Snyder had located the keeper of the fossils, and the two had joined forces. Ch'en decided to give *Lives & Times* a few more days, until the ad had appeared and the second contact had been made, and then to begin tailing Snyder full-time. The end of the hunt seemed in sight.

Waiting for Weitzman to return from the darkroom, Ch'en lit a cigarette and permitted himself a little reminiscing. Almost twenty years . . . how many impersonations? Ch'en, the technician and artist—that was the closest he had come to being himself; Moon, the Korean number one boy in Colonel Kimura's home—Kimura, who had long since received his just deserts as a war criminal; Wu, the self-effacing clerk to Major O'Neill at G-2 in Peking and later a graduate student at Baylor University, thanks to the major's patronage—the naïveté of these Americans was really unbelievable, although the Kempetai hadn't been far behind; Wu Hsien-lu, M.A., native of Szechuan and refugee from the Communists, who had had no trouble being hired for a minor clerical job with the Taiwan Turtles' delegation to the United Nations . . . and now, Mr. Lionel Ling of Hong Kong. Soon Mr. Ling would die a natural death like his predecessors Moon, Wu and the nameless leper. Lionel Ling would die in Hong Kong, and Ch'en and the Peking Man would finally return to their homeland. . . .

Ch'en blinked and shook his head. It was not realistic to dream. The fossils seemed within reach, but they were not yet in his hands.

Weitzman burst in, wildly excited. "Look at this, just look at this! I've had enlargements made right away. I brought one up—it's still wet. The others are drying in the lab; they'll be ready in about fifteen minutes!"

He and Ch'en pored over the damp eight-by-ten. It

226

showed a close-up of an egg-shaped object that fitted closely into a container, possibly a cardboard carton. A few strands of wood shavings showed at the sides and in the one corner that was visible.

The object was not really egg-shaped; it was more like the Greek letter omega, closed at the bottom and lying on its side. The top seemed to be pieced together, like a jigsaw puzzle. One of the puzzle pieces was white, the rest were darker. A jagged, U-shaped projection underneath the bottom line of the "omega" was slightly out of focus.

Ch'en nodded and said evenly, "I think it is one of the Peking skulls." He could have added the number, the date and locus of excavation, and the fact that he himself had joined the pieces together and fashioned in plaster the shape of the missing fragment, which showed up white in the photograph. He kept these details to himself. Weitzman asked, "How can you be sure that this is a photo of the real thing and not one of the casts? How can you tell the difference in a photo?"

Ch'en did not answer directly. Instead he asked, "How many more?"

"There are six clear exposures on the roll. Let's go down to the lab and look at them; the film is now being washed, but I've had the enlargements made after it came out of the hypo. The technician will print more as soon as the film has been properly rinsed and dried—heaven forbid it should spoil."

The film, hanging from a line, was almost dry. Ch'en examined it carefully. It had been shot with a 60 mm reflex camera—a Rolleiflex, a Rolleicord, or one of their Japanese equivalents. The photographer was obviously an amateur. The first and third of the twelve possible exposures were blank, the second blurred. The following six were all right, the last three again blank. A close-up lens had obviously been used, and the cartons had been placed in such a way that the pictures showed very little or no background, nothing to indicate where the pictures had been taken. Ch'en unclamped the film, rolled it up and put it in his pocket.

The enlargements were dry. Weitzman and Ch'en returned to the office and spread the photos out on the desk.

One picture showed a side view of the carton and the edge where the sealing tape had been cut. Another offered an interior view of the empty carton with the skull's impression in the nest of wood shavings. There were front and side views of the skull resting upon a sealed carton, one shot of a stack of five sealed and one opened cartons, and the one with the bird's-eye view of the skull inside the carton, which they had already examined.

Ch'en hid his excitement and said dispassionately, "I have every reason to believe that these are the genuine fossils, in their original packing materials."

"How can you be so sure?"

Ch'en ignored the question. Weitzman had served his purpose. It was none of his business that Ch'en recognized the India ink markings on the bones, which did not appear on the casts, and that he knew the packing materials he had used when assisting in the packing of the fossils in 1941.

Weitzman seemed to be in shock. He finally pulled himself together and poured himself a drink, saying, "I sure need this. What about you?"

Ch'en declined. Weitzman downed his drink, shot a glance at Ch'en and said, "Seems to me we should get the opinion of an expert. I'm going to call Dr. Bernstein, the curator of the museum, ask him to come over and have a look at the photos."

Ch'en said coldly, "That will *not* be necessary, Mr. Weitzman. You may consider me fully qualified to make the identification. I am satisfied. I will take charge of the film and the prints. No further prints will be necessary."

Ch'en scooped up the photographs and placed them in his briefcase. The film was already in his pocket.

Weitzman watched in stunned silence. "W-what is the meaning of this, Mr. Ling?" he stammered finally. "You can't be serious! This is a *sensation*. . . . The pictures must be published. . . . There must be a press conference. . . ."

"No, Mr. Weitzman. These pictures will *not* be published, and there will be *no* press conference. Certainly not at this time. Perhaps at a later date. You will then be notified, and the film and the prints will be returned to you at the proper time."

Weitzman and Ch'en stared at each other for a good minute. Weitzman gave in. He shrugged his shoulders and spread his palms. "Okay, Mr. Ling, I guess you're calling the shots. Well, at least we'll avoid diplomatic complications for the time being. I'll have that ad phoned in to the *Times*."

24

Evvie had not been entirely truthful when she claimed that she knew how to operate Joe's Rolleiflex. Her familiarity with the camera extended to a couple of times when Joe, after having set focus, lens opening and shutter speed, had let her press the button. However, Evvie wished to forestall Snyder's offer to take the pictures. As long as he didn't know where the fossils were, he couldn't double-cross her. The fossils were her ace in the hole in this uneasy partnership. . . . Let him handle the details of this dirty business—he was good at that and it was always useful to have a man around in a critical situation—but she wasn't going to hand the fossils over to *anyone* until that half million was safely in her hands (or perhaps even the whole million?).

She put the camera in a large shopping bag and set out for Willoughby's downtown.

The clerk began by offering to trade her "obsolete" model for a new one with coated lenses and built-in flash attachment; he'd allow fifty dollars toward the price of four hundred dollars. Evvie declined politely but firmly; the clerk didn't seem to mind. He declared himself happy to show the lady how to load her "obsolete" model—he did it for her—how to cock the shutter and wind the film in one movement; how to use the flash: "Set it on *B*, press the button, release the flash, release the button"; and how to take the exposed film out of the camera: "Better do it in the dark." He also sold her a flash attachment, two dozen flash bulbs, a tripod and a cable release.

In the afternoon Evvie placed camera, tripod, close-up lenses, flash attachment and flash bulbs in her laundry bag, piled the laundry on top and went down to the basement. While the washing machine was going, she set up her equipment, unlocked the trunk and removed and stacked the six cartons. She slit the sealing tape on one and lifted out the skull with great care. Horrid-looking thing. She realized that this was actually the first time she had ever seen the famous Peking Man. She arranged her subjects and began to shoot.

The first exposure clicked off before the flash did. On the second, the flash went off before she had set the focus. The third time her movements were well synchronized, but she had forgotten to replace the burned-out flash bulb with a fresh one.

After these mishaps she got into her stride. The camera was easy to operate. The mat glass permitted her to see exactly what the picture would be like, enabling her to exclude the background. After the sixth successful shot, she clicked off the remaining exposures in the dark and wound up the film.

She felt she had done well and was rather pleased with herself. Joe would have been proud of her. . . . Funny, she was thinking and dreaming more of Joe these days than of Pablo. . . . Too bad she wouldn't be able to see the pictures she had just taken. She was sure they had come out, but if not, *Lives & Times* would let her—*them*—know about it in their ad.

Evvie returned the skull to its carton, resealed the lid, replaced the cartons in the trunk and locked it. She gathered up her paraphernalia, collected her damp laundry and returned to her room. In the darkness of the closet she removed and sealed the exposed film, returned it to its aluminum container and then sat down to type the covering letter.

She addressed and sealed the small Manila envelope, affixed a stamp and went down to the corner mailbox. She also mailed her monthly check to the Acme Storage Company on Tenth Avenue. This might be the last time, she thought. Pretty soon she'd be able to get her belongings out—she had already moved the television set to her room on 126th Street—use them to furnish a nice apartment in a nice place somewhere.

Three days later the ad was in the *Times:* "Nellie, let's talk it over."

Evvie read and reread it. So the pictures were okay. She couldn't call Bill till evening; this wasn't something they could discuss over his office phone. She had all day to think about the money. Perhaps she wouldn't call Bill at all. Perhaps she could handle the transaction herself. After all, the fossils were in *her* possession.

All it took was a telephone call to the managing editor of *Lives & Times,* saying . . . what? "Bring a million dollars in small used bills to West 126th Street and pick up the trunk with the fossils in Mrs. Ramirez's basement." They'd be only too happy to oblige. Except, instead of a million dollars in used ten-dollar bills, they'd bring the police or the FBI or both, and perhaps an immigration officer or two for good measure.

How did they handle the payoff in kidnapping stories? They arranged a "drop" for the ransom: "Put the money in the garbage can at the corner of X and Y streets at 1:30 A.M. sharp, and the victim will be released unharmed. Do not bring police or the victim will be killed." But her "victim" had already been dead for 600,000 years; she couldn't just release it unharmed; it couldn't walk off into freedom by itself.

"Send me a million dollars; I'll send you the merchandise by United Parcel Service as soon as the money is received. . . ." Send a million dollars *where?* A post office box? They'd be watching it day and night. . . .

Of course, she could just call the magazine "confidentially," no questions asked, and claim the legitimate reward in return for the promise of immunity. But Evvie had come around to Snyder's way of thinking: fifty thousand dollars was chicken feed, while a million was safety and security for life, worth the risk, as Bill had pointed out, quite correctly.

Reluctantly Evvie came to the conclusion that she needed Bill to bring off the deal. Even half a million

231

was still ten times more, and therefore ten times better, than fifty thousand dollars.

Snyder, also, was pleased to see the ad, which implied that the photos were acceptable. Evvie must have done a creditable job. He'd had his doubts about that, remembering how finicky Joe had been about letting anyone but himself handle his precious Rolleiflex. But Snyder had not wanted to press the point, insist that he help her with the photography. Let Evvie go on thinking that he didn't know where she and the fossils were located. It wouldn't be for long now, as Snyder had no intention of leaving Evvie in possession of the goods one moment longer than necessary. He had all day to plan strategy; she wouldn't call before evening.

Snyder left the house at his usual time, heading for the subway.

His departure was observed by Ch'en, who lingered in the Pierrepont coffee shop across the street until 9:10 A.M. He then called Snyder's office.

"U.S. delegation. Snyder. Can I help you?"

"Sorry, wrong number."

Ch'en went to *Lives & Times* magazine. No contact was made by phone that day. A response by mail couldn't be expected until the next day at the earliest.

Ch'en was back at the Pierrepont in time to see Snyder return at his usual hour. Ch'en watched the brownstone on Hicks Street through the night, but Snyder didn't go out again, not even to dinner. This was a little unusual, but of course it was raining, windy and getting colder. Ch'en neither knew nor would he have cared that the weather was ruining the neighborhood kids' "trick or treat" expeditions on this Halloween evening.

Evvie called at six o'clock. Snyder was ready for her.

"Bill, have you seen the ad?"

"Yeah, sure. You must have done a nice job, Evvie."

"What do we do now, Bill?"

"Now? Now we do *nothing*."

"Nothing! What do you mean, Bill?"

"I mean nothing. We let them stew awhile, soften them up—see what I mean?"

Evvie hesitated, disgesting this. Then, "How long, Bill? And how about the—you know—the payoff?"

"No problem, Evvie. You'll get your five hundred grand. I've got it all worked out. It's foolproof! But we'll have to discuss this face to face, not over the phone."

Snyder held his breath. This was the crucial moment. But Evvie didn't seem to suspect. After a slight hesitation, she said, "Okay, Bill. When shall we meet?"

"Let's make it tomorrow evening, nine o'clock."

That was okay with Evvie.

"Any suggestion where you'd like us to meet, Evvie?"

Evvie suggested the Schrafft's at Forty-second Street and Eighth Avenue. She reasoned, although she didn't say so, that Times Square was a good distance away from West 126th Street, that it was teeming with people and cops at all times, so that Snyder wouldn't dare try any funny business in the street, and the subway station was so crowded and confusing, with all three subway lines crossing, that she could easily give Snyder the slip should he attempt to follow her home.

Snyder agreed without argument. The distance was okay; that was all that mattered. The intricacies of the New York City subway system were irrelevant to his plans.

The morning of All Saints' Day was gray, cold and windy. The rain had diminished to a drizzle, but picked up again during the day. The weatherman predicted "heavy rain, turning into sleet, possible snow flurries and turning much colder" for the evening and night.

Ch'en, having again established that Snyder was at his office, turned up at the *Lives & Times* office at 10 A.M., and left at 4 P.M. He got his black Fairlane out of the parking garage behind the Pierrepont and parked it at the hotel entrance, risking a possible ticket. Snyder's pink-and-gray Chevy was parked in its usual space in front of the brownstone diagonally across the street. Ch'en called Weitzman, who had come in at an unprecedented 8:57 A.M. and was still at the office at 6 P.M., waiting. The waiting was fruitless;

233

no contact had been made by phone or mail, and Weitzman was about to leave for home.

Ch'en saw Snyder come home at his usual time, perhaps a few minutes later because of the weather. He went out again at six-thirty, probably to eat, and was back by seven forty-five.

Ch'en also had dined, off a tasteless hamburger in the Pierrepont's coffee shop. His raincoat, hat and umbrella were in readiness while he sat watching the Chevy across the street.

At 8:10 P.M. Snyder left the house, muffled in a heavy, fur-collared leather coat. Ch'en, grabbing his coat and umbrella, saw Snyder unlock the car door, place something on the passenger seat and settle himself behind the wheel.

Ch'en had the Fairlane started in time to follow the Chevy's taillights. Snyder led him onto the Brooklyn-Queens Expressway, staying in the right-hand lane, obviously bound for the Battery Tunnel.

Ch'en managed to follow Snyder through the tunnel and onto the West Side Highway, although visibility was poor and traffic still fairly heavy at this hour.

Snyder exited at West 125th Street and made a left turn into Amsterdam Avenue, then another into 126th Street. He made a U-turn and parked in front of a tenement. Passing slowly on the opposite side as if in search of a parking space, Ch'en saw Snyder remove a limp object like a rug or a large bag from the passenger seat and enter the building. There were three empty parking spaces behind Snyder's car.

Ch'en made a U-turn and parked behind Snyder's car, hogging two of the available spaces so that no one could squeeze in between his Fairlane and the Chevy. He gave Snyder five minutes, then got out, went to the Chevy and tested the trunk. It was unlocked. Ch'en walked to the tenement. He noted the sign advertising furnished rooms in a first-floor window and, following its instructions, rang apartment 109 for *información*.

The door opened a crack behind a chain. Señora Ramirez peered out behind the crack. In the dim, forty-watt hall light she beheld an Oriental gentleman. The gentleman cleared his throat as a prelude to speech, but before he could utter a sound, Señora

234

Ramirez said rapidly, without stopping for breath, "No spik Englis no buy nutt'n you no go 'way I call polis," and slammed the door. Ch'en heard her shoot the bolt.

Ch'en was an intrepid man. He had no fear of the Kempetai, American majors, or the U.S. Marine Corps in the person of Snyder, any one of whom—the latter specifically and within the hour—he was prepared to take on unarmed. But he was thoroughly intimidated by little old ladies with faces like shriveled brown winter apples and bright black eyes. Señora Ramirez's Indian features reminded him of his grandmother, who had ruled the House of Ch'en with an iron hand and a lashing tongue. Ch'en retreated.

He sat in the car shivering, but dared not run the engine to keep it warm and to operate heater and windshield wipers, lest Snyder return unexpectedly and be warned by the wipers' movement and the engine noise. Slurry accumulated on the windshield, obscuring vision. Ch'en opened the vent window, which created an additional icy draft but enabled him to keep the doorway under observation. It was 9:35 P.M.

The wind was playing clanking soccer with empty garbage cans. The street was deserted. People were glad to stay indoors on a night like this, or to get indoors out of the driving sleet as fast as possible. Nobody came out of the tenement, and only a few people, singly or in pairs, straggled in sporadically as time went by.

Evvie had been sorely tempted to stand Snyder up on this dismal night. But the desire to get the "operation" over with as quickly as possible had won out. Huddled in her black seal coat and well muffled in a mohair head scarf, she had made her way to the 125th Street station of the Eighth Avenue subway.

It was now nine thirty-five; Snyder had not yet shown. She had been sitting in Schrafft's for twenty minutes and had just ordered her second cup of coffee. Was *he* standing *her* up? She went to the phone booth and called his apartment. No answer. So he had left; he must be on the way. Perhaps he was driving? Evvie didn't know whether Snyder owned a car, but this seemed a good night to leave the car in the garage and travel by subway. . . . Evvie finished her second cup of coffee and again called Snyder's apartment. Again there was no answer.

Evvie returned to her table. She decided to give Snyder till ten o'clock, and switched from coffee to hot chocolate.

At ten she left Schrafft's and went down the stairs to the Independent subway.

Snyder had had little trouble in finding and entering Evvie's room on the sixth floor. He had searched the room carefully. It needed very little time to establish that the steamer trunk was not there. The idea that it might be in the basement didn't occur to Snyder. He thought that she probably kept it in the warehouse on . . . where was it?—Tenth Avenue?—where she stored her furniture, had removed it temporarily to take the pictures and then returned it to storage. He didn't remember the name of the company that what-was-his-name?—Briant-Ryan—had given him, but he would get it out of Evvie as soon as she got home. Which wouldn't be long now!

Snyder waited in the dark. It was a tedious wait. He craved a cigarette, but didn't dare smoke for fear that the smell would warn Evvie off. Nor did he want to leave the butt of a Lucky in the ashtray on the bedside table, which was filled to overflowing with the stale leftovers of Evvie's filter-tips. He also suppressed a steadily growing need to visit the communal bathroom at the end of the hall. . . .

Ch'en peered through the curtain of snow at the deserted street. A solitary woman was picking her way through the accumulating slush, her scarved head bent against the wind and the sheets of large, wet snow-flakes. The woman entered the tenement. Ch'en thought nothing of it.

Snyder heard the tapping of high heels in the hall-way over the sounds of radio and television, laughter and staccato Spanish that came through the walls. He tensed and positioned himself behind the door.

The door opened, the light came on.

236

Snyder's gloved left hand went over Evvie's mouth, his right forearm angled hard against her throat. He pulled her, kicking and struggling, into the closet. The fur coat slipped off and fell to the floor.

"Okay, Evvie, where are they!"

Snyder relaxed the pressure of his hand slightly, but the tensing of her throat muscles warned him that she was going to scream.

Both hands went around her throat. "Where are they, Evvie? Where?"

Evvie emitted a hoarse croak. Her hands, which had been clawing at his, dropped; she went limp. Snyder released his strangle hold; Evvie collapsed on the floor. Goddamn broad had fainted!

Snyder began to slap Evvie's face, but she wouldn't come to. He dragged her out of the closet into the lighted room, laid her on the floor. Evvie's eyes were bulging like peeled hard-boiled eggs, her face had a bluish tinge, her tongue was protruding between retracted lips.

Snyder gasped. He felt for the pulse; there was none. He tore the front of her white nylon blouse, put his ear to her chest. Nothing. He grabbed a mirror from the dresser, held it over Evvie's mouth. The glass remained clear.

Evvie was dead! He had killed her! He hadn't meant to, at least not before he had got her to divulge the whereabouts of the fossils.

Never mind the fossils now. He had to get the body and himself out of here!

Snyder was not unduly disturbed by the sight of Evvie's distorted features; he had seen worse in Hokkaido POW camp. He forced himself to think. He would have given the whole million bucks right now for a cigarette and a visit to the bathroom. Well, both comforts would have to wait. Best make it look as if Evvie hadn't come home. . . .

He bent down and stripped the boots off the body, gathered up the damp fur coat from the closet floor.

He dumped boots and coat into one of the plastic leaf bags he had brought with him, thanking his stars that he had had the foresight to bring two in case one wasn't sturdy enough to hold the fossils.

237

He managed to stuff the body into the second leaf bag.

He turned off the light, opened the door a crack and looked out. The hallway was deserted. High decibels of sound issuing from behind closed doors attested that the neighbors were safely glued to their radios and television sets.

Snyder heaved the bag with Evvie's body over his shoulder, praying that the plastic would not rip. He got the bundle to the elevator, which had not moved from the sixth floor since Evvie had got off. Snyder opened the old-fashioned sliding door, pushed the body in and closed the door.

He quickly tiptoed back to the room, grabbed up the bag containing Evvie's coat and boots. The keys lay just inside the door, where Evvie had dropped them. He picked them up, gave a quick look around the room. He had kept his gloves on all along; no fingerprints to wipe off.

Snyder fumblingly locked the door and ran to the door marked "Exit" near the elevator. He made it down the dark stairway to the first floor without encountering anyone. No wheezy creaks, no metallic clanks—the elevator stayed put on the sixth floor.

Snyder emerged into what passed for the lobby. Yells and gunshots behind the door of apartment 109 indicated that M. Ramirez was safely occupied watching what sounded like a Western.

Snyder ran to his car, threw the bag on the back seat, and glanced quickly up and down the street—no one in sight. Taking a risk, he started the engine and hurried back into the house.

He pressed the elevator button. The ancient cage creaked to a stop after what seemed an eternity. Snyder greedily sucked in air, suddenly realizing that he had been holding his breath during the elevator's entire, blessedly uninterrupted, descent.

He got the burden out of the elevator, out of the house, and into the car trunk. He slid behind the wheel, lit a cigarette and inhaled voluptuously. The pressure in his lower abdomen eased suddenly, exquisitely. He made no attempt to control the warm flow as he shifted into Drive and pulled out smoothly.

Ch'en was just getting out of his car in order to confiscate what he felt sure were the fossils on Snyder's back seat, when Snyder returned with his second, apparently much bulkier and heavier load. It seemed reasonable to Ch'en that Snyder had divided the cartons into two separate bundles but had been too nervous to distribute the weights more evenly.

Ch'en tried to decide whether to intercept Snyder and relieve him of both packages, but he hesitated a fraction too long. Snyder had heaved the second load into the trunk. Ch'en saw the flicker of the flame as Snyder lit his cigarette, and before Ch'en could reinsert himself behind the wheel, the Chevy's taillights flashed red. Snyder signaled and pulled away from the curb.

Ch'en turned the key in the ignition. The motor sputtered, then went dead. Frantically trying to start the stalled car, Ch'en fleetingly regretted not having followed Snyder's example and risked a preliminary warm-up. Half a block ahead, Snyder skidded into a right turn and disappeared from sight.

The Fairlane's engine finally caught; Ch'en gunned it, hoping to make the corner light, and immediately went into a skid. The slush on the pavement was rapidly freezing. He regained control of the wheel and rushed the light, but amber changed to red. He braked abruptly, skidding far enough into the intersection to see along Amsterdam Avenue. There was no traffic to block his view of a solitary car signaling for a left turn, waiting for the light to change at the 125th Street intersection.

It had to be Snyder, but Ch'en was puzzled. A *left* turn? The fastest way back to downtown Brooklyn was the way they had come, via the West Side Highway, which called for a *right* turn at the corner.

The lights changed; Ch'en turned right, then left into 125th Street, following what he hoped were Snyder's taillights glimpsed dimly almost two blocks ahead, going east. Snyder appeared to be headed for the Triborough Bridge.

Continuing crosstown, the Chevy was held up by several red lights in succession; the Fairlane made the lights and caught up. But then Ch'en's luck ran out. He

239

saw the Chevy half a block ahead, slowing down, then stopping for the toll booth, but by the time he himself had paid his quarter, and was on the Grand Central Parkway, he had lost Snyder in heavy traffic near La Guardia Airport. It was impossible to tell in the driving sleet which of the red taillights ahead of him belonged to the Chevy.

Ch'en pulled into the right-hand lane, slowed down and considered the situation. He still couldn't understand why Snyder had chosen this long detour to return to Brooklyn . . . unless he was headed for Long Island. For what purpose, Ch'en could not imagine, especially on a night like this.

Ch'en decided to return to Brooklyn Heights by the shortest route. He took the Long Island Expressway, then the Brooklyn-Queens Expressway. Driving had become extremely hazardous. Ch'en went into a heavy skid on the iced-over Kosciuszko Bridge and barely escaped a rear-end collision.

Forty-five minutes later the Fairlane was back in the garage behind the Pierrepont.

The Chevy's parking space in front of the brownstone diagonally across the street was still empty. Ch'en made tea and stationed himself in an armchair by the window to await Snyder's return.

Despite the tea, Ch'en kept dozing off. He jerked awake at lengthening intervals; the Chevy's parking space remained empty. When Ch'en awoke again at 5:30 A.M., stiff and sore and with a fuzzy head, the Chevy still hadn't returned. Ch'en noted blearily that the wind had died down, that snow was falling densely and gently. He dragged himself over to the bed, kicked off his shoes and treated himself to another two hours of sleep.

When he woke again, the parking space across the street, indeed the whole street, was blanketed in a pristine layer of freshly fallen, still undisturbed snow. There were no tire marks to indicate that the Chevy might have pulled in and out again. Snyder had not come home. . . .

Ch'en turned on the radio, listening while he went into the slow, measured motions of his daily *tai chi chuan* exercises. ". . . first snowstorm of the season.

240

High winds, icy roads and bridges created extremely hazardous driving conditions last night. Many accidents were reported on the city's streets and highways. Five people were killed in a four-car smash on Mill Basin Bridge in Brooklyn. A Brooklyn-bound car, apparently skidding out of control and buffeted by high winds, smashed into the abutment of the Marine Parkway Bridge, killing the driver. More news after this important message—"

Ch'en turned the radio off, called room service for coffee and copies of the morning papers, and went to shower and shave.

The *News* had the information he was looking for. It was one of several items listed under the heading SUDDEN ICE STORM CAUSES MANY TRAFFIC DEATHS:

"William Snyder, 48, of 195 Hicks Street, Brooklyn, was instantly killed on the iced-over Marine Parkway Bridge when his Brooklyn-bound car skidded across the opposite lanes, jumped the walkway and crashed into the abutment. Mr. Snyder was associated with the U.S. delegation to the United Nations. A sister in Harlingen, Texas, has been notified."

There was no mention of suspicious bulky objects in the wrecked car.

This explained why Snyder had not come home last night, but not what he had been doing on the lonely Marine Parkway Bridge halfway between Brooklyn and the wind- and wave-swept Rockaway peninsula.

Ch'en called the *News*'s city desk, but was told no, nothing but the smashed-up driver had been found in the "totaled" car. "What were you expecting—who *is* this—what's with that guy Snyder?" But Ch'en had rung off, leaving the city editor to speculate futilely about a possible mystery connected with the squashed William Snyder; perhaps a heroin drop?

Ch'en had not really expected any positive information. The discovery of the Peking Man in a wrecked car in Brooklyn would have rated interruption of the radio commercial and headlines in the *New York Times*.

Snyder must have hidden the fossils somewhere in the desolate swamplands in the Jamaica Bay area of southern Queens. Ch'en consulted the Queens map and tried to retrace Snyder's route.

Snyder had taken the Grand Central Parkway. If Ch'en was correct, Snyder had continued south, and had then turned west on the Belt Parkway, getting off at the Cross Bay Boulevard exit for the Rockaways. Cross Bay Boulevard traversed the Jamaica Bay area west of Idlewild Airport. This whole area, between the airport and Marine Parkway some fifteen miles farther west, was largely a wildlife reserve, totally deserted at this time of year except for some hardy sea gulls and a few straggling flocks of geese and ducks. If Ch'en was right, Snyder had hidden the fossils somewhere in this wilderness, not too far from Cross Bay Boulevard, where they could easily be found if explicit directions were given. Snyder had then continued south on Cross Bay Boulevard, crossed the toll bridge, and turned west, parallel to the Belt Parkway, on the south shore of the bay, then north across Marine Parkway Bridge to regain, but never reaching, the Brooklyn-bound lane of the Belt Parkway.

Having stashed the fossils, Snyder—or his accomplice in Spanish Harlem—would have been ready to contact *Lives & Times,* demanding a ransom payment far exceeding fifty thousand dollars—Ch'en was very sure of *that*—and promising to divulge the fossils' whereabouts as soon as the ransom money was received and the thieves had left the country. Contact and ransom demand were now up to the accomplice, who had no doubt read about Snyder's demise in this morning's *News.*

Ch'en went to *Lives & Times,* but again no contact was made that day. Weitzman reinserted the ad: "Nellie, let's talk it over," arranging to have it run for three consecutive days, but there were no phone calls and no letters in response. Even the crank mail had stopped coming in. The fifty-thousand dollar reward lay unclaimed in Lionel Ling's safety deposit box. Ch'en, who had the only key, would eventually find a use for the money, though perhaps not quite the one that Messrs. Chin, Wei and Liu had had in mind.

As soon as the snowfall stopped, Ch'en went out to

Jamaica Bay and searched the stretches of wilderness on both sides of Cross Bay Boulevard, but he found no trace of the fossils.

25

Señora Ramirez was aggrieved because she felt she had been cheated. Here it was the sixth of the month, and Señora Acevedo still had not paid her rent.

Señora Ramirez dismissed the thought that this omission was highly unusual and that something might be amiss since Señora Acevedo had always been most punctual about her rent payments. Señora Ramirez was too upset by the disaster of having lost forty-five dollars and, in addition, a chance to let the room—she had already had two inquiries.

She took the elevator to the sixth floor and knocked on Señora Acevedo's door. There was no answer. The door was locked. Señora Ramirez opened it with her passkey. There was a strong smell of stale cigarette ashes emanating from the pile of butts in the ashtray on the bedside table. The bed was neatly made and had not been slept in. A pair of pink leather slippers were lined up underneath.

The señora opened the closet. Three dresses, two suits, a few blouses and a raincoat hung in a row. A pair of scuffed but well-polished brown oxfords, and a pair of balding blue suede pumps, both on shoe trees and both with Florsheim labels, stood at the bottom. A crumpled dark-red mohair scarf lay on the floor of the closet, and Señora Acevedo's blue suede purse, gaping open, lay nearby. Señora Ramirez picked up the purse and rummaged. The purse contained a wallet, some papers, lipstick, comb, a gold compact, a checkbook and some crumpled tissues, but no keys. The wallet yielded $8.67 and two subway tokens. Señora Ramirez pocketed the wallet and its contents.

Further inspection of the closet revealed a portable typewriter and two suitcases. A camera and accessory case were hanging from a hook in the back. Señora

Acevedo's black seal coat and her high-heeled, fur-lined leather boots were missing.

A silver-backed hand mirror and matching brush-and-comb set lay on the dresser. The dresser drawers held assorted lingerie, three cashmere sweaters, hose and other small items of apparel, as well as a large green leather folder. The folder contained official-looking documents printed in unintelligible languages, and a passbook.

Señora Ramirez could think only of the missing fur coat and boots. Her lodger had skipped!

Overcome by resentment, the landlady did not stop to consider that a female lodger intent on skipping was unlikely to leave her purse and wallet behind. It did not occur to her that there might be a sinister reason for Señora Acevedo's absence and failure to pay her rent, and that she should notify the police. In Señora Ramirez's circles and neighborhood, one did not invite the police into one's house; one gave the cops as wide a berth as possible. Her threat to call "polis" when Ch'en had rung her doorbell had been pure bluff.

Señora Ramirez felt only, and overwhelmingly, that she had been done out of forty-five dollars and was therefore entitled to compensation.

She dragged the two suitcases out of the closet. One was filled with very nice clothes bearing Fifth Avenue labels. Size eight—they'd just fit her Margarita! The other suitcase was empty. Señora Ramirez swept the mirror-comb-brush set and the contents of the dresser drawers into the suitcase. She added the clothes, the raincoat, the shoes from the closet, and the pink slippers from underneath the bed. She put the green folder on top—this one would go into the garbage compactor —and knelt on the pigskin case to force it shut. She slung the camera and accessory case around her neck—these and the typewriter would go to Goldman's hockshop on 125th Street this very afternoon—and picked up the two suitcases and the typewriter. She locked the door—she'd ask fifty dollars from the next tenant—and carried her burdens to the elevator. She'd send Ramón up for the TV set later on.

Having distributed her skipped lodger's belongings about her apartment, Señora Ramirez bethought herself of the steamer trunk in the basement. Armed with a screwdriver and a chisel, and carrying the green leather folder, she went downcellar.

While the garbage compactor was devouring the green leather folder and its contents, Señora Ramirez pried open the steamer trunk. There were six cardboard cartons inside. She opened one that was loosely sealed and shrieked, *"Jesús María y José!"* when she saw what it contained. She crossed herself rapidly and repeatedly, and opened the rest of the cartons.

Monstrously beetle-browed brown skulls glared and bared enormous fangs at her; disembodied jaws and teeth seemed ready to devour her! It was like something out of a horror movie—only this was *real*.

Señora Acevedo had been a *witch!*

Señora Ramirez dragged the trunk with its grisly contents over to the garbage compactor.

Murmuring prayers and imprecations she fed into it piece by piece five skulls, two humeri, nine femurs one os lunatum, one clavicle, and some 150 assorted teeth and jaw fragments, representing the earthly remains of some forty individuals of *Homo erectus pekinensis,* worth fifty thousand dollars to her, had she but bothered to learn English in the twelve years she had been living in New York City, and thus been able to read *Lives & Times* magazine.

She hunkered by the garbage compactor, saying rosaries, while Peking Man was being crunched to dust. It took a while. The garbage compactor finally ground to a halt. Señora Ramirez said, *". . . ruega por nosotros pecadores, ahora y en la hora de nuestra muerte. Amen,"* kissed the crucifix, crossed herself and collected a large plastic bag full of grit.

She tied the bag and deposited it on the sidewalk in the blackened snow, amid crumpled used tissues, chicken bones, fish heads, dented beer cans, hundreds of cigarette butts, half-rotted apple and potato peels and two peanut butter sandwiches that had spilled from the six overflowing garbage cans in front of the tenement. The Sanitation Department had missed last week's collection because of the snowstorm.

Señora Ramirez was just in time. The garbage truck was already rumbling and clanking two houses away.

Five minutes later it stopped in front of the tenement The accumulated trash, minus the spill on the sidewalk, was fed into its grinding rotary maw.

With sounds like clashing cymbals, the "sanitation engineers" banged the empty metal cans back on the refuse-strewn sidewalk, called cheerfully and raucously to each other and went on down the block, with the truck rumbling after them.

At 9:30 A.M. the next day, the garbage truck noisily evacuated its load onto the reeking hill of New York City refuse south of the Belt Parkway between the Pennsylvania Avenue and Cross Bay Boulevard exits, which would encroach upon Jamaica Bay once the landfill was completed.

A cloud of gulls wheeled overhead, shrieking angry protest at being disturbed in their muckraking. They immediately settled down again to their interrupted meal when the truck, having relieved itself, rumbled away toward the service road.

Epilogue

━─━─━─━─━

RED CHINESE AGENT DEFECTS TO U.S.

NEW YORK, January 27—The *New York Times* learned today that Ch'en Hsu-liang, 48, an agent of the People's Republic of China, has surrendered to the U.S. Immigration authorities, asking for political asylum in the United States. Mr. Ch'en, who has also used the names of Wu Hsien-lu and Lionel Ling, is now being questioned by the FBI and military intelligence. . . .

Author's Postscript

The Peking Man Is Missing is fiction, extrapolated from the fact that the Peking fossils actually *are* missing, having unaccountably disappeared on or about December 8, 1941 (China time), somewhere between the U.S. Marine barracks on Legation Street in Peking and the U.S. naval base at Chinwangtao.

Diligent searches carried out at Emperor Hirohito's orders by the Japanese secret police (Kempetai) during and U.S. military intelligence (G-2) immediately after the war, as well as ongoing, more or less widely publicized investigations by private individuals, have turned up a great many dead ends, mares' nests and red herrings, but no fossils.*

Although the present story's plot is largely fictitious, some of the characters' pronouncements are not, and require documentation:

The Professor's remark that the Piltdown Man *(Eoanthropus dawsoni)* was an "anatomical impossibility" (page 27) was made verbatim to the author by Professor Franz Weidenreich, director of the Cenozoic Research Laboratory, Peking Union Medical College, in December 1940, some fifteen years before the remains of the "Dawn Man" were actually discovered to be fakes. This discovery left many of the Professor's eminent colleagues with a red face, and must have been particularly embarrassing for the gentleman who based his theory of "asymmetric evolution" on Piltdown Man's artificially antiqued modern human skull cap and ape jaw.†

* W. Foley, "A Small Contribution to the Mystery of Peking Man" (*Cornell Medical College Alumni Quarterly*, Winter 1971–72). J. Cox, "Whatever Happened to Peking Man" (*Harvard Magazine*, September 1974). G. G. Janus and W. Brashler, *The Search for Peking Man* (New York: Macmillan, 1975). *People* magazine, March 10, 1975. *Reader's Digest*, September 1976.
† H. L. Shapiro, *Peking Man: The Discovery, Disappearance and Mystery of a Priceless Scientific Treasure* (New York: Simon & Schuster, 1974), pp. 45–46.

Father Lorrain's prototype, Father P. Teilhard de Chardin, would certainly have changed his opinion regarding the negligible scientific value of the Peking fossils at the time of their disappearance (page 109), in view of the recent discovery of the Lake Turkana, Kenya, skull, a spitting image of *Homo erectus pekinensis* with an estimated age of 1.5 million years. It should be noted in this connection that the age of 600,-000 years attributed to the Peking fossils in the story reflects the thinking of the 1930s and 1940s. Contemporary discoveries and improved dating methods indicate that Peking Man and his period, the Pleistocene, are probably much older.

Apart from his remark on page 109, and the nature of his work, the actions ascribed to Father Lorrain in the story, though in character, are fictitious. However, the anonymous attack accusing his prototype of having faked the Peking fossils (pages 185, 223) is factual.‡

Except where they refer to actual historical dates, the events in the story have been contracted or transposed in time, in order to avoid intervals like "Twenty Years Later" of the *Three Musketeers* type. For this reason, however, the author had to take liberties with Canada's recognition of Red China, which in the story precedes the actual event by some twelve years.

The locations and places mentioned in the story are authentic whether in Peking or in New York, although some names have been changed. Street numbers and people living at same are fictitious. There was no Cuban consulate in Tientsin or Shanghai.

Most of the characters cavorting through the story are imaginary, including Ch'en, Kathy, Tom Aiken and Bill Snyder, as well as assorted minor personages. Others have been developed from single individuals or are composites of real people, none of whom were connected with the Peking fossils before or after their disappearance.

The freckled, quadrilingual Captain Omura is a por-

‡ *Social Justice Review*, October 1964, pp. 196–199; ibid. May 1965, p. 72.

trait of an Irish-Japanese Kempetai officer who, however, was not based in Peking and did not commit suicide but, according to rumor, was executed after standing trial for war crimes.